Luke Jensen, Bounty Hunter: Legion of Fire

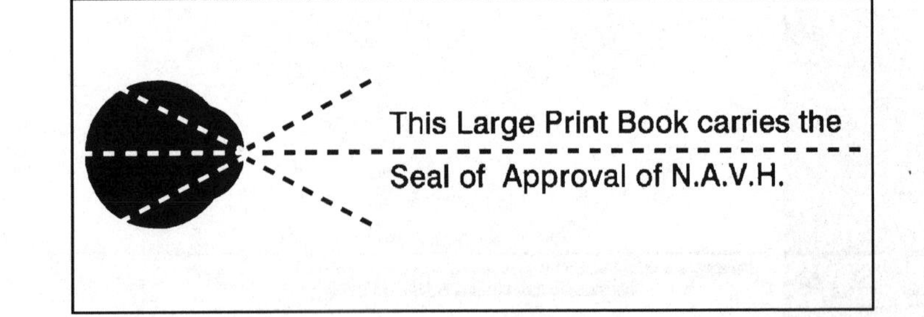
This Large Print Book carries the
Seal of Approval of N.A.V.H.

LUKE JENSEN, BOUNTY HUNTER: LEGION OF FIRE

WILLIAM W. JOHNSTONE
WITH J. A. JOHNSTONE

WHEELER PUBLISHING
A part of Gale, a Cengage Company

Farmington Hills, Mich • San Francisco • New York • Waterville, Maine
Meriden, Conn • Mason, Ohio • Chicago

Wheeler Publishing, a part of Gale, a Cengage Company.

Following the death of William W. Johnstone, the Johnstone family is working with a carefully selected writer to organize and complete Mr. Johnstone's outlines and many unfinished manuscripts to create additional novels in all of his series like The Last Gunfighter, Mountain Man, and Eagles, among others. This novel was inspired by Mr. Johnstone's superb storytelling.
Wheeler Publishing Large Print Western.
The text of this Large Print edition is unabridged.
Other aspects of the book may vary from the original edition.
Set in 16 pt. Plantin.

**LIBRARY OF CONGRESS CIP DATA ON FILE.
CATALOGUING IN PUBLICATION FOR THIS BOOK
IS AVAILABLE FROM THE LIBRARY OF CONGRESS**

ISBN-13: 978-1-4328-6066-0 (softcover)

Published in 2019 by arrangement with Pinnacle Books, an imprint of Kensington Publishing Corp.

Printed in Mexico
1 2 3 4 5 6 7 23 22 21 20 19

THE JENSEN FAMILY
FIRST FAMILY OF THE AMERICAN FRONTIER

Smoke Jensen — *The Mountain Man*
The youngest of three children and orphaned as a young boy, Smoke Jensen is considered one of the fastest draws in the West. His quest to tame the lawless West has become the stuff of legend. Smoke owns the Sugarloaf Ranch in Colorado. Married to Sally Jensen, father to Denise ("Denny") and Louis.

Preacher — *The First Mountain Man*
Though not a blood relative, grizzled frontiersman Preacher became a father figure to the young Smoke Jensen, teaching him how to survive in the brutal, often deadly Rocky Mountains. Fought the battles that forged his destiny. Armed with a long gun, Preacher is as fierce as the land itself.

Matt Jensen — *The Last Mountain Man*

Orphaned but taken in by Smoke Jensen, Matt Jensen has become like a younger brother to Smoke and even took the Jensen name. And like Smoke, Matt has carved out his destiny on the American frontier. He lives by the gun and surrenders to no man.

Luke Jensen — *Bounty Hunter*

Mountain Man Smoke Jensen's long-lost brother Luke Jensen is scarred by war and a dead shot — the right qualities to be a bounty hunter. And he's cunning, and fierce enough, to bring down the deadliest outlaws of his day.

Ace Jensen and Chance Jensen —
Those Jensen Boys!

Smoke Jensen's long-lost nephews, Ace and Chance, are a pair of young-gun twins as reckless and wild as the frontier itself . . . Their father is Luke Jensen, thought killed in the Civil War. Their uncle Smoke Jensen is one of the fiercest gunfighters the West has ever known. It's no surprise that the inseparable Ace and Chance Jensen have a knack for taking risks — even if they have to blast their way out of them.

Chapter 1

Two minutes before the bullets started to fly, Luke Jensen emerged from the Keg 'N Jug Saloon and paused on the lip of the weathered walkway that ran in front of the place. He was feeling frustrated and more than a little puzzled.

Following standard procedure for arriving in a strange town on the trail of a fugitive, he had stopped by the town marshal's office to report his presence and state his business. Trouble was, he'd found only a plump, round-faced old man present, a self-described "part-time deputy whenever the marshal has to be out of town."

The deputy had gone on to inform Luke that the marshal was away chasing rustlers and there was no telling when he would be back. Hardly inspired by the oldster's seeming lack of eagerness for getting involved in anything of significance, Luke hadn't bothered him with the details of his visit, just let him know he was a bounty hunter and passing through.

From there, Luke had checked out first the livery stable and then the town's two drinking establishments. He'd come up empty all the way around. No sign of either the man he was looking for or the horse the man had been riding, as previously seen through the magnification of Luke's binoculars.

Earlier that morning, Luke had unexpectedly spotted the little town of Arapaho Springs from the crest of a tall hill off to the east. He'd viewed it as a stroke of possible good luck following the bad luck of a storm that had kept him hunkered down and drenched for most of the previous day and night. Thanks to that storm, he had lost the trail of Ben Craddock — the hombre whose name and face were plastered on a wanted poster Luke carried in his shirt pocket.

In addition to Craddock's image and description, the poster also displayed the banner **$2,500 REWARD — DEAD OR ALIVE**. That was where Luke came in. As a bounty hunter of considerable renown, he made his living off running down men like Craddock.

He was far from ready to give up in this case. The fact Craddock seemed to have given him the slip was only a temporary setback.

Upon sighting the town, Luke had figured it was probable that the wanted man, who'd been on the trail for a long stretch before also getting caught in the same storm as his pursuer, would stop at least long enough to replenish his supplies and more than likely oil his tonsils some at one of the saloons along the muddy main street.

True, Craddock was a man on the run and therefore somewhat cautious, but he had no idea Luke was on his trail, let alone anywhere close. Since the crimes that had prompted the wanted poster had been committed a whole state away and Arapaho Springs was such an out-of-the-way little place, it seemed unreasonable for Craddock to pass it up.

Yet it appeared he had. Either that or he'd come and gone so quickly that no one Luke had spoken with so far remembered seeing him.

So the man hunter was left with a decision to make. Did he hang around a little longer, check a little closer to make *sure* Craddock was nowhere in town? Or did he ride on, hoping to pick up the fugitive's trail again?

Or did he tarry awhile strictly for his own

purposes — namely, taking in a hot meal at the café down the street and maybe finding a place where he could bathe and change clothes — and *then* move on to once more cut Craddock's sign? Any doubt about accomplishing the latter never entered his mind. Luke was good at what he did, and that included being a keen-eyed tracker. He may have lost his man's trail briefly, due to the rain, but he felt confident it would be just a matter of time before he was able to pick it up again.

With that thought in mind, he made his decision. He would take some extra time for that hot meal and bath, perhaps ask a few more questions to those he encountered in the process. If no trace or remembrance of Craddock continued, it would be time to climb back in the saddle and ride on.

Luke started toward the café that had been tempting him ever since he'd passed it earlier and caught a whiff of delicious aromas. Fortunately, it was on the same side as the Keg 'N Jug, so he didn't have to cross the muddy, sloppy street again.

As he strode along, continuing to take in the sights and sounds of the peaceful little town that surrounded him, Luke received a considerable amount of appraisal in return. He was a tall, solidly built man in his early forties, with rugged facial features built around a prominent nose and neatly trimmed mustache. No one would ever call him classically handsome, yet women tended to find him attractive while men took note for reasons of their own. He dressed habitually in black — boots, trousers, shirt, wide-brimmed hat. Around his waist he wore a brace of nickel-plated Remington revolvers pouched in holsters set for the cross draw and a sheathed knife on his left hip, just behind the gun on that side. He generally earned more than a passing glance.

As he approached the café, Luke again caught scent of the aromas that had first lured him. Only a couple of horses were tied at the hitch rail out front of the establishment, but it being close to the noon hour, Luke expected there would be a good-sized crowd inside. At least there *should* be, if the food was anywhere near as good as it smelled. It crossed Luke's mind that, given his rather bedraggled, mud-spattered condition, maybe he should opt for the bath and change of clothes first, before mingling with other diners.

While he was pondering whether or not to clean up first, the choice was suddenly made for him. A rifle crack came from the opposite side of the street and the accompanying wind-rip of a bullet passed scarcely an inch in front of his nose. His reaction was swift, instinctive as he jerked back a half step and dropped into a low crouch. Even as the bullet that barely missed him was smashing against the side of the building he'd been passing, the Remingtons seemed to leap into his fists.

Staying crouched, his eyes scanned across the street, looking for some sign of the shot's origin. Up and down the boardwalk in either direction and on both sides, citizens who'd been going about their business were scrambling frantically to get inside one of the stores or otherwise find cover.

In the wide-open double doors of a blacksmith shop catty-cornered across the suddenly abandoned strip of muddy wagon and horse tracks, Luke saw what he was looking for. In that doorway, braced against its frame on one side, stood a man with a rifle raised to his shoulder. A haze of bluish smoke from his first shot hung in the air just above the man's head and, as Luke's eyes locked on him, he triggered another round.

The shot tore in low, gouging a furrow and throwing a spray of splinters from the boardwalk planks half a foot to Luke's left. Luke instantly responded by squeezing off a blast from each of his revolvers. The range was pushing the accuracy for a handgun, especially rounds fired without taking careful aim, but at the moment, Luke was only looking to neutralize the advantage of the man who'd opened up on him and buy himself a few seconds to get to shelter.

He got what he wanted when the rifleman ducked back from the .44 caliber slugs the Remingtons had sent screaming through the blacksmith shop doorway. While the shooter was trying to get reset and raise his rifle again, Luke sprang up out of his crouch, spun to one side, and lunged around the corner of the building he'd been caught in front of. A third shot chased him, but too late. It only managed to blow away a fist-sized chunk of wood an instant after Luke disappeared behind the building's edge.

He found himself at the mouth of a narrow alley between two structures. The ground underfoot was wet and sloppy, sucking at his boots, and strings of pooled rainwater were still dribbling down from the buildings' eaves. But all of that was minor discomfort compared to stopping a bullet.

His mind raced, calculating and weighing

his options. At least he had the satisfaction of knowing he'd caught up with his man — for the rifleman across the way was none other than Ben Craddock. The brief glimpse Luke had gotten between bullets was enough to confirm that much.

Damn! The blacksmith shop. *That* was where Craddock had gone after arriving in town. Considering all the miles Luke knew his quarry had recently ridden, he should have thought of the possibility Craddock's horse might need some reshoeing.

As a matter of fact, before leaving his own horse at the livery stable, Luke had taken time to check and make sure its shoes were in good shape since it, too, had traveled a fair stretch of miles and a smithy was close at hand if any repair had been needed. Finding everything okay in that department, he'd dismissed any further thought of the blacksmith.

A mistake, as it turned out. Nearly a fatal one.

As far as Luke knew, he'd given no prior indication to Craddock that he was closing in on him. His name, black-clad appearance, and his line of work were pretty widely known across the frontier. All it would have taken was for the wanted man to have gazed out the open doors of the blacksmith shop when Luke was coming up the street and he would have quickly jumped to the conclusion the bounty hunter was after him. What apparently came next was an equally quick decision to waste no time cutting him down with rifle fire.

Only Luke's swift reflexes had saved him. At least so far.

Chapter 2

Once more dropping into a crouch, Luke leaned out around the corner of the building and fired another shot into the doorway of the blacksmith barn. As before, he didn't take time for careful aim. He meant to accomplish two things. One, he wanted to make sure Craddock was still in place, and two, he wanted to work on his nerves some.

How successful he was at the latter, he had no way of knowing. But Craddock *was* still in the blacksmith's doorway, though pulled back so that only a sliver of him was visible along the edge of the frame. As soon as Luke's shot sizzled well wide of him, the fugitive leaned out and blasted two return rounds into the mouth of the alley.

With bullets again chewing wood in his wake, Luke wheeled about and lit a shuck toward the far end of the alley. There was no sense remaining where he was and continuing to trade lead with Craddock, especially at the range disadvantage for Luke's pistols against the outlaw's rifle.

Luke burst out the rear of the alley, slipping and skidding a bit, then cut hard to his right. Once again, he was headed in the direction of the aromatic café, and it occurred to him that if he came up on the far side of the eatery, it should put him almost straight across from the doorway to the blacksmith shop.

He pumped his arms as he ran, the long-barreled Remingtons flashing in his fists. From out on the street he heard the crack of two more rifle reports, Craddock firing blindly into the alley Luke had just vacated.

Good, let the damn fool waste ammunition.

It also signaled he was holding in place, unknowingly waiting for Luke to get repositioned.

Even as that advantage crossed his mind, Luke reached the back of the café. He slowed as he came to the far corner, allowing his breathing to level off some and then slowly edging around the building to take a cautious look and get his bearings. He quickly saw that he was a little farther down the street than he'd reckoned. Only a portion of the blacksmith shop was visible straight ahead. He'd have to move forward along the side of the café in order to reach a point where he could see into the doorway Craddock was shooting from.

That was okay with Luke. Possibly even a bit better than he'd hoped for. The angle for his line of fire would be reversed — left to right instead of right to left — though at a considerably reduced distance. What was more, if Craddock remained crowded partially behind the door frame on the right, he would be almost completely exposed when Luke reached the front corner of the café.

Luke edged forward, brushing along the side of the building, pistols raised and ready. The street remained empty and silent. The sound of his muddy boots on the soggy ground sounded contrastingly loud.

Reaching the corner of the café, he leaned cautiously ahead and out. His eyes locked intently as more and more of the blacksmith shop's open doorway came into view. All of it was right before him . . . but it was empty! There was no longer any sign of Craddock.

What the hell?

Luke fought the urge to lunge forward and sweep his gaze in all directions. But no, he didn't want to risk exposing himself too completely or too suddenly. Craddock could have merely stepped back deeper into the shop, losing himself in the shadows but still maintaining a full view of the street.

Luke had moved fast but apparently not fast enough to keep Craddock from growing suspicious or for some other reason deciding to shift his own position. Exactly to where and what he next —

A sudden ruckus came from somewhere near the back of the blacksmith shop. What sounded like the clatter of loose boards mixed with the shrill protest of a horse against a man's harsh commands.

"Yah! Yah! Get on through there, damn you!"

It was enough for Luke to realize what was happening. Craddock was attempting to escape on horseback out the rear of the blacksmith shop!

Luke shoved away from the café, and rushed out onto the street, quickly taking in the rectangular, scaled-down, barnlike structure of the blacksmith shop. Through the wide-open front doors, he could see the glow of a forge near the front. Farther back, since the smithy fashioned horseshoes and apparently also did farrier work, Luke reckoned there must be stalls or holding pens of some kind. Speculating that Craddock had his horse in for some shoe work meant the animal was readily available now that the fugitive was resorting to flight after his failure to effectively ambush the bounty hunter.

Luke wasn't inclined to let that happen. Not if he could help it.

Although the alley and the ground he'd passed over behind the other buildings was wet and sloppy, it was nothing compared to the middle of the street. Churned by numerous horses and wagons during and since the prolonged rain, it was a soupy, syrupy morass that seemed almost like a living thing bent on trapping and holding Luke's feet and legs. The slowness forced on him by fighting through the thick muck was infuriating, but he trudged ahead, slogging on, slamming first one foot forward and then the other. He thought he heard the wet thud of hooves out back of the blacksmith barn but couldn't be sure over the puff of his labored breathing and the thick slap of his own feet.

He stayed on a straight course toward the side of the blacksmith building, not veering to the open doorway. The alley on the side was wide and clear, through which he figured he could make better time than threading his way through the crowded, cluttered shop. Plus he didn't want to silhouette himself in the wide doorway, just in case Craddock lingered long enough to try one more shot at him.

The alley running beside the blacksmith barn was as muddy as the previous alleys and the ground behind the other buildings, but it was still a welcome reprieve from the street. When Luke reached it and began racing toward the other end, he finally felt like his feet had been freed and he was actually *running* again.

As he neared the end of the alley, he glimpsed the treeless, grassy, undulating expanse of Kansas landscape behind the blacksmith barn. It was interrupted only by a battered old wooden fence and a deep, weed-choked drainage ditch just a short way beyond that.

Ignoring the view, he came in sight of Craddock again. As expected, the fugitive was mounted on the same horse Luke had previously caught glimpses of through his binocular lenses. They'd already made it past the fence, a pair of wooden rails knocked loose from their posts offering an explanation for the clattering of boards Luke had heard earlier.

Craddock was spurring his horse hard toward the drainage ditch but had to hold up after only a couple of dozen yards in order to negotiate the steep banks of the ditch — too wide to jump and worn deep by decades of hard rain runoff from the surrounding slopes. The horse shied at the near edge of the cut, not wanting to start down the slick, weedy bank, but Craddock's cursing and the insistent pounding of his heels forced the frightened beast on over.

Luke ran past the end of the blacksmith barn just as horse and rider dropped down out of sight. The depth of the ditch and the high growth of weeds running along its rim momentarily obscured them.

Luke spat a curse of his own, knowing that if Craddock made it to the other side of the ditch and broke for open country, he almost certainly would make good his escape.

As suddenly as they'd dropped from sight, the pair reappeared on the other side of the ditch. The horse was gallantly struggling upward, its front hooves pawing and digging through the weeds, trying to find enough purchase in the soft earth underneath to pull itself forward. Craddock was hugging the animal's neck, frantically urging it on.

Luke continued to run toward them. His chugging breath was burning like fire inside his chest, but he didn't let up. Wouldn't let up. It crossed his mind to use his pistols, but the situation didn't yet feel desperate enough to warrant shooting a man in the back, nor did he want to risk hitting the flailing horse.

The distance to the ditch was shrinking. Luke's ears were filled with the hammering of his own heart and, more vague, the shrieks of the struggling horse and Craddock's demanding curses.

For a moment, it looked like the animal had made it. Its hooves reached up over the edge of the embankment, slamming down hard, gouging in, straining to pull its heaving chest and the rider on its back the rest of the way up the incline. But then part of the embankment crumbled away under those slashing hooves and horse and rider backslid amidst a shower of wet, loosened dirt.

An instant later, Luke launched himself from the edge of the near bank and landed full on Craddock's back. Still gripping his two pistols, Luke wrapped his arms and legs around the horseman and twisted with all his might, wrenching Craddock out of the saddle. Tangled together, the two men toppled into the four feet of water that filled the bottom of the ditch.

It was shockingly cold. They rolled under the surface, barely escaping the thrusts and kicks of the horse's hind feet as it continued to struggle up the embankment. The sensation of being underwater was briefly disorienting yet at the same time bracing and somewhat revitalizing. It jolted Luke out of the exhaustion from his run.

Never loosening the clamp of his legs or the grip of his powerful arms around Craddock, Luke twisted the man underneath him and held him there, grinding him into the muck and mud at the bottom of the ditch. Craddock tried to struggle, but he was outmatched. Much of the wind had been knocked out of him when Luke landed on his back, and he was being given no chance to try and regain any of it.

Luke, meanwhile, jerked his face above the surface and sucked in a great mouthful of air while he continued to hold Craddock under.

Only after he felt satisfied all the fight was gone from the fugitive did Luke finally roll off. He stood up, holstering his left-hand gun, and yanked Craddock's head out of the water.

To his surprise, the gasping, choking man showed he had some fight left after all — although only a meager amount. A last-ditch, desperation effort came in the form of a pitifully weak punch to Luke's jaw. It was enough to earn him a ringing clout to the side of the head from the long-barreled

Remington still in Luke's right fist. When Craddock sagged against the muddy bank, it was certain he was out of it. He was knocked cold.

CHAPTER 3

"After chasing rustlers for half the night and through the morning in the damn rain, I was looking forward to coming home to a nice dose of peace and quiet." Tom Burnett, the marshal of Arapaho Springs, spoke the words with a sour twist to his mouth and a mild scowl aimed at Luke Jensen.

"Things *are* peaceful and quiet around here . . . now," Luke replied matter-of-factly. "And you can hardly blame me for my share of the lead that got thrown in the streets of your town. I was defending myself against an ambush attempt that nearly blew my head off."

"Yeah, I guess I have to give you that much," Burnett allowed somewhat grudgingly. "Anybody who saw any part of it agrees with your version. It's just damn lucky that no innocent citizens got caught by any of that flying lead."

"But not everybody escaped harm," Luke

reminded him. "How's your blacksmith?"

"Doc says he'll likely have a headache and maybe a touch of dizziness for a few days, thanks to that rap on the noggin he got from Craddock." Burnett grunted. "Luckily, Swede's got a skull only a little less thick than that anvil he hammers on every day, other wise it might have been a lot worse."

"I'm glad to hear that. I hope it's some consolation for him to know that I paid Craddock back with a smart rap to his own noggin."

"Yeah, I expect Swede enjoyed hearing that," Burnett said. "A lot more, I'm sure, than Craddock enjoyed it from his end. The doc says he has a concussion. Not to mention the three or four cracked ribs you gave him."

"If anybody expects me to express sympathy for his injuries, I'm afraid they're in for a long wait."

The marshal regarded him. Burnett was a husky six footer, somewhere around fifty years old, getting a little thick through the middle as the years crept up. His face was broad and fleshy, featuring an expressively wide mouth, blunt nose, and inquisitive eyes. The hair on his head was thick and wavy, sand-colored, going gray around the temples. At the moment he was dressed in damp, rumpled, mud-spattered trail clothes and clearly not in the best of moods.

As he continued to study Luke, his scowl shifted to a look of curiosity. "Why didn't you just go ahead and shoot this Craddock varmint? Especially since the papers you got on him say **WANTED DEAD OR ALIVE.** Ain't that the way you bounty hunters usually do it — take the simplest route to be able to claim your blood money?"

Luke felt the familiar swell of resentment start to rise in him, but he managed to hold it in check. After all the times he'd endured similar remarks, he guessed he was getting used to them. The unfortunate truth was that too many in his profession *did* take the quick and easy way when it came to dealing with the men they went after. But then, so did a fair amount of lawmen operating on the fringe of the frontier. Luke considered pointing this out to Burnett, but decided against it. Countering one rude comment with another seldom accomplished anything useful.

"The rewards I claim," he responded calmly, "are legal compensation paid for rendering a service long upheld by the laws and courts of our land. I conduct my business in what I believe to be a reasonable and professional manner. Toward that end,

I stopped by this office first thing to let you know I was here in pursuit of a fugitive. You were unavailable. As for not shooting Craddock — it wasn't necessary, so I didn't."

"Well, now," Burnett said, hiking his eyebrows, "you've got that spiel down real pat, don't you?"

"I'm just saying how it is, that's all. I figure it's best if we have an accurate understanding of one another. Including, I should add, my appreciation for you and your deputy allowing me to lock my prisoner in one of your cells for the time being."

The discussion was taking place in the front office area of the sturdy log building that housed the town marshal's office and jail. After apprehending Ben Craddock, it was there — encouraged by a handful of townsfolk who'd reappeared once the shooting was over — that Luke had taken his prisoner. Big Swede Norsky, the blacksmith who'd gotten bashed over the head with a rifle barrel when he'd tried to stop Craddock's attempted ambush, was prominent in the mix of citizens who'd marched with Luke on the walk over. Upon being shown the reward dodger and hearing the eyewitness accounts of the shooting and the assault on Norsky, Fred Packer, the round-faced old part-time deputy, hadn't hesitated to make a cell available for locking up Craddock.

With his man secured behind bars, Luke had been directed to the local barbershop, where he was able to arrange for a hot bath, the cold one he'd gotten in the drainage ditch not counting for much, along with a shave and a hair trim. His soiled clothes were sent to a woman who took in wash and were received with a promise they would be cleaned and ready to be picked up the next day.

While soaking in a steaming tub in the privacy of a cramped room behind the barbershop, Luke had cleaned and oiled his guns and holsters, then carefully wiped dry each cartridge before reloading the Remingtons.

Once he was scraped and scrubbed clean, his intent was to finally pay a visit to that aromatic little café. Those plans, unfortunately, got knocked askew once again before he ever made it out of the barbershop. The disruption had come from Deputy Packer, who'd showed up to inform Luke the marshal wanted to see him right away. The deputy then departed to tend to other matters and Luke was left with little choice but to heed the marshal's summons. After all, he *had* participated in a shooting in the man's town and was responsible for the prisoner currently in his jail.

"Based on everything I heard from Deputy Packer, not to mention the half dozen citizens who waylaid me as soon as I got within the city limits, I got no problem keeping Craddock in our lockup," Burnett said now. "It sure seems to be where he belongs. Hell, that much would be warranted just based on his actions here in Arapaho Springs. But there's no sense going to the trouble of adding to the list of charges already listed on that dodger of yours. There's plenty there" — the marshal made an offhanded gesture to the soggy poster spread out to dry on a corner of his desk — "to stretch the hangman's rope."

"Seems like," Luke agreed. "But once I take him back and turn him over to the authorities down in Amarillo, that will be up to them to decide."

Burnett leaned back in his chair behind the desk and laced his fingers over his stomach. He seemed to relax some, and the scowl was gone from his face as he regarded Luke once more. "Maybe I was a little harsh a minute ago, Jensen. Painting you with a broad brush dipped in the stain of other bounty hunters I've had past encounters with. You seem different, and I recollect now hearing your name mentioned a few times in the past. How you play the bounty-hunting game a lot straighter than many in your trade. So I'll ask you to overlook my unfriendliness and chalk it up to a case of saddle sores, bone weariness, and being wet from my butt both ways after some long hours chasing sneaky, no-account wang-doodles."

"Consider it done. I know a little something about how a long chase can wear a body down."

"Well, at least we got the stolen cattle back." Burnett sighed. "Two of the thieves learned what you might call a hard, permanent lesson about the error of their ways. Three others got away, but I wager they'll think twice about coming back around these parts to try any more of that business in the future."

"I'm glad things turned out okay," Luke said. "But, if you don't mind me asking, isn't it a little unusual for a town marshal to go to so much trouble for a rustling problem?"

"Because of all that jurisdictional crap, you mean?" Burnett made a face. "If we had a sheriff or a U.S. marshal anywhere close by, believe me, I'd be more than happy to stay within the limits of my town jurisdiction and let them handle rustlers. What's more, my aching butt and back would be quick to second that motion by reminding me, the way they're doing right now, just how out of shape I am for gallivanting off into rugged country on such pursuits . . . which, come to think of it, rightfully calls for something else." The marshal leaned forward and reached into a low drawer on the side of his desk. When he straightened back up, he was brandishing a three-quarter-full bottle of whiskey.

Pulling the cork, he announced, "Strictly for medicinal purposes, you understand. To soothe the aforementioned aches and ward off the risk of catching a cold from the damp."

A faint smile touched Luke's mouth. "Understood."

After taking a long pull, Burnett lowered the bottle, wincing slightly as the contents went down. Then he said, "Come to think on it more, I reckon tussling with a hard-case desperado, not to mention getting soaked yourself due to being dunked in a muddy drainage ditch, might also rate a touch of preventative medicine." He extended the bottle toward Luke. "A swig of prevention?"

Luke accepted the bottle. "Don't mind if

I do." A moment later, after throwing down a healthy slug, he handed the bottle back, exclaiming, "Whoa now. That is *not* for the young and innocent."

Burnett grinned. "Too true. It's local moonshine." He took another nip from the bottle, then recorked it and returned it to the drawer.

"Now then. Back to the matter of your prisoner." Burnett leaned back in his chair once more, again lacing his fingers. "You said you plan on taking him to Amarillo. Not to sound pushy, but when did you have in mind to do that?"

"Just as soon as possible," Luke answered. "Ordinarily, since it's getting late in the day and you've agreed to keep him in your jail, I'd wait and head out first thing in the morning."

Burnett frowned. "Something about this make it *not* ordinary?"

"Not as far as I'm concerned," Luke told him. "But your town doctor made it a point to state pretty emphatically in front of several onlookers that it would be inhumane of me, considering Craddock's condition, to put him on the back of a horse and ride him any distance for at least a couple of days."

"That sounds like Doc Whitney, cautious

to a fault some of the time. Leastways in my opinion." Burnett twisted his mouth ruefully. "But he's been doctoring in this town for a lot of years and has managed to save more than he's let slip away, so folks tend to pay attention to what he says."

"Where does that leave me as far as *not* paying attention?" Luke wanted to know. "In other words, if I was to decide to go ahead and ride out tomorrow with Craddock in my custody, would you object based on the doctor speaking out against it?"

"Meaning no offense but, speaking honest, I personally would be glad to get rid of both you and Craddock. The sooner the better," Burnett said. "The thing is, though, my personal opinion and my legal obligation might be at odds."

It was Luke's turn to frown. "How so? You *are* the law in Arapaho Springs, aren't you?"

"Be nice to think so. Time was, that was the long and the short of it. But times change, Jensen. For the better, some say." Burnett's tone clearly conveyed a lack of conviction on that point. "One of those improvements, believe it or not for a little town like Arapaho Springs, is the addition of a lawyer in our midst. A real ambitious fella by the name of Jules Mycroft. He's an almighty stickler for the letter of the law —

especially for the law as applied to those sworn to uphold it."

"You sound like somebody who's found Mycroft to be more of a thorn in your side than an ally," observed Luke.

"Those are your words, not mine," replied Burnett, though not exactly disputing them. "Let's just say that any minute now, as soon as he hears I've returned to town, I expect Mycroft to be showing up here. First, I expect he'll lecture me and take issue with me having left town and ventured beyond my jurisdiction to go after those rustlers we discussed earlier. He'll be disappointed that I failed to arrest any of them so he could provide representation to defend their rights. I'm sure he'll also be primed to look into the matter of your Mr. Craddock and the circumstances of him being behind bars."

"I can fix that in a hurry. I can take Craddock out from behind bars and head for Amarillo right now."

"Uh-huh. You see, that's where my personal feelings and my legal obligation might have to butt heads. With Dr. Whitney saying it wouldn't be fitting and proper to move the injured prisoner and Mycroft poised to swoop down like some kind of legal eagle if I was to ignore that advice and let you go ahead and haul him off —"

The door to the marshal's office burst open before Burnett could finish or Luke could begin to state his objections. A very pretty young woman came quickly through it. Trailing rather timidly behind her was a tall, lanky young man wearing an uncertain expression.

"Father! Thank heaven you're back safe from chasing those rustlers," the young woman exclaimed, rushing past Luke and going straight to Burnett. The marshal managed to rise up out of his chair and meet her in a mutual embrace. In the midst of this, the girl's tone turned half-scolding as she added, "You left so suddenly and were gone for so long, I was worried half sick!"

When the embrace ended, Burnett's eyes cut back to Luke and he said somewhat sheepishly, "In case you haven't figured it out, Jensen, this is Millie, my worrywart of a daughter."

Chapter 4

Millie Burnett turned to look at Luke as if noticing his presence for the first time. In the moments she took to regard him, Luke also had the chance to appraise her more closely. And the pleasure was all his.

Not more than twenty years of age, Millie already possessed a very full set of womanly curves displayed nicely by her simple attire of a hip-hugging corduroy riding skirt and an amply filled white blouse. Above this was a delicately featured face highlighted by a wide, lush mouth and luminous brown eyes, all framed by a tumbling spill of wheat-blond hair. Luke had encountered many lovely women in his travels but few, if any, more stunning than the young beauty facing him.

"I beg your pardon, Mr. . . . Jensen, is it?" Millie said in a voice as lilting and pleasant as the rest of her. "I didn't mean to barge into the middle of your discussion with my father. I just got back into town myself and I was so anxious about . . . well, I guess I already blurted that part. Please forgive my interruption."

"Certainly," Luke said. "Think nothing of it."

Placing a hand on his daughter's shoulder, Burnett said, "But I have a question for you, missy. If you were so concerned about my well-being, what were you doing out of town yourself while I was away?"

"I explained that to you two days ago, Father. Don't you remember?" Millie replied. "I told you that Russell had been tasked with delivering some very important legal documents to Mr. Ramsey out at the R-Slash as soon as they were ready. Being relatively new to the area, he wasn't sure of the way out to the Ramsey ranch, so I volunteered to guide him. As far as going with him today, I figured I could worry about you just as well out of town as I could staying here fretting."

The lanky young man who'd arrived with Millie stepped forward. He was dressed in a gray suit with a matching vest and maroon bowtie. The hat he'd removed from his head upon entering, revealing a thatch of straw-colored hair, was a gutter-creased homburg with a silk band that matched the color of his tie.

"Millie insisted on fulfilling that commitment, Marshal Burnett," he said, "even though I told her it wasn't necessary in light of you being away and all. I offered to find someone else to show me the way or attempt to manage it myself, but I'm afraid your daughter is . . . well, rather headstrong when she makes up her mind about something."

Burnett arched an eyebrow. "Tell me something I don't know."

"Never mind that," Millie said. "How did it go with your attempt to catch the rustlers, Father? Did you have any success?"

"In a manner of speaking. We got Whitey Mason's cattle back. I guess that's the main thing." Burnett paused, frowning, then added, "We shot and killed a couple of the thieving skunks, but the rest got away."

"How unfortunate," Russell said.

The marshal turned his frown on the young man. "Unfortunate how? That we killed some or that some got away?"

"Why, the whole event," Russell managed to answer, though clearly caught off guard by Burnett pinning him down with the questions. "I mean, it's unfortunate that kind of lawlessness still takes place — the stealing of cattle and whatnot — and that violence has to be the answer for it."

"Yeah, you've the outlook of your boss ingrained in you real good, don't you?" Burnett said, half sneering. "But you're right about one thing — violence *is* the only answer for lowlife scum who make their way preying on others. Whitey Mason and his whole family have worked hard for a lot of years to make a go of their little ranch. I wasn't about to stand by and let a bunch of thieving bastards rob them blind just when they're starting to get a leg up on things!"

"Father! Your language," Millie objected.

Burnett ignored her, keeping his attention focused on Russell. "And speaking of violence — did it happen to occur to you, Mr. Quaid, that with the rustlers on the prowl it was hardly a wise decision on your part to pick such a time for a ride out of town? And especially to drag my daughter along, no matter how headstrong she can be?"

"Father, that's not fair," Millie said. "Russell was given a job to do. He could hardly refuse. And as far as me going along, you're the one who taught me that a commitment is a commitment. As it turned out, it was a good thing I *did* accompany him. The bridge over Yellowtail Creek is washed out and he would have never known about the old north ford if I hadn't been there to show him."

Burnett scowled. "Maybe so, but were these legal documents so blasted important they couldn't have waited another day or two? You both knew that rustling had been taking place. Curly wolves who'll stoop to robbing cattle are capable of other things, especially where a pretty young gal is concerned. What if you'd crossed paths with them?"

"That's a rather silly notion and you know it, Father. You told me the rustling was taking place on the Mason spread, to the west. The R-Slash is well to the east. I don't see where there was much chance of us encountering any trouble out that way."

"And in the event there *had* been any kind of trouble, I assure you, sir, I would have defended Millie with my life," Russell stated firmly. "As to the legal documents I delivered to Mr. Ramsey, they represented the resolution to a long-contested matter involving some false claims by distant relatives on a portion of his property. Mr. Mycroft deemed it important I present the good news to Mr. Ramsey posthaste, especially after yesterday's rain delay, in order to finally relieve his distress over the matter."

"If it was so important, why didn't Mycroft deliver the papers himself?" Burnett wanted to know.

"Mr. Mycroft's time is best spent addressing complex legal matters," Russell said rather stiffly, worrying his hat in his hands. "It falls to me to take care of more mundane things like serving as the occasional courier."

"By the way, Mr. Jensen," Millie said, suddenly addressing Luke, "please allow me to belatedly introduce my friend Russell Quaid. Russell is the legal clerk for our town's most prominent lawyer."

"Our town's *only* lawyer," Burnett was quick to correct. "Don't make Mycroft out to be more than he is — he does a good enough job of that all on his own. Besides, I already gave Jensen here the lowdown on him."

Luke acknowledged Russell with a tip of his head. He felt a little sorry for the young man, standing there enduring the remarks of the annoyed marshal. The father in Burnett certainly had every right to worry about the safety of his daughter. Still, expecting two grown people to halt their going and coming from town because of some outlying rustling problem seemed a bit much. And to expect Russell or any other red-blooded male to cancel plans of going for a long, leisurely ride with the likes of Millie was even more so.

"If you want to know about violence and the kind of trouble that can be found out on the trail," Burnett added, "then you need to talk to Jensen here. He's a bounty hunter. He deals with the worst owlhoots to be found. Hell, he goes *looking* for 'em."

Millie's widened eyes bored into Luke. "My goodness. Is that true?"

"It's true that I'm what most people refer to as a bounty hunter, yes," Luke conceded. "But I don't exactly see it as going looking for trouble. More like I seek to *remove* trouble by hunting down wanted men who've demonstrated their disregard for the law and their willingness to harm others who get in their way."

"My goodness," Millie said again. "Does that mean you're here in Arapaho Springs on . . . business?"

"He sure is," Burnett answered. "Or, to put it more accurately, he was. So happens his business here is concluded and the result is locked up back in one of our cells."

Millie's eyes fell to the wanted poster spread out on the corner of her father's desk. "And this is the fugitive he apprehended?"

"None other."

Russell moved forward to examine the paper along with Millie. "Wanted dead or alive," he read aloud. His eyes lifted to Luke. "Does that mean you shot him?"

Luke shook his head. "You heard the marshal say he's back there in a cell. When I shoot a man, there's seldom any need to lock him up afterwards."

"Not that Jensen didn't have every right to shoot the varmint and settle his hash permanentlike," Burnett said. "In addition to the crimes listed on the dodger there, this Craddock tried to ambush Jensen right out on Main Street. Nearly blew his head off — after he'd already brained Swede Norsky, I might add, so he could use the door way of Swede's blacksmith shop to do his shooting from."

"Good lord," Millie said. "When did all this take place?"

"A little before noon, while I was still out of town," her father answered. "By the time I got back, it was all over. Jensen had captured his man in that drainage ditch out back of the blacksmith shop and Fred Packer, acting as my deputy while I was away, made a cell available for the prisoner."

"Has Mr. Mycroft heard about this?" Russell asked. "Has the prisoner received proper representation?"

"I'm his representation — me and that wanted poster," Luke said. "That's all that's necessary. Until I get him back to Amarillo, that is, where he'll go before a judge."

Russell looked concerned. "But in the meantime . . . When do you intend to take him to Amarillo?"

"Heading out tomorrow, I hope. Just as soon as the doctor says his injuries are healed enough for him to travel."

"Injuries?" Russell's look of concern deepened. "I thought you said you didn't shoot him?"

Irritation starting to become evident in his tone, Luke said, "In order to get Craddock to stop trying to kill me, I had to be a little more forceful than just asking him politely."

Russell blinked. "Yes. Yes, I suppose so."

"According to everything listed here," Millie said, continuing to study the wanted poster, "this Craddock is one dangerous character."

"Nevertheless, due process is owed everyone," Russell said stubbornly.

"Due process," Burnett groaned, rolling his eyes. "Jesus Christ, son, I'm afraid you may already be past helping. You've spent so much time hanging around Mycroft and breathing in the ink fumes from his musty old law books that you're coming down with a serious case of lawyeritis!"

Russell lifted his chin. "You're entitled to your opinion, Marshal. But I would argue that there certainly are worse things to aspire to than becoming a good lawyer."

"A good lawyer — maybe," Burnett allowed. "But that's not the same as becoming another Jules Mycroft."

At which point, as if responding to some silent, invisible cue, the front door to the office opened and a tall, dapper-looking man strode in. One glance, well before any introductions could be made, was all it took for Luke to know the newcomer was Jules Mycroft.

CHAPTER 5

"Well now. How fortunate," said the dapper man. "Everyone I hoped to have words with is present here in one spot. Providing, that is, that you, sir" — he turned his attention to Luke — "are the rather notorious bounty hunter, Luke Jensen."

"I'm Jensen," Luke agreed. "Can't say I lay claim to the notorious part."

"Oh, trust me. You are all of that. Your escapade in our town earlier today was proof enough, even if your name wasn't already familiar to several of our citizens. Inasmuch as I do not share your wide recognition, however, and since introductions seem to be slow in coming, allow me to handle it personally." The man's right hand was extended. "I am Jules Mycroft, attorney at law."

Luke hesitated slightly before taking the offered hand. Mycroft was a bit above average height, fiftyish, trim and solid looking, with a thick head of brown hair shot with streaks of gray around the temples. He, too, was dressed in a three-piece suit, pale blue in color, though much better cut than that of his young clerk.

The strength of his grip came as something of a surprise to Luke, who said as they shook, "As a matter of fact, I've heard of you also."

Mycroft's eyes cut automatically to the marshal. "Yes, I can imagine," he said coolly. Then, abruptly, the lawyer shifted his gaze to his subordinate. "Before getting to the business that brought me here, Russell, I must say that I am somewhat surprised to find you present. I should have thought you would report directly to me upon returning to town."

"I only just arrived a few minutes ago, sir," Russell was quick to explain. "If you recall, Miss Burnett accompanied me to show me the way to the R-Slash ranch. When we got into town and she saw her father's horse at the hitch rail out front, she was anxious to stop and see how he'd fared with his investigation of rustling activity. I'll admit I tarried a bit extra when I heard about the street shooting and the apprehended fugitive, but I was just about to —"

"Never mind. I understand," Mycroft

said, cutting him off.

Looking on, Luke judged that the lawyer's main purpose had been to show his authority by making his subordinate squirm a bit in front of the others. Having accomplished that, he didn't really care about the explanation or even the fact the young man was tardy with his report. He showed all the signs, Luke concluded with his hackles prickling, of being not only the pompous ass Burnett had painted him as, but also a bully.

"It really was my fault Russell got detoured from reporting to you right away, Mr. Mycroft," Millie said in defense of the young man. "But, like he said, we've only been in town a few minutes."

"I understand," Mycroft said again, smiling at her. "I understand furthermore how reluctant anyone in Russell's position would be to part company with your lovely self, Miss Burnett."

Russell's face turned bright red. "It wasn't anything like that, sir. It wasn't that I wanted to prolong my time with Millie . . . That is to say I didn't want to *not* spend time with her, either . . . But when we — or rather she, that is —"

"For crying out loud, son, put a sock in it." This time it was Burnett who cut him off. "Stop. Stop, before you get your tongue tied in a knot you'll never get untangled. How will you ever be a lawyer then?"

The color in Russell's face stayed bright, but he knew when to quit. He made as if to lift his hands only to let them drop loosely to his sides again in an exasperated gesture.

Burnett's eyes went to Mycroft. "You say you came here to discuss some business matters, Mr. Attorney-at-Law. I doubt we've covered any of them so far so I suggest you get to it. And I'll warn you right up front that I've had a long, wet night and a dry but equally long morning, which has left me full of no sleep or hot food or coffee . . . meaning I'm in no mood for any of your long-winded prattling."

"Very well." Mycroft harrumphed. "Let us start with the reason for your uncomfortable night and morning. Once again you were engaged in activities far beyond your legal jurisdiction. Activities which, to my understanding, left two men dead. Do you deny this?"

"Yup. Wrong on every count. For starters," Burnett said through gritted teeth, "the only things that got killed were two lowdown cattle thieves. Only by the flimsiest definition could anybody call them men."

"You place such low value on human life

that you can make light of it?"

"Like I said, they were lowdown varmints. So, yeah, I place a lowdown value on them," the marshal growled. "As for that jurisdictional bull crap we've been through a dozen times before, I wasn't out there acting in the role of a lawman. I was out there lending a neighborly hand to Whitey Mason in order to help him protect his cattle herd from rustlers trying to pick him clean. A man has a right to protect his property, doesn't he?"

"Of course he does."

"And if he asks some friends and neighbors to help him, don't they have the same right?"

"You're playing games with the law, Burnett, and you know it. You're supposed to uphold the law, not twist it around to suit your personal need."

"Isn't that what shysters like you do every day of your lives?" Burnett demanded. "Twist and manipulate the law with your fifty-dollar words and long-winded legal mumbo jumbo so that a common man can't follow the right or wrong of half of what you spout? Well, I'm not twisting anything. I'm saying it straight out, plain and simple. If a decent, honest man needs my help against a bunch of damn crooks, then by

God, I'm going to help him — jurisdiction be damned! So you might as well get it through your thick skull, Mycroft, because I'm getting sick of having this conversation and I don't intend to waste my time with it ever again."

"One of these days you aren't going to have any choice," Mycroft told him. "The days of relics like you who merely 'keep the peace' however they see fit are coming to an end. Nothing short of strict adherence to the letter of the law — by miscreants as well as those who wear a badge — will be tolerated."

"When that day comes, you be sure and let me know," Burnett said sarcastically. "Now what else is stuck in your craw that you came here to hack out? Get to it and get it over with."

Mycroft glared at him for a long moment. Then, clearing his throat, he said, "All right. I want to have a meeting, in private, with the prisoner you're holding back there in one of your cells. I want to make sure he understands he has the right to counsel and I'm prepared to represent him if he so chooses."

In almost perfect unison, Luke and Burnett said a loud and firm, "No!"

Mycroft looked stunned. "What do you

mean no? That's the right of every citizen. It's due process. You can't refuse —"

"I can," Luke said. "That man is my prisoner. The marshal here is doing me a favor by letting me use his lockup merely as a holding facility. But Craddock remains my responsibility and until I turn him over to the authorities in Amarillo, the only rights he has are the ones I give him. You want to talk due process, counselor?" Luke jabbed a finger at the wanted poster on the desk. "Based on the authority provided me as an enforcer of that warrant, I could have made due process for Craddock — and still can, if I choose — as simple as a bullet. Now I suggest you get out of my face without any further noise I might interpret as trying to interfere with me and the job I have to do."

Chapter 6

Forty miles to the east and a bit south of Arapaho Springs, Sam Kelson stood smoking a cigarette on the front porch of what had once been a well-appointed ranch house. In its current condition, however, the house and surrounding grounds of the Split D ranch headquarters showed little remaining evidence of the tidy, orderly run operation it had long taken pride in being. The fine glass windows of the main house were all broken to nothing but jagged shards with tattered curtains streaming out from within like panting tongues through uneven fangs.

On the ground outside each of these windows lay scattered, mostly broken items — lamps, dishes, candle-holders, slashed couch cushions, and various brightly colored pillows — all hurled from inside. Before the front door that hung crookedly open on twisted hinges was more wreckage strewn across the width of the porch and onto the front yard. A few larger items were contained in the mix — broken dining-room chairs, a collapsed table, more lamps and dishes, an ornate cuckoo clock split open with its brightly painted little bird dangling twisted and forever stilled.

Outlying from the main house, a handful of short-horn cattle milled and bawled nervously in a small holding pen. Just outside the fence, three of the critters lay as hastily butchered carcasses with large chunks of meat removed. In a nearby corral, twenty or so cow ponies trotted restlessly back and forth, blowing and whinnying uneasily at the scent of blood filling their nostrils.

Not far from the corral, the cookshack and bunkhouse for the ranch wranglers also showed signs of disarray. Their doors and windows stood open, too, with items from within strewn out on the ground. The only difference was the meager belongings of the punchers didn't make for much to be tossed out.

That left the half dozen other items littering the ground between the main house and the outlying structures . . . the bodies of men lying in still, lifeless sprawls on the muddy ground.

Puddles from the previous night's rain had collected in shallow depressions close to a couple of bodies, the water in them showing a red tint due to blood leaking from the bullet wounds that riddled the fallen men.

Sam Kelson calmly took all of this in as he drew deeply on his cigarette and then released the smoke in a long, slow plume. He was a tall man, solidly built, with large, powerful hands and a head that seemed a shade too big even for his broad shoulders. He had a strong jaw, thick brown hair that fell over his collar at the back of his neck, and deep-set brown eyes that many had commented looked perpetually sad, except for the occasions when they flashed with near-maniacal rage.

As Kelson smoked and dispassionately surveyed the wreckage and carnage around him, two men emerged from the bunkhouse and started in his direction. One was a couple of inches over six feet, rangy in build with notably bowed legs and the rolling walk of a man who'd spent years on the back of a horse. His beard-stubbled face was deeply seamed by wind and weather and he had piercing dark eyes sandwiched between crow's-feet as sharp and permanent as if they'd been carved by a scalpel.

The second man was as many inches

under six feet as his companion was over. He was sparely built with quick, precise movements, a pugnacious thrust to his chin, and alert blue eyes set under shaggy blond brows that matched the unruly thatch of hair on his head. Like Kelson, each man had a red bandanna tied around his right arm above the elbow.

As the pair trudged toward the main house, they skirted around puddles and bodies without appearing to notice much distinction between the two. In the sinking afternoon sun, they cast grotesque, writhing shadows on the ground ahead of themselves.

Upon reaching the front edge of the porch, Elmer Pride, the taller of the two men, squinted up at Kelson and said, "The boys are ready to ride as soon as you give the word, Sam. Horses saddled and pack animals all loaded and waitin' out behind the bunkhouse."

"How many packhorses?" Kelson asked.

"Five, all told," the shorter man, Henry Wymer, answered. "We already had the two we've been traveling with since that last job, and now we've made an especially good haul here. Lot of good supplies to take on to our winter quarters, Sam. Appears they were stocking ahead, making their own plans for the upcoming cold months. Plenty of salt pork, flour, beans, rice, big batch of canned goods. All stuff we can put to good use."

"Not to mention a heap of grain we found in a bin. We filled seven or eight sacks from it to take along for our horses," Pride added.

Kelson nodded. "That was real thoughtful of old man Delmonte's crew to have all of that on hand for us, wasn't it? Money-wise, the skinflint old bastard didn't have nothing but a few hundred dollars stashed in his safe. And hardly anything in the way of jewelry or fancy geegaws for his wife and daughter. Glad to hear those other goods still make this a worthwhile haul for our trouble."

"Hell," Wymer said, "we even found half a case of dynamite in the toolshed. Don't know what they had in mind to use it on but they're past having any need for it now. I had our boys load it up, too."

Kelson arched an eyebrow. "What need you figure we got for it?"

"You never know." Wymer shrugged. "Could be a time when something like that comes in handy. Maybe we should even take a few sticks along the next time we hit a town."

"We never needed dynamite to take a town before," Kelson pointed out. "And since we usually run into a few good citizens not liking us wherever we show up, I don't care for the idea of having a stick of dynamite in a saddlebag that might get hit by a stray bullet."

Wymer made a sour face. "I guess I never thought of that. Should we leave the dynamite here then?"

It was Kelson who shrugged. "Since you already got it loaded, might as well bring it along. Like you said, could come a time when it'll be useful for something."

"Speakin' of things to bring along," Pride said, "what about Delmonte's wife and daughter? You have anything in particular in mind to do with 'em?"

Kelson's brows pinched together. "You mean they're still alive?"

Pride and Wymer exchanged glances.

"Well . . . yeah," Pride said. "The boys drug 'em out to the bunkhouse last night and, you know, used 'em to pass the time whilst we was hunkered in outta the rain."

"That's what led to the question of what to do with 'em now," Wymer explained. "Since we're headed for winter quarters and figuring to lay low for a spell . . . well, some of the men were asking about maybe taking the women along. To help pass the time some more, once we get there."

Kelson made a distasteful face. "Good God. I didn't pay much attention while they were being dragged out, but from the glance I got, the wife looked plenty old and used up to begin with, and the daughter was so homely I can understand why the old man didn't waste money on fancy geegaws for her. Yet *that's* what the men want to keep around for company?"

"Ain't nobody sayin' it's exactly what they *want,*" Pride said. "It's more a case of what they got. Poor pickin's though they may be, those Delmonte gals are better than nothing."

Kelson chuckled dryly. "I guess I can't argue that." He flipped away the smoldering remains of his cigarette then added, "But consider this. What if, before settling into our winter quarters, we made a stop somewhere where the pickings are likely to be much better?"

Now it was Wymer's turn to squint up at him. "You got something in mind. What is it?"

"Chewed on it some during the night. Decided on it a little while ago," Kelson said. "To the west and a piece north of here is a little town by the name of Arapaho Springs. Ain't much of a place. Normally wouldn't be worth our time. But since we're going to ground for the winter and it's practically on our way, I figure why the hell not. There's a bank and a few stores, so there's bound to be some money for the taking. More supplies, too. And since they got next to nothing in the way of law — only one marshal last I knew — it'd be an easy grab."

Wymer frowned. "We already got a nice pile of loot stashed away, don't we, Sam?"

"So what? You think there's such a thing as *too much* money?"

"No, of course not. I'm just thinking the men are pretty strung out. We've covered a lot of ground this past month, hit two other towns already and then this ranch." Wymer shrugged. "There's such a thing as wringing too much out of a body of men. I learned that during the war. Comes to that, they can start getting sloppy and careless and it can lead to things not going so smooth."

"Didn't I make it clear what a piece of cake this amounts-to-nothing place is going to be?" Kelson's face reddened and took on an annoyed scowl. "So our boys are a little strung out. I could take Arapaho Springs with a Sunday School picnic class that didn't get any sleep the night before. How much risk can there be in that?"

Wymer spread his hands. "You're the

leader of this outfit, Sam. You make the call. I'm just tossing in something to think about, that's all. We've been riding together long enough, I thought I had that right."

Some of the color drained from Kelson's face almost as fast as it had appeared there. "Of course you have the right to speak your thoughts, Henry. You and Elmer both. You're my right-hand men. Maybe I'm a little strung out, too. I guess we all are, like you said. Chalk up me snapping at you to that. But, damn it, I still think hitting this town ain't a bad idea. For all the reasons I said. Plus, now that it's been brought up, one more."

One corner of Elmer Pride's mouth lifted. "Better pickin's for some women to take to our winter quarters."

"There it is," Kelson said. "Hell, ain't I human, too? You think I wouldn't like to have some gals around to pass the time with when we go to ground? You'll just have to excuse me if I'm particular enough to want 'em to be a little better looking than the rump end of my horse." He cut his eyes to Wymer. "Come on, Henry. The chance to rake in some more money and supplies *and* some decent looking belly-warmers for the cold months ahead — don't you think that's enough to motivate the men for pulling one more job?"

Wymer tried to maintain a stony expression, but after only a couple of seconds his mouth twisted into a rueful smile. "You and that persuading damn tongue of yours. You should've been a politician instead of an outlaw, Sam."

"You say that like there's a difference," Kelson replied.

"Well, if it's settled then let's get to it. Let's ride for Arapaho Springs," Pride said. "How far is it?"

"If we ride through the night, we can hit there early in the morning before they get woke all the way up. But we can't cover ground that fast with packhorses. So pick out two or three men — Grogan as one of them, I'd say, on account of how good he is with horses — and send them and the loaded animals on ahead to our hideout. The rest of us will take care of the Arapaho Springs job and then either meet up with them there or on the way."

"We going to torch this place before we go?" Wymer asked.

"Why would we do any different than usual?"

"What about these women then?" Pride wanted to know.

Kelson swung a cold gaze in his direction.

"Be a mighty cruel thing to leave a poor widow and her homely, ruined daughter with nothing but a burnt-out shell of a home and their dear husband and daddy and ranch hands laying dead all around them, wouldn't you say? Seems plain enough to me it'd be a kindness to make it so they never have to live through that kind of misery and suffering."

Chapter 7

Tom Burnett couldn't seem to stop chuckling. "I tell you, that was a performance it was a privilege to see. Hell, I would have paid good money to watch. Mycroft actually turned purple. Purple," he repeated for the third or fourth time. "I never knew a person's face could take on a color like that."

His daughter seemed less amused, though she couldn't entirely hide a guarded smile. "It's pretty rare for anyone to get the last word on Mycroft, that's for sure. What I'm not so sure of, is whether it was a good idea. I think he is capable of being a very spiteful man who would relish the chance to try and get even at some point."

"What chance is he going to have for that? Luke will be leaving tomorrow or the day after at the latest," Burnett said. "Besides, he's dealt with a lot more dangerous characters than Jules Mycroft looking to settle a score with him. Ain't that right, Luke?"

Just the three of them were left in the marshal's office. Mycroft — with a glum-looking Russell obediently in tow — had stormed out immediately following his exchange with Luke. Outside, the lengthening shadows of late afternoon were starting to reach in toward the middle of the street.

A brief smile curved Luke's mouth, not so much over the thought of his dressing down lawyer Mycroft as for the marshal's sudden familiarity in using his first name. He thought of the old saying *The enemy of my enemy is my friend.* It was clear that the animosity between Burnett and Mycroft had been simmering for a while, and the exchanges of a few minutes ago had done little to make any difference except give the marshal a temporary ally in Luke.

"Your daughter makes a valid point all the same," Luke said. "I may be moving on shortly, but Mycroft strikes me as the type who's not above harboring his spiteful feelings and taking them out on somebody else if and when it becomes more convenient. And, for however long I *am* around, I don't exactly need any more enemies. As you just pointed out, Marshal, I already have plenty of those."

"Well, I wouldn't lose no sleep having that

pipsqueak as one of them," Burnett said. "I know I sure won't, and he's been a thorn in my backside ever since he graced our town by hanging out his blasted shingle." He paused long enough to let an exaggerated frown tug at his face. "And speaking of sleep, I don't mind saying that I am damned well overdue for some. Right after I peel off these wet clothes, do some soaking in a tubful of hot water, then have me an early supper . . . providing a certain young lady is finished gallivanting all over the countryside and takes a notion to get home and fix something."

"All right. I can take a hint," Millie replied. "Getting you fed and put to bed will be a welcome relief from hearing you bellyache, you old grouch."

"How would you know how much I bellyache? You're never around."

"Maybe there's a connection there. Did you ever think of that?"

Luke recognized good-natured banter between two people who were obviously very fond of one another.

Millie's expression shifted, turned more serious. "But wait a minute. What about the turn around town you usually take after supper? And won't you be bunking here at the jail tonight, like you usually do when you have a prisoner in the lockup?"

"Not this time," Burnett said with a shake of his head. "I've already arranged with Fred Packer to take care of both those things for me. He'll make the evening rounds and then come back here to grab whatever sleep he can while keeping an eye on things until I get in come morning."

Millie's gaze went to Luke. "What about you, Mr. Jensen? Where are you staying tonight?"

"To tell the truth, I don't have that planned quite yet," Luke answered. "It occurs to me, though — since Craddock is technically my prisoner — maybe I ought to be the one to stick close and keep an eye on him. If it's all right with the marshal, I could sleep on the cot in the other cell."

Burnett nodded. "You know, that ain't a half bad idea. I'm sure Fred wouldn't mind not having to give up his comfortable bed at home. He could go ahead and still make the evening rounds for me, and then head home."

"It should be my responsibility to see to it the prisoner gets fed, too," Luke said. "Since I've been planning on taking a meal at the little café down the street, I figured I'd bring him back something from there."

Burnett's forehead puckered. "That's

good thinking, except for one thing — the café is closed by now."

"Closed?" Luke echoed, the emptiness in his stomach suddenly faced with only disappointment to fill it.

"That's right. Lucinda, the gal who runs the café, opens early for breakfast and keeps serving a while past lunch. By two or three in the afternoon, she closes," the marshal explained. "She tried staying open later but found she didn't do enough business on account of most folks around town prefer to take their supper at home. The two saloons lay out an evening spread, though. The Brass Rail's the best of the two, in my opinion. You could get some sandwiches for you and your prisoner there."

"He will not!" Millie objected. "Isn't it enough that Mr. Jensen comes to our town, gets nearly shot, and then is left to sleep on a jail cot? The least we can do is see to it he doesn't have to go without a decent meal."

"It's all right, miss," Luke assured her. "Your father is doing plenty by allowing me to keep Craddock here and also giving me a place to bunk with a roof over my head. He doesn't owe me anything more. Nobody does."

"Well, I don't see it that way," Millie insisted. "I have a mound of already cooked roast beef at home — way more than just Father and I can eat, even after we've already made one meal out of it. I will be heating it up and serving it with some side dishes and dessert for our supper. After I've fed the old grouch and put him to bed, I'll prepare plates for you and your prisoner and return here with them. I will be highly offended if you do not accept this offer of hospitality."

Luke wanted to refuse, wanted her not to go to that much trouble, but the depth of her imploring brown eyes and the anticipation that knifed through his stomach at the mention of roast beef was a lot to overcome.

An appealing look in the direction of Burnett didn't help at all.

"If you were paying attention earlier, I believe you heard ample warning about my daughter's headstrong tendencies," the marshal said. "My advice to you, friend, is to accept the offer and get yourself set for a fine meal."

"It's about damn time somebody came around to check on me. I been hearin' voices yammerin' out in the other room, folks comin' and goin', but not a damn one gave a peep to me. I ain't seen nobody since that rickety old horse doctor who wrapped this bandage around my head and announced I had a busted skull. Like I didn't already know that much on my own." Ben Craddock sat on the edge of his jail cell cot and glared at Luke on the other side of the bars.

The outlaw was a huskily built specimen, late thirties in age, with a ruggedly handsome face and piercing blue eyes. At the moment he had a thick bandage wrapped around the top part of his head, just above his bristly eyebrows, leaving his longish, unruly dirty blond hair to poke out around the edges.

"Yeah, I probably could have diagnosed the cracked skull part, too," Luke said dryly. "I ought to know, since I'm the one who gave it to you."

"You're damned right you did." Craddock rose to his feet. "If that mangy nag I was ridin' would have had some sand in her instead of too much lead in her ass to climb a lousy hill, it would have been a different story. You'd have never got close enough to get your hands on me and I'd be ridin' free and clear right about now."

Luke shrugged. "If you're going to blame somebody, why not yourself? You had a wide-open shot when I was walking unprepared down the street. You should have taken care of business right then and there."

"You bet I should have!" Craddock balled his fists and came closer to the bars. "How I missed, I'll never know."

Luke's mouth formed a thin smile. "Well, you've got plenty of time ahead of you to think about it. It's a twelve-day ride to Amarillo and then, once there, you'll have another stretch in a cell before you eventually take your walk up the gallows steps. Trouble is, none of it will provide the chance for you to improve your aim any."

Craddock unclenched his fists and wrapped them around the bars. "Don't you count on it, bounty hunter! Like you said, it's a long way from this godforsaken town to Amarillo. A lot can happen. I ain't at the top of those gallows steps yet."

"Keep dreaming," Luke told him. "You had your run, but now you're in my custody. And if you know anything at all about me, you know I'm not in the habit of losing prisoners."

"Yeah. Luke Jensen, the big bad bounty hunter in black," Craddock sneered. "I don't know how you caught up with me, but that still don't mean it's over. I might've made a mistake by missin' that rifle shot, but it just might be you made a mistake, too, by not finishin' me when you had the chance."

"Thanks for reminding me. I'll be sure to keep that in mind in case you try anything cute when we're out on the trail."

Craddock's sneer faded. Turning sullen, he said, "We ain't out on the trail yet. What about the here and now — am I gonna get anything to drink or eat? And is that doctor ever comin' back? My head's poundin' like there's somebody with a hammer inside tryin' to beat his way out."

"You'll be getting some food and water in a little while," Luke replied. "The headache you're going to have to live with. Consider yourself lucky it's not a bullet hole."

Chapter 8

It was after dark when Millie Burnett returned to the jail bearing a large picnic basket with a red checkered cloth draped over the top.

In the interim, following his brief session with Craddock, Luke had killed some time by again stripping down his pistols, cleaning them, and then once more carefully wiping each of the cartridges from the cylinders and his gunbelt before reassembling and reloading. If he was somewhat fastidious in his appearance and mannerisms, he was even more so when it came to his weapons. They were, after all, the difference between life and death in his line of work.

Deputy Packer also helped pass some time by stopping by for a bit of small talk in the midst of his rounds. Luke obliged him by recounting a couple of "bounty huntin' adventures," without too much elaboration or exaggeration yet enough to satisfy the oldster before he drifted on. After he was gone, Luke took the liberty of going through the stack of wanted posters on Marshal Burnett's desk.

Nothing in particular piqued his interest, especially since he was going to have his hands full with Craddock for the next couple of weeks, but he did note that three or four of the unfamiliar faces staring back at him all carried, as part of their descriptions, the phrase "Reputed member of the Legion of Fire." That was a new term to Luke. Obviously a gang of some sort operating in the region.

The fact that he hadn't heard of them wasn't surprising, considering he'd been busy down in Texas for much of the past year, mostly along the border until he drifted north to take up the trail of Craddock. Seeing the size of the rewards attached to the suspected Legion of Fire members, however, was enough to make him muse about coming back this way again to maybe try for a slice of that pie.

A slice of pie, in the literal sense, was far more easily attained once Millie showed up. The plates of food she had prepared were heaped with thick slices of roast beef, mashed potatoes, buttered carrots, and a fat wedge of apple pie for dessert. She'd even brought a pitcher of lemonade.

All of this she withdrew from the basket and laid out on one end of her father's desk. "I hope you find this to your liking. Father is the only one I ever get the chance to cook for. He says I do a good job, but I can never be sure if that's truly the case or if he's just being kind. Mother was an excellent cook, but she passed away when I was only fourteen and just starting to learn her ways in the kitchen. On top of that, Lucinda Davis, who runs the town café, often invites him over for supper at her place." She smiled. "She seems to have taken a romantic interest in him. You can imagine how intimidated I am by having that kind of competition."

Looking down at the fare spread out before him, Luke said, "By the looks and aroma of everything you've prepared here, I have a pretty good hunch you can hold your own against any competition."

He could have added that, in addition to the food itself, the same could be said about the preparer. Millie had changed from the riding attire she'd had on earlier and was wearing a full-skirted dress, lemon yellow in color, with short sleeves slightly puffed at the shoulder and a modestly scooped neckline trimmed in white lace. Her ample bosom nevertheless filled the front of the dress to the point of showing an intriguing hint of cleavage and a flow of creamy flesh leading up to her long, graceful neck. She'd pinned up her cascade of blond hair with ornate hairpins that glittered silver-blue above each ear and exposed more of her finely chiseled facial features. Once again Luke was reminded that she was as striking as the finest beauties he'd ever been in the presence of.

"I hope so," Millie responded to Luke's comment on the food she'd laid out. "But the proof, as they say, is in the pudding — or more accurately, in the *taste* of the pudding."

Luke frowned. "I don't need any proof to know one thing. This second plate you made up is too good for the likes of Craddock. You definitely shouldn't have gone to so much trouble."

"Once the meal was ready, it wasn't that much trouble to fill one more plate. Your man may be a scoundrel and a varmint, as my father would say, but he's still a human being. He deserves to eat something, too."

"I suppose," Luke allowed grudgingly.

"So you sit down and dig in before everything gets even colder," Millie directed. "I'll go ahead and take his plate back to —"

"Whoa. No, you won't," Luke said, interrupting her and placing his hand on the plate of food she'd been about to pick up. "I'll be the one to deliver Craddock his grub."

Millie blinked. "It's really no big deal. I take meals back to men in the lockup all the time."

"Maybe so. But Craddock's not going to be one of them. I'll take care of him."

"I appreciate you being cautious for my sake, but it's really not necessary. There are heavy bars all around and a narrow slot to slide the food through. I can't possibly come to any harm by —"

"Think what you like, but I prefer to handle this myself," Luke said, picking up the plate and turning toward the heavy door that led back to the cell block. "In addition to being a robber and a killer, Craddock has a lousy attitude and a foul mouth that I'd just as soon not have any part of exposing you to." He brushed past Millie and passed through the door into the cell block.

Craddock rose from his cot at the sight of him. At first the prisoner's mouth curled automatically into a sneer, but then, spotting the plate of food, his expression mellowed. Moving closer to the bars, he said, "I would say it's about damn time, but seein' what all you got there, maybe it's gonna be worth the wait. Damn, that looks fine."

"Go ahead and feast your eyes, but don't even think about getting used to it," Luke told him. "Once we get out on the trail, I can guarantee you're not going to be eating this high off the hog."

"I wouldn't expect otherwise," Craddock replied. With his eyes taking on an eager gleam as Luke slid the plate through the narrow vertical opening in the bars, he added, "Which is why I always say, reach with both hands and take everything you can get while you can get it."

"Yeah, and we all know how well that particular philosophy of reaching and grabbing has worked out for you," Luke said, releasing the plate into his hands.

Craddock took a step back and held the plate under his nose, closing his eyes and inhaling deeply. When he opened his eyes again, his gaze immediately darted past Luke's shoulder and his bristly brows lifted high with a new show of heightened appreciation.

"Say now. This keeps gettin' better and better, a plateful of delicious food for my belly and now some added dessert for my eyes!"

Luke looked around and found Millie moving up behind him holding a tin cup in her hand. "You forgot to bring him anything to drink," she said innocently. "So I poured him a cup of lemonade."

Gritting his teeth, Luke took the cup from her. Turning back to Craddock, he saw that the prisoner was staring brazenly at Millie with a lewd grin spread across his face.

Craddock said, "Thank you ever so kindly, darlin'. You mind stickin' around just a minute longer? In case this lemonade is a bit too tart, maybe I could get you to sweeten it up a mite by dippin' one of your pretty little fingers in it."

"Put your eyes back in your head and shut your mouth or I'll pour this lemonade down your boot," Luke growled.

Craddock's grin only widened. "How about you pour it in the boot of that lovely little thing instead? Then I'll take it from there — be like sippin' champagne from the slipper of an elegant lady."

Luke snorted. "What do you know about champagne or an elegant lady, either one?" Over his shoulder he said to Millie, "Okay, you've brought him his drink. Now go on back in the other room. I'll join you in a minute."

Still grinning, Craddock said, "Better do like he says, darlin'. He's soundin' kinda ornery. I hate to see you leave, but I'll sure enjoy watchin' you go."

Millie looked somewhat puzzled by the remark yet turned and departed as Luke had instructed.

Gazing after her, Craddock murmured, "I may not know about champagne, but I damn well know how to drink in the sight of fine womanhood when I see it sashayed in front of me."

"She's barely more than a girl," Luke said, shoving the tin cup through the slot and into Craddock's grimy paw. "And on the best day of your miserable life, you never rated getting anywhere close to the likes of her."

Finally tearing his eyes away from the doorway Millie had disappeared through, Craddock cut his eyes to Luke. "Then where does that leave you, bounty killer? You goin' in the other room to have a friendly little session with her? You think *you* got any kinda chance with an overripe young piece like her?"

Luke felt his ears burn and his jaw muscles tighten. "If I was a bounty *killer,* you wouldn't be alive to be making crude remarks like that. And if you say any more, I may decide to come around to the other side of these bars and show you the difference."

CHAPTER 9

"He *is* a rather nasty man, isn't he?" Millie said when Luke came back into the office area.

Luke scowled at her. "I tried to tell you that. But you just had to find out for yourself, didn't you?"

Millie blinked her big brown eyes in what Luke was beginning to recognize as a well-practiced bit of histrionics staged to deflect ire by conveying innocence. "What do you mean? I was just bringing his drink to save you making a second trip."

Deciding it was time somebody called her on it, Luke said, "That Little Miss Headstrong Yet Innocent routine might wash with your father and your suitor, but I find it neither convincing nor particularly attractive."

Bright red color flared in Millie's cheeks. "What a terribly rude thing to say! And after I went to all the trouble of —"

"What I said in no way negates these fine meals you've prepared," Luke cut her short. "That was da— er, darn nice of you, and I appreciate it greatly. But it was at your own insistence, I'll remind you. And if *I* was rude, then barging into the lockup after I'd asked you explicitly not to was equally rude on your part."

"I told you. I was just trying to help you."

"You could have called out to me or waited and handed the cup to me when I started back through the door. What you were really doing was using the lemonade as an excuse to get your way when it came to having a peek at the big, bad prisoner."

"So now you're calling me a liar?"

The challenge made Luke pause. He wasn't prepared to go quite that far and measured his words. "What I'm saying, is that I suspect you're so used to getting your own way that you probably no longer even notice the different little tricks you use to go about it. Me, I don't like being manipulated . . . not even by a gal as pretty as you."

Millie glared at him for several beats. Gradually, the color faded from her cheeks and she said, "I'm not sure I like being called a manipulator any better than a liar."

Luke sighed. "Look, miss. I'm obliged to your father and his deputy for their cooperation, and I'm truly obliged to you for these meals you fixed. The last thing I want is any trouble with anybody. I've already got enough of that lined up in the days ahead, getting Craddock back to Amarillo."

After some consideration, Millie said, "I'll accept that as the closest thing I'm likely to get as far as an apology out of you. Now, you'd better start eating before your food gets any colder and you offend me some more by not digging in."

Luke settled into the marshal's chair behind the desk and pulled the plate of food over in front of him. He hesitated with a forkful of mashed potatoes raised partway to his mouth.

"What's wrong?" Millie wanted to know.

"It's just that I'm worried I might dig in a little too eagerly, so much that I forget my table manners," Luke explained. "Plus, I feel rather awkward eating in front of you when you're not having anything."

"Don't worry about me. I ate with Father."

At that, Luke proceeded to go after his food with all the eagerness he had prophesied.

After pouring him a cup of lemonade, Millie took a seat in a chair in front of the desk and sat back to watch him eat. "My father is a hearty eater, too. I think one of the things my mother loved about him the most was the way he gobbled up her cooking. She always said that a man who's a skimpy eater is either a poor cut of a man or there's something wrong with the food put in front of him."

"Well, there's certainly nothing wrong with this food," Luke assured her. "It's delicious."

Millie's lips curved into a pleased smile. "Father certainly seemed to like it, too. He ate so much I was afraid for a while there might not be anything left for me to bring you and the prisoner. It helped, I'm sure, that he was so hungry after being out all night chasing rustlers." She paused, arching one pretty eyebrow before adding, "Of course, in his case, like I said, he always praises my cooking . . . you know, because I'm so good at manipulating him."

Luke's brows pinched together. "I thought we were past that."

"We are. But it was a remark I'm not likely to forget. Nobody ever said anything like that to me before."

"No, I suppose not."

Millie leaned forward in her chair. "You said my 'routine' might wash with my father and my 'suitor.' Did you mean Russell

Quaid?"

"That's the one."

"He's not really my suitor."

"Maybe not. But he'd sure like to be."

"You really think so? That he feels that way, I mean."

Luke gave her a look. "You're doing it again."

"Doing what?"

"Your routine. The overly innocent one. You might be young and inexperienced, but surely you're old enough and smart enough to know that you are extremely attractive. I'd wager there isn't a man in Arapaho Springs — young or old — who doesn't crane his neck when you walk by. And it would be that way wherever you went. It sure doesn't start and stop with Russell Quaid."

New spots of color appeared on Millie's cheeks, a pure blush this time. "You are a very direct-spoken man, Mr. Jensen."

"I've found that, in most cases, it's the best way to be." He took his final bite of apple pie then laid his fork down on the emptied plate and pushed it away.

As she watched him, Millie said, "It might be, however, that the things you state so directly are not always as accurate as you think."

"Possible, I suppose," Luke said with a shrug.

"For example," Millie continued, her gaze taking on a bold directness, "it might interest you to know that I am not nearly as inexperienced as you claimed a minute ago."

Luke felt a warming of his own cheeks and all of a sudden that last bite of pie needed an extra swallow to keep it down. "Under different circumstances, miss —"

"Millie."

"Okay. Millie. Under different circumstances, Millie, I might indeed find that interesting to know."

"What's wrong with the circumstances that we have right now?" she wanted to know, the boldness of her gaze not subsiding. "You're a man. I'm a woman. You said you find me attractive. And I admit to finding you very intriguing, far more so than anyone else I'm likely to meet here in Arapaho Springs."

"That's flattering to hear," Luke said, frowning. "But I'm also nearly old enough to be your father. And your actual father happens to be someone who's shown me professional courtesy and a measure of friendship. I can hardly —"

"There it is again!" exclaimed Millie, making a frustrated gesture with her hands. "It's always my father. That's the problem with the rest of the men around town. I thought you were different. Just because my father wears a badge, it's like I'm unapproachable and untouchable. You said I'm attractive, but what difference does it make? I might as well be a leper or an old hag for all the good it does me!"

Luke's frown turned into a tolerant smile. "I doubt it's really that hopeless. You *are* pretty, and you know it. Beautiful, in fact. It's just a matter of time and not a very long one, I'd be willing to bet, before you'll have more beaus knocking on your door than you can turn away. And that's regardless of the fact your father wears a badge. What's more, if that's enough to scare them off then, as your mother might say, they're a poor cut of a man to begin with."

"There must be a lot of poor cuts of manhood around these parts," Millie said wryly, "because there's sure none of them knocking on my door so far."

"What about Russell?"

"Russell's just a boy."

"Appeared to me he was man enough to stand up to your father. And he said he'd be willing to defend you to the death in case of trouble," Luke reminded her.

Millie went quiet, seeming to consider this.

Before anything more could be said, the office door opened and Deputy Fred Packer came in. "It's just me again, Jensen," he announced. Noticing Millie for the first time, he quickly pulled off his hat. "Oh, hi, Miss Millie. Didn't expect to run into you here."

"Millie was kind enough to bring some supper to me and our prisoner," Luke explained.

"Then somebody was lucky enough to get some good eats, accordin' to the way the marshal brags on Miss Millie's cookin'."

"That was definitely the case," Luke confirmed.

Millie stood up. "Well, having successfully accomplished my task, I'd better be getting home. I left Father asleep in his easy chair in the parlor. That was as far as he made it after eating his own supper. Now I'll have to try and roust the old bear and get him to go the rest of the way to bed."

"In that case, maybe I'd better walk with you. It's gettin' kinda late for a young lady to be out alone," Packer said.

"That's really not necessary. It's not that late and it's not that far to the house."

Packer shook his head. "Nonsense. I only stopped by to grab my pipe that I forgot to take with me earlier." As he said this he shuffled over to the windowsill and retrieved the old clay pipe he'd previously left behind after his fat-chewing session with Luke. Turning back, he clamped the stem between his teeth and said, "There, that's better. Now, I insist, Miss Millie. I couldn't forgive myself if I didn't see you home properly. Besides, you wouldn't deny an old codger the pleasure of strollin' for a ways in your company, would you?"

After tossing a brief, somewhat plaintive glance in Luke's direction, Millie relented, turning a beaming smile on Packer. "Very well, Deputy. Let us stroll."

CHAPTER 10

Though it wasn't uncommon for him to sleep soundly under conditions that ranged from trailside bedrolls to sumptuous beds in fine hotels, Luke was surprised by how well he rested that night at the jail. What was different on this occasion was the unsettled feeling he'd been left with after Millie Burnett's departure. Her bold overtures had stirred things in him he didn't want to allow yet had been unable to completely ignore.

His head kept reminding him she was too young and the circumstances were all wrong, but other parts of him remained keenly aware of her distinct beauty and all-woman body. For a time he worried that, after Deputy Packer was out of the way, she might come back. If she did, he wasn't altogether sure his willpower would hold up.

To his relief, Millie hadn't returned and after a while he was able to relax. It helped that a well-padded couch in a corner of the office was available as an alternative to the cot in the empty cell. It also helped that he took the liberty of sampling a couple more pulls from the bottle of moonshine Marshal Burnett kept in his desk drawer. These, combined with the accumulated weariness of several days on the trail and especially the toll taken by the recent drenching rain, before long had a lulling affect that soon turned to deep, welcome slumber.

It was daylight when Luke woke to the sound of a door being opened and the heavy thud of boots entering the room. His eyes flew open and he sat up, all senses alert and one of the Remingtons gripped in his right fist.

"Hold your fire," a familiar voice was quick to say. "Take it easy. It's only me." Tom Burnett momentarily filled the doorway as he stepped the rest of the way through and then heeled the door shut behind him. He looked considerably refreshed from yesterday, clean shaven and dressed in a different set of clothes complete with a string tie knotted loosely at his throat.

"Appears you slept okay," he said to Luke as he strode toward his desk, sweeping a broad-brimmed hat from his head and hanging it on a wall peg that he passed by.

"I reckon so." Luke stood up, holstered the Remingtons, then ran the fingers of both hands through his rumpled hair and rolled his neck and shoulders, working out the kinks.

"There's a little room off one end of the cell block," Burnett said, motioning. "Inside is a washbasin and a bench pump. You can use it to wash up, if you've a mind. By the time you get back out, I'll have some coffee brewing."

Luke nodded. "Sounds good. Obliged."

When he returned to the office a handful of minutes later, it was indeed to the scent of bubbling coffee. Before quitting the cell block, he checked on Craddock and found him stretched out on his cot, propped up on one elbow.

"I sure would be obliged for a taste of that coffee I can smell," the prisoner said.

Luke gave him a look, made no promises.

Back out in the office, Burnett was seated behind his desk. "Mud'll be ready soon and not long after that, my daughter should be coming by with some breakfast for you and your prisoner."

Millie had left behind her picnic basket from last night. After she was gone, Luke had gathered up his plate and utensils as well as those of Craddock and stacked everything neatly inside, placing it on the corner of the marshal's desk.

Burnett gestured to it. "I reckon the feed she brought you last night was satisfactory?"

"And then some. It was delicious," Luke told him. "I wish she hadn't gone to so much trouble, and she surely doesn't need to do it all over again this morning. The café's open now. I can get something for Craddock and me from there."

"I tried to tell her as much. Most days I take my own breakfast at the café. But Millie was up early this morning, fixing mine and insisting she would be fixing something for you right after I was out of the house." Burnett shrugged. "As I believe you heard me and her friend Russell discuss yesterday, she has a mighty headstrong way about her. I know there are times when I need to put my foot down more. But over breakfast ain't one of 'em. Not when she cooks as good as she does."

A corner of Luke's mouth quirked up. "No, I suppose not."

Burnett leaned back in his chair. "Now. Much as I hate to jump to a considerably less pleasant subject, it's only fair to warn you that on the way over here I ran into certain parties who were going to stop at the diner and then they, too, will be heading this way."

Luke regarded him, said nothing, and waited for him to continue.

"One of them is Doc Whitney, coming to check on your prisoner," the marshal said. "He ain't so much a problem. But accompanying him will be lawyer Mycroft and his tag-along clerk. Mycroft went to some trouble to inform me that he is coming in the interests of your prisoner and if the good doctor still advises that Craddock should not travel, then the legal eagle will insist you abide by what he says. Apparently Mycroft didn't learn a damn thing from the way you pinned his ears back yesterday."

"Too bad for him," Luke said, setting his teeth on edge. "Because I'll tell you right now, no matter what the doctor says, I fully intend to ride out of here with Craddock today. He's feeling well enough to run his mouth and eat and stomp around his cell. In my book that makes him fit enough to travel. I've delivered men with bullet holes in them, and they survived. Hell, I've traveled good distances with bullet holes in *me,* and I'm still kicking."

"Anybody can see that," Burnett conceded.

Luke frowned. "My only question is — where does that leave you? As far as your own feelings and as far as where you'll stand with the doctor and the lawyer?"

Burnett got up and went over to the stove where the coffeepot was bubbling. Hooking a pair of tin cups from nearby pegs, he began pouring the black steaming brew. "I've had the chance to think on it some since we first talked yesterday. What I concluded is that Craddock is your prisoner and the only thing you have to abide by until you hand him over to the Amarillo authorities, just like you already told Mycroft, is what it says on that wanted poster. Means I got no say in the matter." He handed Luke one of the cups. Grinning wryly, he added, "Don't take this wrong but, like I told you before, when it comes to you hauling your trash out of here — the sooner the better, is how I see it."

Luke matched his grin. "Same way I see it. Not meaning for you to take it wrong, either, you understand."

As the two men took their first tentative sips of the coffee, the door opened and Millie came in. This morning she was wearing another full-skirted dress, pale blue with a higher neckline but a snug bodice that only accentuated the swell of her breasts. Her hair was pulled back into a loose ponytail, tied with a ribbon that matched the dress. One look at her and Luke couldn't help but mentally question how big a damn fool he was for turning her away last night.

"Good morning," she said, carrying a carefully balanced cloth bag that bulged with roundish contents and from which wafted the unmistakable aroma of bacon and eggs. To Luke she said, "I trust Father warned you that I was at it in the kitchen again this morning?"

Luke nodded. "He did. I told him I wished you hadn't gone to still more trouble but now, having gotten a whiff of what you've got there, I take it back. I am suddenly very grateful you did."

Smiling, Millie marched to the desk, where she placed the bag beside the picnic basket already setting there.

"I gathered the plates and everything from last night and stacked them in the basket," Luke told her. "I didn't know there was a washbasin in the other room or I would have cleaned them up first."

"Don't be ridiculous. I'll take the whole works back home after you've finished eating this morning and clean it all there." She reached into the bag and carefully withdrew a plate heaped with scrambled eggs and bacon. "All you need to worry about is eating this before it gets cold. I've brought a plate for your prisoner, too, but since I know you don't want me going back there we'll impose on Father to deliver it so you can start right in on yours."

"I don't know if I can be trusted," Burnett declared. "I thought I was full from what you fed me at home. But this looks so tempting I think I might be ready for seconds."

"From the look and smell, I can understand why," came a voice from the doorway. "Even though I just came from the café, I suddenly have the urge for some of that delicious-looking fare as well."

Luke, Burnett, and Millie turned to see Dr. Whitney entering. Behind him trailed Jules Mycroft and Russell Quaid.

"Millie is just delivering breakfast for Mr. Jensen and his prisoner," Burnett explained.

Mycroft lifted his eyebrows at that. "Well, there's a morsel of encouragement . . . knowing at least that much civility is being shown the unfortunate incarcerated wretch."

Ignoring him, the doctor said, "I don't mean to interrupt, but as I told you earlier, Marshal, I'd like to take just a couple of minutes to examine the injured man before I start the rest of my day." He was a leathery-faced old gent of sixty or so, snow-white eyebrows and hair, physically stocky with stooped shoulders. He held a black doctor's bag in one heavily veined hand, swinging it beside him as he started toward the thick door leading back to the cell block.

Luke edged over so that he was partly blocking the doctor's path. "You can go ahead on back if you like, Doc, but since you're a man whose time is obviously very valuable, might I suggest not wasting any of it? You see, just as soon as I've finished eating and have had time to put together some provisions for the trail, I have every intention of riding out of here this morning with my prisoner. With all due respect, I'll do so no matter what your evaluation is. I've been observing Craddock all night and I see no reason he's not up to traveling."

Mycroft huffed like a steam engine. "There! Just as I suspected. This ruffian, this gunslinger who *pretends* to be on the side of the law, has nothing but contempt for it and especially for any poor unfortunate who stands merely accused of being on the wrong side of it!"

Luke cocked an eyebrow in his direction. "I warned you once about getting in my face, mister. You keep it up, the doc isn't going to have to go into the other room to find an injured man to check on. We can arrange for one right here."

"Come now, Mr. Jensen," Dr. Whitney said with a tolerant smile. "Is it really necessary to —"

Whatever the doc was going to say was lost to the interruption of a sudden commotion out in the street. Men shouted, voices quickly rising in intensity and volume to frantic wails. Next came the distant scream of a woman, followed by another from somewhere closer. And then could be heard the unmistakable pop and crack of gunfire.

Burnett surged to his feet, right hand falling to the pistol holstered on his hip. "What the hell?" He went around the desk and headed for the door in long strides. Luke fell in beside him, both of his Remingtons already drawn.

Mycroft and Russell, momentarily in their path, sprang to either side to clear the way.

Just before Burnett and Luke reached the open front door, a man with wild eyes and an anguished expression on his face appeared there. "My God, Marshal!" he cried. "The Legion of Fire is hitting our town!"

CHAPTER 11

An instant after blurting his warning, the man in the doorway was knocked sideways by a bullet slamming into his shoulder. He spun away, staggered a half step, then was hammered by another slug pounding into his back. He pitched forward and sprawled with outstretched arms onto the edge of the muddy street.

Instead of continuing out the open door, Luke and Burnett peeled off to either side and pressed themselves to the wall just back from the edges. The marshal had his own gun drawn. Out on the street, the air was alive with the roar of increasing gunfire and flying lead.

To the others in the office, Burnett shouted, "Get back! Crowd over in the corner by the cell block door. Better yet, get all the way back in there where it's even safer."

"We can't do any good back there," protested the doctor. "Where are the keys to your gun rack?"

"You know how to handle a gun, Doc?"

"I had a gun in my hands long before I ever picked up a medical bag," came the gruff answer. "Now where's the damn keys?"

Before Burnett could answer, Millie said, "In the middle drawer of the desk. I know where they are!" She lunged to yank open the drawer and from within seized a ring of keys.

While this was taking place, Luke was peering around the edge of the door frame, trying to assess whatever the hell was going on. His line of sight was limited to an angle extending north along Main Street, past the two saloons that sat on opposite sides from one another, and other adjacent businesses. A dozen or so riders were thundering right down the middle of the street, throwing lead wildly to either side, shooting at anything that moved. A couple of horsemen up near the front of the group seemed to be concentrating especially on the jail building, peppering it with shot after shot. It seemed evident that one of them was responsible for planting the slugs in the man who'd appeared briefly to give warning.

Luke took careful aim and pulled a trigger

on one of those riders. The man jerked from the impact and went tumbling off the rear of his horse. In response, a heightened hail of bullets came pouring at the jail. The open door rattled and shook on its hinges, shedding slivers and chunks of wood from the chewing lead. A handful of slugs came through the opening, some sizzling low to gouge into the floor, others angling high to dislodge dust and wood chips from the ceiling.

Luke realized some of the shots were coming at an angle from the south, not just from the pack of riders he'd gotten a fleeting view of. More shooters were also opening up from the other end of the street!

"We're getting riddled here," the black-clad bounty hunter said through clenched teeth. "It'd be suicide to try and go out this door, but we need to get out there on the street for any chance to fight back effectively. Is there a back way out of here?"

"A bolted door leads out the rear end of that room where the washbasin is," Burnett answered. "I know the way better than you. I'll go. You stay and —"

"No, I'll go." Luke was already in motion as his words cut off those of the marshal. "You stay here, guard your daughter and the others. I'll come around from the back and cover you so then you'll have a chance to make it out, too."

Luke ran to the back wall of the office, careful to stay out of the direct line of the doorway. The gun rack was on his side of the room. Millie and the others were crowded into the opposite corner, near the heavy door that led back to the cell block.

Doc Whitney held up the ring of keys Millie had pulled from the desk drawer, shouting, "One of these unlocks that gun rack. Use it to grab us some weapons!"

The chaos out in the street was increasing. Bullets continued to batter the front of the jail building. Every once in a while one sailed in through the open door with a menacing whine ending in a loud *whap!* as it made contact with an inanimate object. Crouched just back from the door frame, Burnett had begun throwing some return fire.

"No time for sorting through keys," Luke called back to the doctor. "Stand clear!" A moment later he'd placed the muzzle of one of his Remingtons against the links of the chain that secured the rifles lined up in the rack and pulled the trigger. The links blew apart, adding a metallic ring to the roar of the gun.

Momentarily holstering his pistols, Luke

quickly yanked the broken chain free from the way it was threaded through the trigger guards of the gun row. The selection consisted of two double-barreled shotguns, three Winchesters, and two Henry repeating rifles. Luke tossed one of the Winchesters to Doc Whitney, followed by a box of ammunition.

"Throw another one to me. I know how to shoot!" called Millie.

"And me!" echoed Russell.

Not taking time to question or argue, Luke tossed the remaining two Winchesters. It didn't pass his notice, though, that only the pasty-faced, trembling Jules Mycroft, pressed deepest back in the corner, failed to request any weapon.

Turning briefly to the doorway, Luke called, "How you fixed for ammunition, Marshal?"

"I got enough for my handgun," Burnett replied over his shoulder. "But slide me one of those shotguns along with some shells!"

Luke did as requested, giving one of the shotguns a hard shove across the floor so that it came to a stop against the heel of the marshal's boot. He followed suit with a box of shells.

"It's pure hell out there on the street!" Burnett called anxiously. "We need to get out there and try to turn the tide!"

"I'm on my way!" Luke paused only long enough to shove a box of shells behind his belt and grab the second shotgun for himself, then he darted to the opposite side of the room, crossing the area aligned with the front door between any incoming rounds.

At the door leading back to the cell block, Luke paused again, long enough to say to the group huddled in the corner, "Somebody needs to go up to the front and help the marshal in that doorway."

The bulky old doctor started in motion. "I'll go."

Russell suddenly crowded past him. "No, I will. I can move faster. You stay here and guard Millie."

"I'm not some helpless baby, you know," Millie protested, jacking a shell into her Winchester. "I told you I know how to shoot, too!"

"Knock off the damn arguing," Luke barked. "When I'm able to cover the marshal so he can join me out on the street, there'll be plenty of opportunity for more of you to take over up front. In the meantime, somebody come rebolt this back door behind me."

As he started through the cell block door, he saw, out the corner of his eye, Russell making his dash to the opposite side of the room and then moving up to join Burnett at the front. By God, Luke thought, maybe there was still hope for the kid not being irreversibly influenced by the gutless Mycroft.

While the majority of his gang was raising hell throughout the rest of the town — a dozen riding in from each end, mowing down hapless citizens, starting to loot the smaller stores and businesses, and a select handful located near the jail, pinning down the marshal — Sam Kelson and four handpicked men concentrated on the Arapaho Springs bank. The establishment had been open for the day's business for only a few minutes when the five barged in with drawn guns.

The bank guard, a frail-looking, elderly gent sitting in a chair near the front door with a cup of coffee balanced on one bony knee and his shotgun leaning against the wall beside him, was gunned down immediately just to make a statement on the seriousness of the matter at hand.

When one of only two customers present, a local businessman with a pouch of deposit money still in hand, tried to protect his interests by going for a nickel-plated hideaway in his vest, he met the same fate. The other customer, a rather handsome woman on the good side of middle age, emitted a startled peep and then fainted. As did one of the female clerks. The two other clerks, both soft-looking middle-aged men, immediately froze and stood with raised hands and nervously bobbing Adam's apples, trying to swallow their fear while all the time trembling and dripping sweat with gun muzzles staring them in the face from mere inches away.

Kelson moved around behind the partition and confronted the bank president trying to crawl under his desk. Kelson dragged him up by his sparse hair, swatted him alongside the head a couple of times with the barrel of his Colt, then bent him backward over the desk and snarled in his face, "You know what this is. And you know what these red bandannas on our arms mean. So lead me to your biggest bills and make it fast. All we want is paper. You can keep the change. How fast and how thoroughly you cooperate will decide whether or not we leave it behind with your blood splashed all over it!"

Chapter 12

Luke emerged cautiously from the rear of the jail, making sure none of the raiders had worked around to pose an awaiting threat. Once he'd determined none had, he quickly checked each corner of the building to decide his most effective option for gaining the street in order to start fighting back against the attackers.

The jail building was located toward the south end of town, about three quarters of the way down Main Street. The higher-volume businesses — bank, hotel, stores, saloons — all lay to the north. The closest building that way was a saddle shop, separated by a cluttered alley. Immediately to the south of the jail was an open space choked with chest-high underbrush and a few scraggly trees.

Luke opted for the south side. He'd gotten his fill of alleys yesterday, plus the underbrush provided a fair amount of concealment. He picked his way forward, shotgun gripped in his left hand, Remington in his right. When he drew even with the front of the jail, he crouched momentarily where he had a good view through the bushes without revealing hardly any of himself.

A quick scan showed that most of the action had shifted to the north. Gunfire, curses, shouts, and screams filled the air, mingled sporadically with the sound of breaking glass and the occasional shrill protest of a horse. Though some of the raiders still remained mounted, a number of others were now on foot, forcing their way into the stores and shops. For the first time, Luke noted that each of the attackers wore a bright red bandanna tied above the elbow of his right arm.

Near his end of the street, four raiders remained for the clear purpose of keeping the marshal pinned in place while his town was being pillaged. Two of these were positioned in front of the livery stable catty-cornered across the street. They'd dismounted and taken cover behind each end of a long wagon heaped with loose straw. From there, they were pouring a steady stream of rifle fire on the jail building.

To the north, on the same side of the

street, a raider was ducked behind a corner of the saddle shop, throwing his share of lead with a handgun. Directly across the street from him, a fourth man was shooting from inside a small, cottage-style building with a sign over the door that read QUILTING NOTIONS & FINE POTTERY. He'd busted out one of the windows and was working with a long-barreled Henry repeater.

Luke took all of this in in a matter of mere seconds. From there, it took only another second for him to decide what his course of action would be.

Each time one of the men behind the straw wagon fired on the jail, he would lean out and expose himself momentarily in order to do so. Each man guarded the brief exposures against the return fire from the jail, but since neither was aware of the position Luke had taken up, they were leaving themselves wide open to him.

He chose the shooter on the farthest end of the wagon for his first target. The next time the man leaned out, Luke was ready. His Remington spoke twice and both slugs the long-barreled pistol sent screaming across the width of the street hit their mark. The first bullet jerked the rifleman up and back, seeming to balance him for a fraction of an instant on his toes, and then the second one slammed him the rest of the way back and down, his rifle spinning away from outflung arms.

Luke immediately swung his aim to the man on the other end of the wagon. Given all the noise and shooting that filled the street, the rifleman appeared not to notice his closest cohort had gone down. Nevertheless, for some reason he chose the very instant Luke fired on him to drop a little lower in his crouch behind the corner of the wagon. Luke's shot passed a fraction of an inch above the man's head, doing no harm except to a fistful of straw that was blown to shreds.

The near miss was enough to alert the man to Luke's presence, causing him to drop back farther behind the wagon so that Luke's follow-up shot missed, too. At the same time, rounds fired from the jail doorway also pounded the end of the wagon, driving the rifleman even farther back.

Luke saw this as an opening. Shouting "Cover me to the north. I'm going over!" to Burnett and Russell, the black-clad bounty hunter sprang from the underbrush and started across the street in a full-out run. Yesterday afternoon's sunshine and a low, moaning wind through much of the night had considerably improved the muddy street. There was still a layer of slop deeper down, but it was covered over by a dried crust that gave Luke decent purchase as he ran.

Crouched forward ten feet from the straw wagon, Luke spotted the movement of feet passing between the wheels on the back side of the wagon. He immediately went into a dive, pitching onto his stomach with the shotgun extended forward in his left hand. As he landed, he triggered both barrels simultaneously and sent a devastating blast ripping under the belly of the wagon.

The feet on the other side caught the brunt of the blast and were instantly shredded to bloody stumps. As the rifleman back there went crashing to the ground, his feet and the lower part of his legs literally blown out from under him, his agonized scream was shrill enough to cut through the twin roars of the shotgun.

After triggering that devastation, Luke immediately went into a roll and scrambled back to his feet. Even with Burnett and Russell providing him cover fire, he knew he couldn't afford to make himself a stationary target for the shooters up the street, behind the corner of the saddle shop and in the window of the quilting and pottery store. Proof came as the wind-rip of bullets passed mere inches behind his head just before he reached the far end of the straw wagon and lunged behind it.

In back of the wagon, Luke quickly sought out the man whose feet he had blasted away. The former shooter was still alive, though in such horrible agony he likely wished he wasn't. Luke wasted no time sending a bullet to put him out of his misery.

Moving up to the north end of the wagon and dropping in low behind a wheel, Luke began reloading his shooting irons — shotgun and handguns alike — as he called across the street to Burnett. "Two down, but there's still two more to deal with before we can move up the street — one by the saddle shop on your side, another in the window of that quilting store on my side!"

"Not anymore," the marshal called back. "While you were making your dive behind the wagon, Russell got the one in the store window."

"Good job!" Luke responded.

"I'm coming out," Burnett said. "I mean to rush that bastard behind the saddle shop!"

"Make your move. I'll follow your lead," Luke called back. He barely finished saying those words before Burnett came barreling out the front door of the jail.

With his shotgun thrust ahead of him, the marshal turned hard to his left and ran straight for the saddle shop. Luke broke from behind the wagon and started at an angle for the same spot.

Perhaps the gunfire and chaos from only a short distance up the street had sufficiently drowned out the exchange between Luke and Burnett so that the shooter at the corner of the saddle shop hadn't heard or understood. Or maybe he'd heard but was just a crazy brave damn fool bent on holding his ground and doing the job he'd been assigned no matter what. For whatever reason, hold his ground is what he tried to do.

From his angle, Luke caught sight of the shooter first as he leaned away from the building. Firing a Remington as he ran, Luke's shot went wide of his intended target. It came close enough, however, for the shooter to shift his attention from firing toward the jail as he originally intended and swing the muzzle of his pistol in Luke's direction. That caused him to lean out further still — directly into the line of fire for Burnett's shotgun, which the marshal triggered as he continued his rush. The blast raked the side of the building and pounded into the man's chest and shoulder, hurling him backward as if he'd been yanked by an invisible wire. He hit the ground four feet away, a bloody, lifeless heap.

Burnett halted, his gaze sweeping northward up the street. Over half of the raiders still delivering hell up that way had dismounted. Most of those had forced their way into stores and shops, where they were looting and killing. Shooting continued in a seemingly endless roll of noise, some of it return fire from shopkeepers and frantic citizens trying to rally against the attack.

Flinty-eyed, Burnett looked over at Luke. "This is my town, my fight, Jensen. You don't have to make it yours."

"Seems to me I already staked out a piece of that claim, Marshal," Luke replied. "Looks to me like a big enough fight for each of us to have a share."

Burnett gave a curt nod. "Anybody with a red bandanna on his arm, shoot to kill. It's that simple."

"Easy enough. Got it."

Burnett turned back to Russell, who had emerged from the jail doorway and stood thumbing cartridges into his Winchester. "You did a good job in that doorway, son. Keep at it. Stay here, guard this end of town and keep Millie and the doc safe."

Russell tried to protest. "But there's only two of you. I should —"

"You should do as I say! Stay here. Keep my daughter safe." The marshal held out his shotgun. "Here. Take this. Give me that Winchester. You can grab one of the Henrys off the rack when you go back inside."

The guns were exchanged. Burnett pinned Russell in place with a final hard look, then turned north again, brandishing the Winchester. He started up the street. On the opposite side, Luke moved forward as well, keeping pace.

CHAPTER 13

After Doc Whitney had shown Luke out the jail's rear door and then bolted it behind him, the doctor inadvertently left the connecting door to the cell block ajar when he hurried back to the front office area. Cowering in the corner only a few feet away, a trembling, terrified Jules Mycroft cast his eyes on this and recalled the marshal's words from earlier. *"Get all the way back in there where it's even safer."*

None of the others had taken heed of the suggestion. Not only that but they had each appealed to arm themselves rather than seek safety. Even his own clerk had moved to the front door to take the place of Jensen and actually began exchanging gunfire with the marauders. As if the din of all the shooting and screaming from outside wasn't enough, the shattering reports of those doorway guns — from practically *inside* the office — made Mycroft wince and recoil with each blast.

He badly wanted to retreat as far as possible from the noise and violence. At first, not wanting to appear the utter coward he truly was, he'd refrained from ducking back into the cell block. But with the door so close and hanging so invitingly ajar, he could no longer resist.

Once into the cell block, Mycroft found it cooler and more dimly lighted than the office. And while the noise from without wasn't completely muffled, it was diminished considerably. The wave of relief he felt was only short-lived, however.

"What the hell's goin' on out there?"

The harsh demand startled Mycroft. Somehow, in all the other excitement, he had forgotten there was a man in one of the cells. The very individual, in fact, whose fate had brought him there. Mycroft turned sharply and got his first look at Ben Craddock.

Pressed close to the bars of his cell, gripping them tightly, the outlaw insisted, "What's with all the shootin' and runnin' around? I got a right to know."

Recovered from his original surprise, Mycroft adjusted the lapels of his suit coat and automatically donned some semblance of his lawyerly manner. "Yes. Yes, of course you do. Though it's not very good news, I fear. The Legion of Fire, it seems, is attacking our town."

Craddock's eyebrows shot up. "The Legion of Fire! Why would they be messin' with this little pissant of a town?"

"That I do not know," Mycroft replied. "All I know, reportedly at least, is that's what is occurring. And what I know for certain is that it sounds like a veritable battlefield out on the street."

"Yeah, that fits the Legion, all right," Craddock said, grimacing. "They don't just ride in and rob. When they get done with a town there's nothing left but empty cash drawers, bullet-riddled bodies, and ashes."

Mycroft shuddered. "What a dreadful image!"

Craddock scowled at him. "Who are you, anyway?"

"My name is Mycroft. Jules Mycroft." The lawyer pushed back his shoulders and struggled to compose himself. With a somewhat rueful smile, he added, "You might be interested to know that my purpose in coming here this morning was on your behalf, to determine that you were being treated fairly by the marshal and especially by Jensen, that ruffian of a bounty hunter. Although I dare say all of that is now of secondary concern."

"The hell it is! Not to me it ain't," Craddock protested. "What if the Legion picks this place as one of the ones they decide to put a torch to? That'd be their idea of big fun. Burn down the marshal's office and jail on their way out of town. They don't call them the Legion of Fire for nothing. Don't you see where that would leave me, trapped behind these bars? I'd be roasted alive!"

"Good Lord," Mycroft said, his expression aghast. "That would indeed be . . . But no, the marshal will never let that happen. His daughter is in this building, too, out in the other room. Besides, as you just saw with Jensen departing out the back, he and the marshal are planning a counterattack on the marauders."

"Counterattack! Two men against the Legion?" Craddock scoffed. "They'll be lucky to survive, let alone do any good as far as curbing the raid until the Legion is good and ready to ride on. I'm in terrible jeopardy here, I tell you! You've got to do something to help me!"

Mycroft recoiled at the suggestion. "Me? What can I do?"

"You can let me out of this damn cell, that's what! I'm a fightin' man. I know how to use a gun and I ain't afraid to jump into the middle of a battle. I'd be fightin' for my own skin, true, but I'd also be fightin' for the town." Craddock lowered his voice, his tone turned coaxing. "Look, I'll admit I don't really give a damn about your town, but if I went out there shootin' against the Legion of Fire, it would amount to the same thing, right? I won't insult you by pretendin' to promise I won't try to escape if I get the chance . . . but I'd still have to fight through the raiders in order to do it. And hell, there's at least a fifty-fifty chance I might stop a bullet. Even that's a helluva lot better than bein' trapped in here and riskin' bein' burned alive!"

"You make a compelling case for your dilemma," Mycroft responded, appearing shaken and sincere. "But surely you must understand mine as well. I . . . I can't just *release* you. It would go against everything I —"

"Yes, you can!" Craddock jerked futilely on the bars he was gripping. "The others will never even notice. Hell, they may all end up dead anyway. The cell keys are hanging on the other side of the door. I saw them there when they brought me back. All you have to do is reach around and grab them. For God's sake, man, have some mercy!"

Mycroft backed away, suddenly feeling threatened in a different way — by his own temptation. He shook his head. "No. No, I can't do that."

Craddock sagged against the bars as if in defeat. He groaned. When he spoke again his voice was barely above a hoarse whisper. "I know it was too much to ask. But, oh God, how I wish . . ." His voice trailed off. And then, after a moment, his face lifted. "One thing more I will ask, though. Can you get me a drink of water? I haven't had anything since last night. I asked for some this morning but they never got around to it. I was parched then, and after thinkin' and talkin' about burnin' up, I'm even more so."

"Surely. Of course I can do that," Mycroft replied.

"There's a pump of some kind there in that side room," Craddock said, pointing. "I heard Jensen usin' it to wash up this morning. I expect there oughta be a cup in there, too."

"That's all of it," bank president Gerald Epps said, turning from the vault he was kneeling in front of with a fistful of bills and stuffing them into a large canvas money sack. He looked plaintively up at Sam Kelson and added, "Except for a little more in the tills at the clerk stations."

"My men will have taken care of those," Kelson said. He smiled over the muzzle of the Colt he held trained on Epps. "You did real good, mister. It's nice to meet a fellow who knows how to be smart and cooperate."

"Just don't hurt any more of my people. Please," Epps said.

"We're here for money," Kelson told him. "There's no profit in killing unless it's defense or to make a statement in order to help the job go easier. Now stand up."

As Epps rose rather stiffly to his feet, Kelson called over his shoulder to the lean, handsome, narrow-eyed man who was standing watch at the front door. "How's it going out on the street, Cisco?"

"Everything's under control," Cisco Palmer answered. "Except maybe down by the jail. Looks like the marshal and one of his deputies have gotten past the men you sent to keep 'em pinned down. They're trying to work their way up this way but some more of our boys have spotted them and are turning to deal with 'em."

"They'd damned well better," Kelson growled. "Get on out there and give the signal for everybody to start wrapping things up. And tell them to break out the torches!"

The bank president's eyes went wide.

"You're not going to burn my bank, are you?"

"We'll burn whatever the hell we feel like. Besides, what difference does it make to you now?" Kelson sneered. "There's no money left in the joint." Again calling over his shoulder, he addressed a sinewy, broad-shouldered man with the coppery skin and facial features of an Indian. "That female customer who passed out when we first came in — she coming around yet, Smith?"

"Yeah, looks like she's stirrin' some," answered No Nation Smith.

"Get her on her feet. Find something to tie her hands with," Kelson ordered. "She's coming with us."

"No. Please! She's done nothing to you," Epps protested.

Kelson grinned lewdly. "Not yet she hasn't. But I guarantee she'll do plenty for me and the boys before we're through with her."

Epps' lips peeled back. "You filth!"

Kelson hoisted the money sack, still with his Colt leveled on the bank president. "You go ahead and hold that thought. But, even more important, you'd best hold your disrespectful damn tongue!"

Epps shied back, his anger fading even faster than it had flared. "I . . . I . . . You promised you wouldn't shoot me if I co-operated. I've done nothing but."

"Yeah, but now I'm starting to think your heart wasn't really in it. Besides," Kelson said, obviously taking great pleasure in Epps' fright and discomfort, "I didn't promise anything. What I said was, if you cooperated it might spare you having your blood splashed all over some coins. As you can plainly see, there aren't any coins close by."

Kelson's Colt roared one time, spitting flame and a lead slug that made a red-rimmed hole in the middle of Epps' forehead as it took him to a place where he was beyond worrying whether or not his bank burned around him.

CHAPTER 14

"Can you see them? Is Father still okay?" Millie Burnett asked anxiously, crowding up close behind Russell Quaid and Doc Whitney as they maintained their vigil in the jail office doorway.

"Yes. He and Jensen are both okay," Russell answered. "They're working their way up both sides of the street. They're playing it smart, keeping to cover by going from building to building, doorway to doorway."

"It looks like they already picked off a couple more of the raiders," Whitney added. "But they've been noticed now and are starting to draw heavy return fire."

"But they'll stay safe as long as they keep to cover. Right?" The concern in Millie's voice was barely controlled.

"They can't do it all on their own, though," Whitney said. "Thank God it looks like there's some fighting back going on inside some of the stores, too. That's what it's going to take to turn the tide."

Suddenly Russell went very rigid.

Seeing this, Millie said, "What? What is it?"

"Flames. Smoke. See it, Doc? Some of the buildings have caught fire."

"Caught fire, hell!" Whitney exclaimed. "They're being *set* on fire. That's the way the damn Legion does it. They're aiming to burn down our town!"

Millie caught her breath. "Oh, my God."

Whitney turned from the doorway, his expression agitated. "I can't remain here. I've got to go out there and do something to help."

"But the marshal insisted we stay here," Russell said.

"The fight is out there, not here!" Whitney barked back.

Russell thrust out his chin. "All right, then I'll go. Somebody has to stay here with Millie and Mr. Mycroft. You're too important to risk your life out there, Doc. Plus, like I said before, I can move faster and —"

"Enough of that, you young pup!" Whitney cut him off. "Yes, you may be younger and more limber. But I'm craftier and have the experience of dodging more bullets in the late war than you've ever imagined.

What's more, I have *this*" — he seized his medical bag and held it up — "and in addition to whatever good I can do with a rifle, there's bound to be folks out there who will need the immediate care and aid only I can provide."

"But, Doc. If anything happens to you —" Millie tried to say.

Once again Whitney interrupted. "I don't intend to *let* anything happen to me, my dear. Like I said, I'm a crafty old dodger." With his medical bag in one hand and a Winchester in the other, he turned back to the front door and to Russell standing there. "Don't try to stop me or follow me. It falls to you to look after things here. You've done a fine job so far this morning, son. Keep it up."

Then he was out the door and turning up the street.

Luke was pressed into the recessed doorway of a confectionery shop, trading lead with two raiders who were across the street inside the Keg 'N Jug Saloon, one firing back from the busted-out front window, the other from behind the edge of the batwing doors. Burnett had worked his way up to the near corner of the saloon, at first intending to come around and surprise the pair inside while their attention was drawn by Luke.

That plan had to be abruptly altered, however, when a trio of still-mounted raiders from farther up the street spotted what was going on and came riding down to aid their cohorts. Rifle fire from the marshal and a shotgun blast from Luke halted the riders before they got too close, causing them to abandon their horses and scatter to cover on either side of the street.

The situation had turned into a stand-off, with Luke and Burnett occupying these five, preventing them from participating in any more looting at least. At the same time, it kept them from progressing on to engage the main body of raiders. In other words, it was almost like being pinned down back at the jail all over again.

To make matters worse, licking flames and rapidly increasing plumes of smoke could be seen rising from several of the buildings up the line.

"You see that?" Burnett hollered over.

"I see it," Luke replied through clenched teeth.

"That means they must be regrouping, getting ready to ride out, but they aim to leave the town aflame behind 'em," the marshal said.

"We may not be able to do anything to

stop them from here," Luke called back, hating to admit it. "But we can sure as hell stop these five from riding out with them."

"Go ahead and give it your best, big talker," shouted the raider in the saloon window. "The only thing you're going to stop is a bullet — and I'd be more than happy to be the one to give it to you!"

Luke responded with a rapid-fire volley of shots that sent three slugs sizzling through the saloon window. But the man there had immediately ducked safely out of the way after shouting his taunt.

Cursing under his breath, Luke pressed back into the doorway recess as a return barrage from the other raiders was unloosed in his direction. In spite of bullets hammering close all around him, it was with steady hands that he reloaded the discharged cylinders in his Remington.

All the while, up the street the fires were crackling louder and the flames were rising higher.

Moving slowly, cautiously up Burnett's side of the street, Doc Whitney paused behind a thick old cottonwood tree crowding the back edge of the walkway. This was partly to catch his breath and partly to assess the situation he saw just ahead. The marshal and Jensen were pinned down from advancing any farther. To his added distress, the doctor also saw how chaos and shooting were continuing to rage farther up the street and how the menacing fires were spreading. Burnett and Jensen were halted from continuing on, and that meant he was, too.

For a moment Whitney considered moving to the back side of the buildings and working his way up that way. He figured he had a good chance of moving from his current position since he hadn't been noticed yet by Burnett or Jensen or the raiders firing on them. After all the years he'd lived and practiced in Arapaho Springs, he reckoned he knew the back alleys and ins and outs of the town as well as anyone, probably better than most.

But then what? Did he move *past* where the marshal and Jensen were pinned down and try to accomplish something on his own in the thick of the chaos? If so, what would that be? Yes, he might happen on some wounded citizen to whom he could render aid . . . but without cover fire, that would mean a greater risk of revealing himself and catching a bullet, or ten, of his own. Despite his braggadocio back at the jail, Whitney was a realist. He wasn't afraid, but at the same time he knew his limitations. And moving past the marshal and Jensen without trying to help their situation didn't set right to begin with.

Again in spite of his earlier assurances of being good with a rifle, it had been years since he'd fired one. Still, he'd been pretty damn good at one time.

As these conflicting thoughts raced through the doc's mind, a sudden realization hit him. From his vantage point, he had a good angle on two of the raiders who'd abandoned their horses and taken to cover on the opposite side of the street, just up from Jensen's doorway. They were ducked down behind a long watering trough in front of the barbershop. Every time one of them popped up to throw some lead, he left himself momentarily wide open to Whitney's line of fire.

The doctor made his decision. He'd quit the jail to find a way to do more good than he could from back there, to administer healing if possible, to fight if necessary. Right now he had the opportunity to do more good by fighting.

Placing his medical bag on the ground at the base of the cottonwood tree, Whitney adjusted his stance slightly and brought up the Winchester. He braced the barrel in a notch between two branches. It was a fair distance, fifty or so yards. But hell, as a lad in his teens he'd hunted jackrabbits from that far and more, and bagged them regularly. A man-sized target, even if he was a bit rusty, ought not be too much of a problem.

The doc waited, concentrating on slowing his breathing. When one of the men popped up from behind the trough, he was ready. He pulled the trigger.

Chapter 15

"He-e-elp! For God's sake, somebody — help. He's going to kill me!"

The frantic wail coming from the cell block spun Russell Quaid and Millie Burnett away from the office doorway where they'd been watching Doc Whitney make his way up the street.

"Help!" the voice hollered again. When it attempted to say something more, whatever it was going to be came out as merely a strangled, elongated gargling sound.

With a Henry rifle thrust before him, Russell rushed over in response to the plea. Millie was right on his heels. At the doorway leading back to the cells, he said over his shoulder, "Stay back!" even though he knew it likely wouldn't do any good.

After pausing to slowly push the door all the way open with the muzzle of his rifle, Russell followed it cautiously into the cell block. His eyes made an alert sweep and then locked on the source of the cry for help. From behind him, he heard a sharp intake of breath from Millie, who of course had stubbornly refused to listen and stay in the other room.

In front of Ben Craddock's cell, facing outward with his back yanked tight against the bars, stood a wild-eyed Jules Mycroft. One of Craddock's scarred fists was wrapped in Mycroft's thick hair, pulling his head hard into the gap between two of the bars. The prisoner's other fist was reached through the bars and clamped viciously on the lawyer's windpipe, explaining the abrupt gurgling sound and the cessation of the further wailing. A tin cup lying in a puddle of spilled water near Mycroft's feet offered further mute explanation of how he'd gotten himself in such a predicament.

"In case it ain't clear enough, sonny boy," Craddock grated, his eyes burning into Russell, "let me make sure you understand that one wrong twitch from you or the sweetie with the Winchester will result in me instantly crushin' this Fancy Dan's windpipe and leavin' him to choke to death in a real unpleasant way. I've done it before on bigger, stronger men. In a soft, flabby throat like this one it'd be as easy as squeezin' a pimple."

Fighting to keep his voice steady, Russell replied, "And I could squeeze the trigger of this rifle just as easy and you'd end up just as dead."

"I don't think you got the guts," Craddock sneered. "But if you do, go ahead and shoot. My hand will still convulse and kill this weak bag of wind, so you won't accomplish savin' him, if that's what you think."

"What would that gain you?" Russell wanted to know.

Craddock continued to sneer. "Nothing. But then, the way it is now I got nothing to lose. Either I risk bein' trapped and killed in this cell by the Legion of Fire or I end up gettin' hung later on in Amarillo. So what the hell?"

"What alternative are you seeking, then?"

Craddock frowned. "What's with this *alternative* and *seeking*? You some kind of damn lawyer, too? If so, you ain't a very smart one. What I'm *seeking* is a deal where you let me out of this damn cell as a trade for Fancy Dan's life."

"I can't do that!"

"Sure you can. All it takes is just a little twist of the key. Then I head for the tall and uncut and nobody has to get hurt. Otherwise Fancy Dan here gets hurt permanentlike. Whatever happens next, that much is gonna be on your conscience as well as mine." Craddock emitted a nasty chuckle. "No, I take that back. It wouldn't weigh on my conscience one damn bit. But you, you'd have to live with it for the rest of your days."

All this time, Mycroft had remained perfectly still in the desperate prisoner's grip. Only his wildly bugged eyes had moved, darting and rolling about in terror. Now they became focused solely on Russell, silently imploring, begging for his life.

Sensing Russell's resolve starting to weaken, Millie whispered urgently from behind him, "You can't give in to his demands. You can't trust him!"

"Don't listen to that coldhearted little lady, sonny boy," Craddock warned. "I mean what I say — all the way around. You unlock this cell, I'll be gone with no more trouble to you. You don't, I guarantee Fancy Dan will die a real ugly death. Better hurry and make up your mind. My hand is gettin' kinda tired, clamped on his throat this way. Be a shame if it all of a sudden went into a cramp or a spasm like, and I ended up throttlin' him even if I didn't mean to."

Russell's shoulders slumped and the muzzle of the Henry he was aiming at Craddock from waist level drooped some also.

"We've got to give in," he said over his shoulder to Millie, his voice suddenly a hoarse whisper. "I can't just stand here and let him kill Mr. Mycroft. Not even if I shoot him afterward. I don't see any other way."

"I'm warning you, he can't be trusted," Millie said.

"Don't listen to her! My way is the only way without somebody dyin'," Craddock said.

Russell swallowed. "Get the key, Millie."

She hesitated, her pretty face clouded by conflicting feelings, but then she gave in and did as he asked. Thrusting the key ring into Russell's hand, she murmured, "I still think this is a bad idea."

"Think what you want. But here's how it's gonna work," Craddock said, his eyes flinty while in no way easing his grip on Mycroft. "First, both of you are gonna push your rifles into that empty cell where you can't quickly get your hands on 'em again. That way, we'll all be unarmed. Next you're gonna walk over here and unlock this door, sonny boy. Then you and sweetie will move back out of the way."

Russell stood gripping the key ring in a white-knuckled grip, not moving right away. Then slowly, he turned and pushed his Henry rifle through the bars of the empty cell. Even slower, more reluctantly, Millie did the same with her Winchester.

Moving woodenly, Russell covered the handful of steps to Craddock's cell. Mycroft's eyes never left him. Russell could hear a single weak, wheezing whimper escape the lawyer's chest as he drew nearer.

Once the door was unlocked and open, Russell edged back along with Millie until they were at the far end of the cell block, past the connecting door to the office, their backs against the door that opened to the side room.

Craddock slipped quickly out of his cell, releasing Mycroft for only a fraction of a second before reaching around and grabbing him again once he was on the outside. He pushed the lawyer ahead of him, reapplying grips on hair and throat, and started moving forward.

"You promised to release him!" Russell protested.

"That's right. I did, didn't I?" Craddock said, his mouth twisting into a nasty grin. "Okay, here he is!" With that, he lunged suddenly and gave Mycroft a hard shove, hurling him straight into Russell and Millie.

The impact of the lawyer crashing unexpectedly into them slammed the pair back against the side room door. A tangle of flailing arms and legs resulted as Mycroft lost his balance completely and fell heavily into Russell just below his knees. This bowled the young clerk's legs out from under him and all he could do was spill forward — directly into a smashing left cross thrown by Craddock as he rushed in behind Mycroft.

The blow landed just above Russell's right cheekbone, square on the temple, and knocked him sideways to collide with the bars of the empty cell. Craddock was on his already sagging form in an instant, seizing him by his hair and the nape of his neck. He pulled Russell back a foot and a half and then rammed him forward, driving his forehead viciously into the bars of the cell.

Millie screamed and tried to break for the connecting door to the office.

Growling, "Oh no you don't, sweetheart!," Craddock pivoted sharply and lashed out with a clubbing backhand to the side of her face that cut short her attempted flight and dropped her in a heap.

Although the sprawled, whimpering form of Mycroft clearly posed no threat, Craddock nevertheless decided he wasn't done until he'd tended to him as well. First he slammed the toe of his boot in a crushing kick to the lawyer's ribs. After that, he leaned over and grabbed him in the same manner as he had Russell, hair and the nape of his neck, lifted him partially, then rammed the top of his head hard into the cell bars, too. Mixed in with the solid thud of flesh and skull meeting iron, there could also be heard a loud cracking noise issuing from Mycroft's neck.

Craddock straightened up and stood with his feet planted wide, taking a minute to catch his breath. His gaze swung to a stunned Millie, who was weakly attempting to push herself to a sitting position. The side of her lovely face was reddened and already starting to swell.

Craddock smiled. "Now the fun is really gettin' ready to start, sweetheart. You're comin' with me!"

Chapter 16

Doc Whitney's shot was true. The lead pill it administered might not have gone down very easy for the patient who received it, but his discomfort was brief and the end result was that he was cured forever of any future ailments.

What was more, the second raider who'd taken cover behind the watering trough was so startled by his comrade hitting the dirt beside him that his reaction left him momentarily exposed to Burnett's position at the corner of the saloon — something the marshal did not fail to take advantage of. As a result, the second man was cut down a moment after the first.

Once he'd made his shot, Burnett twisted partly around and spotted the telltale haze of smoke drifting away from Whitney's cottonwood tree. "Damn it, Russell, is that you?" he shouted. "I told you to stay back at the jail!"

"I'm not Russell, you ungrateful cuss," Whitney called back. "And, in case you didn't notice, me not staying where I was has suddenly untied two of the knots you were tangled up in."

"There's no denying that," Luke said from his doorway. "You got my gratitude, Doc, even if the marshal is too stubborn to say it."

"Okay, I'm grateful, I'm grateful," Burnett said. "But don't get too cocky, Doc. Keep your head down or one of these Legion varmints, who I guarantee *ain't* grateful to you for showing up, will punch a hole through it."

"You think I don't know that?" Whitney said. "And another thing I know is that unless we do something to untangle some more of those knots, we're not much better off here than we were penned up back at the jail."

Burnett scowled as he thumbed his last cartridge into the Winchester. "I'm pretty damn sick of it, too." After straightening up out of his semicrouch and rolling his shoulders to loosen them, he looked across the street at Luke and made a gesture toward the front of the saloon, indicating *cover me.* With Luke's side of the street cleared, at least in the immediate vicinity, all the firepower of the remaining three raiders who had them pinned down was in a straight line from the marshal's position. With no one positioned to fire at him from across the way, any of the three who were left would have to lean out to shoot in his direction and vice versa.

If he stayed put, that was. But Burnett was tired of going nowhere with everybody popping in and out from cover like a bunch of damn prairie dogs. He meant to flush some of the other dogs once and for all. The maneuver they'd used back down the street had worked once, he told himself, there was no reason to figure it couldn't again.

Roaring, "Let's untangle some more knots!," Burnett suddenly shoved around the corner of the saloon and began running along the front, straight for the batwing doors. At the same time, Luke shoved out of his doorway and started at an angle across the street toward the same spot. Just before Burnett reached the doorway, Luke triggered both barrels of the shotgun he was wielding in his left hand, blowing a melon-sized hole in the batwings and blasting wide open what was left of them. Half a second later, the marshal plunged in with a diving roll through the smoke and wood slivers still swirling in the air.

Dropping the shotgun and drawing his second Remington, Luke shifted his course slightly, veering toward the saloon window. As he ran, he triggered rounds through the window with the pistol in his left fist. The other bucking in his right sent bullets sizzling into the mouth of the alley at the far end of the building where the third raider held a position.

Inside the saloon, Burnett came out of the roll and spun on one knee to face the surprised occupants wheeling to face him. The one who'd been manning the doorway was the closest and slowest, having jumped frantically away from the shotgun blast that preceded the marshal. He never got close to aiming his gun before Burnett levered two Winchester slugs square into his chest, slamming him back against the wall, where he went into a slow, limp, lifeless slide to the floor.

While that one was still sliding down, Burnett swung to face the one over by the window and had only a fraction of a second to realize that there was the man he should have fired on first. The realization came simultaneous with the discharge of the man's gun. But, amazingly, given the close quarters, the bullet failed to score a clean hit, only burning a crease on the outside of the marshal's right arm just above the biceps. His turning motion after downing the doorway shooter had inadvertently spared him anything worse, a piece of luck he did not share when he managed to get off a shot of his own. His round drilled low into the gut of the raider, causing him to lurch and bend forward slightly as he staggered back a step. This placed him directly in front of the open window and, before Burnett could fire again, another bullet coming from outside, courtesy of Luke, struck the side of the raider's head and knocked him off his feet. He was dead before he ever hit the ground.

Sam Kelson mounted his horse in a smooth motion, hanging the bank's money bag over the pommel as he settled into the saddle. The men who'd accompanied him into the bank were also back on their horses, as well as other raiders who'd temporarily dismounted to invade additional stores and shops. All milled around him in the middle of the street. Most of the shooting had ceased, with only a few sporadic reports popping here and there, largely muted by the roar and crackle of the numerous buildings being consumed by fire.

"Everybody accounted for and ready to

ride?" Kelson asked Cisco Palmer as the latter reined up next to him.

"All ready, except for a few men we lost — mainly the ones who went down the street to take care of that marshal and his deputy. Looks like they're not farin' too good." Palmer squinted. "I say we make a sweep in that direction on our way out and blast those damn law dogs once and for all."

"Scratch that. Our way is north. We got what we came for and we're not in the revenge business," Kelson said with a scowl. "No sense risking more men to do a job that should've already been taken care of."

Palmer set his jaw, clearly not liking the decision, but all he said was, "If that's the way you want it."

"It is," Kelson said firmly. Then, raising his voice, he shouted for all to hear. "Any of you men who grabbed a woman, prop her up on your saddles in plain sight to serve as shields against any potshots that might be taken at us on the way out. We're headed north. Let's ride!"

Luke emerged from the alley where he had chased down and dispatched the fifth and final shooter who'd had him and the marshal pinned down. He paused on the edge of the walkway to reload his Remingtons, his gaze swinging north as his hands deftly, automatically performed the task. Through the churning, billowing smoke of the flaming buildings, he saw the raiders forming up and getting ready to ride off.

Burnett came out of the saloon and stepped onto the edge of the street. His eyes also tracked north and his response was to instantly go rigid with alarm and anger. "The sonsabitches are getting away!" he bellowed as he took another step and then braced himself as he raised his Winchester and got ready to fire.

"No!" Luke barked, his head snapping around. "Hold your fire! Don't you see several of them have hostages — women? You can't risk a shot from here for fear of hitting one of them!"

Slowly, numbly, Burnett lowered the rifle. His shoulders sagged. "God help us," he said in a hoarse voice.

Luke turned to look up the street again, watching helplessly as the raiders galloped away, the horde quickly fading beyond the flames and swirling sparks and boiling smoke they left in their wake. Not quite under his breath, the black-clad bounty hunter added, "And God help those women . . ."

Chapter 17

It hadn't taken long for Ben Craddock to realize that his escape plan was a little short on details. Real short, as a matter of fact. At first, all he cared about once he was out of the cell block was getting clear of town before anybody spotted him making a break for it. The commotion up the street and the already-saddled horses left out front of the livery stable by the two raiders who'd been cut down there made that almost too easy. All he had to do was grab one of the nags and ride.

The girl was a complication right from the beginning. But he was hell-bent on taking her with him, no matter what. For one thing, having her as a hostage could be a valuable bargaining chip in case he was pursued and caught up with too quickly. But even more — he just plain *wanted* her.

It had been a long time since Craddock was with a woman. He'd gone through such spells before and endured them well enough. Hell, everybody knew it wasn't that hard to get a woman if you wanted one bad enough. But he'd been biding his time, staying on the move to make sure he was putting plenty of distance between him and the trouble back down in Texas. He hadn't been aware that damned human bloodhound Luke Jensen was on his trail, but he'd always felt an itch like *somebody* might be, so he'd kept on the move, kept to himself, and hadn't stopped long enough to dally with even the easiest kind of woman. Something like that at the wrong time and place could get a fella killed quicker than anything. But then he'd seen Millie last evening when she showed up in the cell block against Jensen's wishes.

Damn!

All the holding back caught up with Craddock in a rush. The sight of a woman so ripe and lovely had nearly taken his breath away like a punch hard and low to the gut. After she was gone, after he was alone in his cell, the yearning wouldn't leave him. It writhed inside him all night like a restless, hungry thing clamoring to be released.

And then, this morning, after he'd duped that simpering, stupid lawyer into stepping within his reach so he could make his bid to bust free, there she was again. He knew in an instant that once he was on the other side of those bars, he was going to take her with him. Hell, otherwise he might have kept his bargain with that tall, gangly young fool who coughed up the key . . . But no, probably not.

At any rate, he had her now and harbored no intention of letting her get away from him, complications be damned. The first thing he'd done was clamp a set of handcuffs on her that he found when rummaging through the marshal's desk. He'd also uncovered his own gunbelt and Colt during that search. Thus armed, along with some extra boxes of cartridges from the office gun rack and the discarded Winchester grabbed out of the empty cell, he quit the jail building and hurried across to the livery stable, dragging a still half-stunned Millie with him. The chaos up the street kept anyone from noticing them.

For a moment, Craddock had debated putting her on her own horse, still secured by the handcuffs, of course. He knew that riding double, even with her additional weight being fairly light, was bound to slow him down. But her grogginess from being backhanded made it somewhat questionable if she could even sit a saddle on her own. Plus, the thought of having her snugged tight up against him while they rode was mighty tempting. Too tempting, it turned out, especially given the pressure he felt to flee from there as fast and far as he could while the Legion of Fire was still raising hell in the rest of the town.

He picked the sturdiest-looking of the horses available to him, mounted, dragged the girl up in front of him, then spurred hard away.

After about an hour of hard riding, some concerns started creeping into Craddock's mind about how ill prepared he was for his escape run. For starters, there was his lack of familiarity with the state. All he knew for sure, based on previous information he'd come by, was that the landscape to the north supposedly turned more rugged, a stark change from the rolling, seemingly endless hills of little besides grass and a few scattered trees. That was the direction he'd been headed to begin with, before his ill-fated stop in Arapaho Springs and the encounter with Jensen. He'd meant to lose himself in that less hospitable setting and come out the other side hoping finally to be able to breathe a sigh of relief from having anyone tight on his back trail.

So, after making a wide loop to the east in order to get clear of the burning town, Craddock again headed north. So far so good.

But the question of provisions started to weigh on his mind. Not only as far as food, except for what odds and ends might be found in the saddlebags of this strange horse he'd climbed onto, but also the matter of shelter gear.

It was going to get cold. That much was certain. Hell, winter was just around the corner. It wasn't even impossible that a freak early dusting of snow might crop up. Craddock could feel the moisture in the air. And it was only recently when that cold, drenching rain had kept him holed up for most of a day and night. But he'd had his own horse and gear then, everything he'd needed to endure bad weather.

He didn't know *what* he had to count on. His confiscated horse had belonged to a member of the Legion of Fire, notorious long-riding outlaws, so it stood to reason that his saddlebags and bedroll would be decently stocked. But there was no way to be certain, not without stopping to check, and it sure as hell wasn't the time for that, Craddock told himself. Whatever he found, regardless of when he dug into it, that's what he was going to have make do with.

On top of everything else, there was the girl. He was almost, but not quite, ready to question the wisdom of bringing her along. True, there remained the chance she might prove valuable in bargaining himself out of a tight spot, if it came to that. And it was double-damn sure she was going to come in handy for warming his bedroll later on, no matter what he found in the way of gear. He was really looking forward to that. Pressing her warm, soft curves against him as they rode was a steady, pleasant reminder of how much. Otherwise, though, it went right back to her being a complication. Still, for the time being, one he was willing to put up with.

For the first time, and so abruptly it gave Craddock a bit of a start, the girl spoke. Over her shoulder, she said, "If you keep riding him so hard, you're going to kill this horse. You need to give him a breather."

"You let me worry about the damn horse," Craddock growled in her ear. "I ain't about to ease up and give some damn posse a chance to close the gap on us."

"You're never going to make it anyway, not as long as you've got me," Millie responded. "Let me go and continue making a run for it, you might have a chance. But as long as you have me, my father will chase you to the ends of the earth!"

Craddock snorted derisively. "In case you forgot, sweetheart, we left your ol' man tanglin' with the Legion of Fire. They get done with him, there might not be anything *left* to give chase."

They continued to ride hard, back to silence after that. Craddock thought he might have heard the girl emit a sob at one point, but wasn't sure. For a brief time she seemed to sag in his arms, as if in defeat.

But then her body stiffened, grew more rigid. He sensed she was steeling herself, willing herself not to give in. He remembered how mouthy she'd been back in the cell block, warning against handing over the key. So there was some fight in her, he told himself; he'd have to keep that in mind. It made him smile slyly. Good, he liked his women to show some spunk.

Before much longer, Craddock became increasingly aware of how hard the horse beneath them was working, how labored its breathing was becoming. He thought about the girl's words. He hated to admit she'd had a valid point, but he was forced to face it. The horse did need a breather. And then he remembered his own words, about how they'd left the Legion of Fire devastating the town and its citizens. Given that, the formation of a posse to pursue either them or him would likely be delayed for hours, maybe days.

Having reached that conclusion, Craddock at last drew back on the reins and allowed the horse to slow down. First to an easy jog, then a walk. After a ways, he brought it to a standstill.

"We're gonna get down now. Stretch our legs, maybe walk for a bit. Let the horse cool. Then we'll all have a drink." The one thing he'd taken time to make sure of before riding away from the livery stable back in Arapaho Springs was that he had two full canteens — the one on the horse he chose, plus the one off the other horse that had belonged to a fallen raider.

Wrapping one fist in Millie's hair and giving it a yank before climbing down from the saddle, Craddock added, "Look around. We're out in the middle of nowhere. If you try to run, I'll damn certain catch you. After that, I'll hog-tie you so tight you'll barely be able to breathe. Keep that in mind."

It was true they appeared to be in the middle of nowhere. Several miles north of Arapaho Springs yet still in an ocean of rolling, grassy hills and the occasional cluster of trees. Now and then thrusts of jagged, sun-bleached rocks had begun to appear, but they were still few and far between.

"Sit down and rest a spell. No sudden moves," Craddock ordered once they were on the ground. He loomed over Millie, glaring, until she obeyed. After she'd settled onto the grass, he edged to the side of the horse and, always keeping one eye on her, began rummaging through its saddlebags. The items he unearthed included a handful of beef jerky, a couple of plugs of tobacco, a clasp knife, three boxes of .44 caliber cartridges, some matches wrapped in oilskin, a thin stack of letters and pictures tied with a shoestring, and a greasy red bandanna knotted around several hardtack biscuits.

After examining these and returning them to where he'd found them, Craddock muttered, "Well, we may not be eatin' high off the hog tonight, but I guess we ain't gonna starve neither."

"No thanks to your brilliant planning," Millie remarked acidly.

Craddock took a step toward her. "You got a real sassy mouth, don't you?"

"You expect me to *compliment* you for dragging me off like this?"

"Oh, I'm expectin' a lot of things from

you, sweetheart," Craddock said with a lewd smile.

"Having you even look at me makes me want to gag."

"Maybe you'd like another cuff alongside the head to knock some of the sass out of you."

"I'd sooner that than the other," Millie sneered.

Craddock took another step toward her. Then he abruptly stopped. Not because his intentions changed, but rather because he was distracted by something else. A faint sound, a low rumble. And also a faint trembling in the ground under his feet.

Millie heard and felt it, too.

Both of their heads turned to look back up the long slope they had descended only a few minutes earlier. The sound seemed to be originating from beyond that grassy crest. The rumbling grew louder. So did the vibration in the ground. A haze of dust boiled up above the crest.

Horses. Several in number. Headed directly their way, Craddock realized. His heart pounded, his mouth dropped open in stunned disbelief. Had a posse caught up with them after all? So quickly? How was that possible?

Then the riders, a score of them, came

over the crest and started down the slope. After a second, amidst the swirl of dust engulfing them, Craddock could see red bandannas fluttering on the arms of the individual horsemen.

He didn't know whether to rejoice or be even more fearful. It wasn't a posse at all. That was the good news. The bad news was that he had inadvertently ridden directly into the path of the Legion of Fire as they thundered away from their raid on Arapaho Springs.

CHAPTER 18

For the balance of the day, the surviving citizens of Arapaho Springs fought the raging fires. Personal pain and grief over the injuries and deaths that the Legion of Fire also left in its wake had to be put aside for the sake of trying to prevent the town's total destruction. In the end, the toll was still severe. Seven downtown businesses and buildings, including the bank, general store, and the Brass Rail Saloon, were turned to nothing but piles of ash and a few scorched timbers. Added to that was considerable damage done to another half dozen nearby buildings and homes.

And then there was the human toll. Fifteen lives lost — shopkeepers, tradesmen, shoppers, and ordinary citizens cut down ruthlessly in the act of going about their daily routines. Another dozen with bullet wounds and/or injuries due to getting kicked or gun-whipped. And too many cases to count of burns, scrapes, and near-exhaustion from the struggle to keep the fires from spreading. Doc Whitney's own tireless efforts to address all of this had been nothing short of awe-inspiring.

But as bad as or maybe even worse than any of this, was the terrible weight of the unknown . . . the fate of the five women who had been hauled off by the Legion raiders.

No one suffered under the crushing weight more than Marshal Burnett, for, on top of the townswomen who'd been taken, one of them being Lucinda Davis, the café owner with whom he'd become romantically involved, came the belated discovery that his own daughter was also gone, evidently at the hands of the escaped prisoner Ben Craddock.

As evening descended on the beleaguered town, hastened and heightened by the thick layers of smoke that still hung in the air over everything, its gloom was more than matched by the mood that filled the jail office where Luke, Burnett, and Doc Whitney sat in weary sprawls. Each man remained coated with a thick layer of soot, streaked by tracks of dried sweat. Additionally, Whitney displayed spatters of blood on the sleeves of his formerly white shirt. The marshal's bottle of confiscated moonshine was perched prominently on the end of his desk.

"After today," Burnett was saying in a low, dejected tone, "I'll never again worry about facing Hell in the afterlife. I've already been there."

"I imagine a lot of folks in our town are feeling that way right about now," Whitney agreed.

Burnett slowly shook his head. "I heard all the stories about the Legion of Fire. I just never figured they'd bother with little Arapaho Springs."

"Tell me about them, this Legion of Fire," Luke said. "What's the story behind them?"

Burnett took time for a swig of the moonshine. Then, passing the bottle to Whitney, he said, "Nobody knows for sure. They sprung up not quite a year ago. First showed up off to the east, then worked their way west and all across the state. They don't just rob banks or trains or stagecoaches, they plunder whole towns, as you saw here. They leave 'em in flames and so devastated that it takes days, or never in some cases, for any kind of posse to be formed to give chase. By then the Legion has scattered to the four winds. Some have speculated they have a hideout up in the Pawnee Badlands where they regroup and then ride out to strike again. There's also been some claims that Sam Kelson, the fella who supposedly leads 'em, used to ride with Quantrill in the war."

"Every pissant outlaw gang that crops up west of the Missouri is laid at the feet of Quantrill," Whitney said. "I wore the gray in the late war and can't say I'm proud to have that association with some of the things Quantrill and Anderson and the rest did. But it's generally accepted that they seldom rode with more than a couple of hundred men, and usually not even that many. By my rough calculation, if all the outlaw leaders who have since been labeled as being former Quantrill men actually *were,* that would have put Quantrill at the head of an army equal to Lee's."

Burnett shrugged. "Maybe so, but you can't deny that the fierce way the Legion of Fire hits has all the earmarks of Lawrence, Kansas. The red bandannas tied to their arms might be an original touch, but all the rest makes them nothing but pure savages. And they get better and better — or worse and worse, I guess I should say — every time they strike."

"Sadly, you're all too right about that," Whitney said as he passed the bottle to Luke.

Burnett frowned at the bounty hunter. "I can't believe you never heard about the Legion before this."

"I'm a little surprised myself," Luke admitted. "But until I set on the trail of Craddock and it led me up this way, I spent most of last year down along the Texas border. There were plenty of other bad hombres down that way to keep a fella in my line of work occupied."

Further discussion was interrupted by a loud groan from across the room. All three men turned their heads to look that way. Russell Quaid, who had been stretched out on the couch where Luke had slept the night before, sat up suddenly and emitted another groan. He raised one hand and held it to his thickly bandaged head, appearing disoriented as well as in considerable pain.

Doc Whitney rose from his chair and hurried over to the young man. "Take it easy, lad. You'd best lie back down. You've received a powerful blow to the head and ought not be trying to move around too much."

In spite of the warning, Russell remained stubbornly sitting up. He tried to swing his legs over the side of the couch but appeared to have trouble getting them to do what he wanted. With his hand still pressed to his head, he said, "Wha . . . Where am I? What happened?"

He clearly had forgotten that when Burnett and Luke first returned to the jail to find him sprawled unconscious in the cell block, he'd come to long enough to spill a rush of words, telling them what had taken place. How Craddock had tricked Mycroft and then used the threat of killing him to con Russell into unlocking the cell in return for sparing the lawyer's life. After that, he quickly faded again, his final words a mumbling jumble that trailed off unfinished. "He tricked me, too . . . he promised . . . I never should have trusted . . ."

He'd never mentioned Millie at that time, but as he struggled to clear his head, his eyes widened as she leaped to his mind. "Where's Millie? Where's Mr. Mycroft?"

Whitney put a hand on his shoulder. "Calm down, son. Mycroft is dead. Millie is . . . gone. It appears Craddock took her with him."

Russell's chin quivered, horrified at what he'd just heard. "My God! What did I do?" His eyes swept the room, touching on Burnett, then Luke, then back to Burnett. "Why are you all still here? Hasn't anyone gone after her?" he demanded, his voice turning strident. "How long was I out?"

"You've been unconscious for several hours, except for a few minutes when the marshal and Jensen first found you," Whitney explained. "In the meantime, nearly the whole town was in flames thanks to the Legion of Fire. We, along with every other able-bodied person, have been involved since then in saving what we could. Many more besides Mycroft are dead, and five other women were abducted by the raiders."

Russell dropped back on the couch, clamping both hands to the sides of his face. He groaned again. "Oh dear Lord, let this be a nightmare! Let me wake up and find this is all some horrible, ghastly dream."

"It's a nightmare right enough," Luke allowed. "But it's one there is no waking up from. The only thing that's left is to forge ahead and salvage as much as possible out of the ashes."

Russell lunged to a sitting position once more. His eyes again went to Burnett. "I know you can never forgive me, Marshal. But I am so incredibly sorry. I let you down and I failed to protect Millie. She warned me not to trust Craddock, but he had Mr. Mycroft by the throat . . . I couldn't let him . . . I thought . . ."

"Don't do that to yourself, kid," Burnett

said. "Heaping blame ain't gonna change a damn thing at this stage, and if we get started with it there's plenty to go around. I'm a father, and I wear a badge for this town. That means I'm supposed to protect my daughter *and* my town. I failed at both!"

"And if you stretch it far enough you can blame me for not shooting Craddock when I had the chance," Luke said. "You see how pointless blame can get? The marshal's right. It accomplishes nothing except to waste time. And if we have any hope of getting those women back, we can't afford to lose any more of that."

Burnett eyed him sharply. "You dealing yourself in on going after 'em?"

"You'd expect any different?" Luke replied. "After all, Craddock was *my* prisoner. And those Legion of Fire skunks gave him his opening to get away. Call me petty, but I take all that kinda personal."

"In addition to the bounty you're looking to claim for Craddock, are you aware there are substantial rewards riding on the heads of several members of the Legion of Fire?" Burnett asked.

A corner of Luke's mouth quirked up. "Let's say I'm not *un*aware of that particular fact. But if you're implying that's my main motive for getting involved, I might have to ponder on feeling insulted."

A tired smile came and went on Burnett's haggard, soot-streaked face. "Trust me. I didn't mean to imply anything. It don't matter what your motives are. As long as you're willing to ride out with me on this thing . . . well, all I can say is that I'd be grateful."

Chapter 19

The morning sun shining down on Arapaho Springs only seemed to amplify the ugliness and ruin left by the previous day's ruthless attack.

A small group of somber-faced men stood before the jail building. A slightly larger, more loosely assembled group, including a few women, stood some distance behind them. Farther up the street, a scattered handful of individuals milled about, gazing with half-stunned looks still on their faces as they surveyed the damage. The stink and haze of smoke remained heavy in the air.

Marshal Burnett was planted in front of the jail, facing out at the five men assembled directly before him. To his left stood Luke. To his right was Doc Whitney and part-time deputy Fred Packer.

"Men," Burnett said, "the task we're setting out on is going to be hard, dangerous, and long. We'll be gone for days, maybe weeks. Other posses who've gone after the Legion of Fire have fared poorly. Capturing or killing a significant number of the gang or getting back the bank money — that's probably too much to hope for. Our main goal is to rescue our women."

He paused, letting the words sink in, letting his gaze rest for a moment on each of the faces looking back at him. "Now, I want to make something totally clear. As all of you know, we're actually dealing with two abductions. That of my daughter by the escaped prisoner Ben Craddock and that of the five townswomen taken by the Legion raiders. After chewing on it all night and talking it over with Doctor Whitney, who needs no introduction, and Luke Jensen, here on my left, a highly skilled bounty hunter who'll be riding with us, I reached a decision on how best to proceed.

"We're going to start by first going after my daughter. The odds are reasonably good for us to catch up quickly with one horse carrying two riders who, from every indication, took off with next to nothing in the way of provisions. After that, we'll immediately turn our attention to the raiders. Reports from posses who've gone after them in the past are that they'll likely break up into smaller groups in order to make the chase more difficult. That also means that catching up with any one bunch would be only be a partial success and only a partial chance to regain anything that was stolen."

Burnett paused again, his eyes flinty, his mouth set in a grim line. "So you see what we're up against. Make sure you understand. And one more thing — if any of you think that going after my daughter first is playing favorites and not decided on strictly for reasons of getting the quickest, surest results, speak up now. It won't change anything, but I'm giving you the chance to get it off your chest. And if it means you decide not to ride out with us . . . well, then so be it."

The five men he was addressing stood silent and still, their expressions unchanging. Until Swede Norsky, the blacksmith, spoke up. "We trust you to make the right decision for the right reasons, Marshal. And even if you were to lean a bit in favor of Millie . . . how could any man fault you for it?"

The others grumbled a general assent.

In response, Burnett nodded silent appreciation. Then he raised his voice and addressed the rest of the gathering, saying, "As for the rest of you, you're being left in the good hands of Doc Whitney and Fred

Packer here, who'll be representing the law in Arapaho Springs while I'm gone. There's burying, grieving, and healing to be done. And then rebuilding to get started. I wish I could be here to participate in all of that with you. I trust you understand why me and these men who'll be riding out with me can't. Our best, maybe only chance to get my daughter and the other women back is to go after their abductors as soon as possible.

"Frank Barley's son Dan rode out at first light for Fort Baker. When they hear what happened, I'm confident they'll respond with aid and supplies to help get our town back on its feet." The marshal's gaze drifted for a moment to the ashes and ruins farther up the street and then slowly came back to those before him. "We've all lost something in the past twenty-four hours. Some of us more than others. Some of it there's no way of ever getting back. The way I see it, those of us who've survived owe it to the ones who didn't make it to carry on and put Arapaho Springs back together again. I hope all of you feel the same."

Five minutes later, the posse was mounted and ready to ride.

Luckily, with Barley's Livery located at the south end of town, it had escaped the raid mostly untouched except for a few bullet holes from when two of the raiders were using the wagon parked in front of it for cover while trying to keep the marshal and Luke pinned inside the jail building. A good selection of horses remained. For those who didn't have adequate horses of their own, Frank Barley, the livery proprietor, had given them complete freedom in making their picks as well as providing a good measure of grain to take along for each.

A choice of provisions for the men, unfortunately, was not so readily available. With the general store, the café, and one of the saloons all burned to rubble and additional looting having been done to several homes, there simply wasn't a lot to choose from. Some of the housewives had put together a few sacks containing biscuits, jerky, two or three slabs of bacon, and a smattering of canned goods — but they'd had to take care to hold back enough for rationing out to their families until supplies arrived from Fort Baker.

The posse would have to do some hunting and foraging as they proceeded with their pursuit.

The five men accompanying Luke and Burnett were Swede Norsky, the blacksmith who'd had a previous brush with Craddock;

Harry Barlow, a bartender at the now destroyed Brass Rail Saloon; Pete Hennesy, a cook at the café run by Lucinda Davis, one of the kidnap victims as well as being Burnett's lady friend; Whitey Mason and his oldest son Keith, ranchers from outside of town who'd been drawn by the smoke of the fires and who'd insisted on joining the posse as payback to the marshal for his recent help in running rustlers off their spread.

At the last minute, an additional posse man made his appearance. Russell Quaid came striding out of the jail, where he'd spent the night on the couch like Doc Whitney had ordered him to do. But he was refusing any more of that. He'd stripped the bandage from his head and wore a wide-brimmed Boss of the Plains hat that he'd taken off the body of one of the raiders temporarily piled out back of the jail. Additionally, acquired from the same source, a gunbelt was strapped around his waist with a .44 caliber Colt Frontier pouched in its holster. In one hand he carried the Henry repeater he'd gotten from the gun rack yesterday.

On the walkway outside the jail he paused momentarily beside Whitney, looking at the doc, clearly expecting strong objection.

Whitney held his eyes for a second and then simply gave a bob of his head.

Crossing the street, Russell paused again beside where Burnett sat his horse. Looking up at the marshal, he said in a firm voice, "I'm coming along."

Burnett regarded him. "You took a helluva blow to the head. You sure you can hold up?"

"I'll hold up," Russell replied, his voice remaining firm and strong. "Nothing short of a bullet is going to stop me."

The marshal grunted. "What we're setting out to do, there's a good chance of running into plenty of those. But if you're sure it's what you want . . . hurry up and saddle a horse."

CHAPTER 20

Ben Craddock hadn't slept well that night. Hardly at all, as a matter of fact. He wanted to relax, to believe that everything was going to be okay, but that was pretty damned hard to do with all that was running through his mind as he lay surrounded by twenty hard-eyed members of the Legion of Fire in the camp they had pitched at dusk.

Not that he wasn't a hard-eyed outlaw in his own right. But he was vastly outnumbered and he wasn't comfortable with being part of this group, not as far as his own feelings nor as far as sensing he was fully accepted by them. It had all happened so fast and such a relatively short time ago.

As the Legion raiders rode down on him and Millie, Craddock figured he was good as dead. He fully expected them to waste no time filling him full of lead, taking the girl, and leaving his remains to be picked clean by the buzzards and coyotes in that empty draw.

Only one thing prevented that from happening. One of the raiders who had ridden with Craddock a few years earlier down in Arizona recognized him. It turned out Elmer Pride held a position in the Legion as a sort of lieutenant to the leader Sam Kelson. In his slow Texas drawl, Pride told Kelson and the rest of the gang of his past association with Craddock; how he was certainly no friend of the law, that he was a good gun hand proven capable of being able to keep a cool head when the lead was flying thick. Further, Pride pointed out, the Legion had just lost nearly a dozen of their members during the raid on Arapaho Springs, and Craddock would be a good start toward filling that void.

For his part, Craddock promptly and sincerely expressed an eager willingness to join the Legion. He went on to explain his current circumstance — how he was on the run from a noose down in Texas, had suffered a fluke capture, and had been jailed back in town. Then he used the distraction of the Legion's strike to break out.

Some of the raiders who'd initially shown skepticism toward Pride's suggestion to bring him into the fold started to look more accepting of the notion.

Of course, the only thing that really mattered

was what Sam Kelson thought of the idea. After listening silently to what Pride had to say and then what Craddock added on his own behalf, the Legion chieftain scrutinized Craddock for another stretch of silence before finally saying, "I put a lot of stock in the opinion of Elmer Pride. That alone stacks high in your favor. On top of that, finding a way to use our attack on the town to your advantage was pretty slick thinking."

His gaze drifted from Craddock to Millie. The raw hunger that shone in his eyes as they lingered there was unmistakable. The corners of his mouth peeling back into a wolf's grin, he added, "But taking the marshal's own daughter as your hostage — that's the cherry on the cake that definitely makes you Legion of Fire material!"

A flood of relief surged through Craddock that, for a moment, almost left him feeling weak in the knees. Just like that he was in. Just like that he changed from being nothing but a lone fugitive. One fleeing desperately with no clear direction or plan and hardly anything in the way of provisions — oh yeah — and with a hostage who would only be of value for a few minutes of pleasure or if a situation arose where she could be used as a bargaining chip, but otherwise loomed as a complication of growing concern. From there, suddenly, he became part of a feared, successful outlaw gang, the scourge of the state with a reputation for being untouchable.

There was one final and important proviso that Kelson insisted be clearly understood. "When you ride with the Legion of Fire," he intoned solemnly, "you saddle up for the duration. When the time comes for us to disband, we do it together. No one peels off on his own before then. You clear on that?"

Within minutes of Craddock answering in the affirmative and Kelson declaring him to be acceptable, Craddock was back in the saddle with Millie in front of him and they were riding away in the thick of the Legion, continuing north at a steady, miles-eating pace.

During periods when they slowed to dismount and walk for a ways, resting the horses, and again when they made a brief early afternoon camp to feed and water the mounts as well as themselves, Craddock had the chance for snatches of further talk with Elmer Pride. He learned their destination was the gang's winter quarters up in the Pawnee Badlands near the Nebraska border, where they would mostly be lying low for the duration of the winter snows.

By the time dusk descended and they stopped to make night camp, the terrain had turned more broken, with sharper, choppier hills covered by coarser, shorter grass. Frequent rock formations thrust up in ragged, sometimes grotesque shapes. It was where two of these moderately tall, spine-like formations angled close together, forming a wedge-like barrier to the cold wind increasing out of the northwest, that they made their camp.

It was also where Craddock got his first real taste of having become a subordinate and no longer calling his own shots. It came as they were first setting up camp.

Kelson ordered all of the captive women, including Millie, to be grouped together and kept under close watch slightly apart from the main body of men. "There'll be no messing with them. Not tonight. Not by me and not by any of you," the gang leader announced to all. "There'll be plenty of time for that after we get to our hideout and turns can be settled and scheduled in an orderly fashion. We'll have all winter, so everybody will get their share of romping. I don't want no hard feelings or petty jealousies cropping up right off the bat. There's no time for it. We've still got to keep an eye on our back trail and make sure we get where we're headed, undetected and with no trouble."

Several of the men displayed obvious disappointment, but none voiced any kind of protest.

"Naturally," Kelson added, "that goes double

for you men assigned to watch over them. Keep your eyes peeled sharp to make sure none of 'em try to run off. Otherwise, it's strictly hands off. Any funny business — by anybody — you'll answer to me damn quick."

As a result, Millie was taken from Craddock and herded with the other women to a spot over against one of the rock walls where three men with rifles were posted to stand guard over them. Also, at Kelson's insistence, Millie's handcuffs were removed. None of the women were bound. It seemed to be assumed that, even if one of them could somehow get past the guards, the locale was so remote and barren that it presented an added deterrent of its own.

Craddock spent the night alone in his bedroll, denied the pleasant interval he'd been counting on so much. Yeah, by most other measures he was better off in the company of the Legion than when he'd been wandering alone and aimless and underprovisioned . . . but, damn, he'd really been looking forward to a night's worth of dallying with the curvaceous Millie.

It shook out that he not only didn't get that particular dalliance but, if the picture he took away from Kelson's words was accurate, when they got to winter quarters it sounded like he would end up sharing her with the rest of the gang members. Not the least of whom, judging by the hungry way he'd looked at Millie back in the draw, would be Kelson himself.

Thoughts like those, in addition to his uncertainty over being fully accepted into the Legion at the early stage, had kept him from getting any decent shut-eye throughout the night. With the beginning of a new day, he sat up in his bedroll and remained there for a few minutes, looking over the camp as the rest of the men were beginning to stir, and wondering just what the hell he'd gotten himself into. Was it for the better or worse?

He had ridden with gangs a few times in the past, but much smaller ones and always with himself as either the single or coleader of the bunch. He'd never much cottoned to taking orders from somebody else, not even as a youngster, and the passage of years surely hadn't done anything to mellow that outlook. On one hand, he liked the thought of the security and added safety gained from being part of a well-organized gang. Especially with winter coming on and finding himself in strange territory with no prospects on the horizon other than keeping on the run. Christ knew that the last few years of being mostly on his own hadn't been very easy or very lucrative. At the same time there was no getting around the fact that being just *part* of this or any outfit, having little or no say in the way of things, was going to be hard to swallow.

And then there was the girl. *Millie.* His possession. Right or wrong, complications and all, that was how Craddock had come to think of her. His to use and then discard on his own whim. Not on the say of Sam Kelson or anybody else. Right off the bat, he was already finding such an intrusion to be something that stuck in his craw. Under the circumstance, he knew it wasn't smart to feel that way, and certainly not to contemplate any resistance to it, but it was there all the same. It was how he felt and he was having trouble getting past it.

He was still sitting up in his bedroll and wrestling with his thoughts when Elmer Pride came walking over with a steaming cup of coffee in one hand.

"You made it that far up," the gnarled old Texan drawled as a corner of his mouth lifted. "You might as well crawl the rest of the way to your feet. They've got coffee ready at the big middle fire over yonder and there'll soon be some pan biscuits to pass around. You don't want to miss out on gettin' yourself some."

"No, that's for sure. Especially not the coffee," Craddock said, managing a brief smile of his own.

Pride squatted down beside him. "How'd you sleep?"

"So-so," Craddock admitted. "Big change. Lot to take in, you know?"

"Reckon so."

"Not that I'm complainin', mind you," Craddock was quick to add. "I'm sure a sight better off than I would've been if you fellas hadn't come gallopin' up when you did. I wanted out of that jail and that town so bad I'm afraid I didn't take time to plan very good as far as food or gear to last me on the trail."

"It happens," Pride said. "Fella in a situation like you was ain't got much of a chance for any fancy plannin'. Just bustin' free is the main thing."

"All the same, your bunch showin' up was a real stroke of luck. And, if I ain't already said it enough, I'm mighty grateful to you for speakin' up for me the way you did."

"It only made good sense. We took a heavy toll as far as the loss of men back in that little town. Way more than usual." Pride frowned. "Got to start buildin' our force back up and so runnin' across you, somebody I already know to be cut from the right cloth, was a stroke of luck for us, too."

Craddock's gaze drifted across the camp and then came back to Pride's weather-seamed face. "You sure the other fellas are convinced of that?"

"If I vouch for you, they'd damn well better be," Pride said. "And with Sam givin' the go-ahead, too, what more convincin' do they need?"

Craddock nodded. "That's good to hear. Again, I appreciate your vote of confidence." He paused, considering his words, while Pride took a drink of his coffee. "This Kelson. I take it he runs things with a pretty strong hand?"

"That he does. He wants things a certain way and don't suffer much in the way of contrary thinkin'. Me and Henry Wymer, we're two who've ridden with him since the beginnin'. We can question him now and then. But even we know not to take it too far." Pride gave a one-shoulder shrug. "Then again, there ain't much call to question Sam. He may be cold and rough in his ways, but he's made us a lot of money that's socked away safe in our badlands hideout along with plenty of provisions to see us comfortably through the hardest winter. Come spring, we'll ride out for some more."

"How much farther to this hideout, these winter quarters we're headed for?" Craddock asked.

"Another two or three days. Dependin' who gets what route when we split up."

"Split up?" Craddock echoed.

"That's right. Whenever we return to our hideout," Pride explained, "we never go there in a straight line and never all of us in one bunch. We separate and take a couple of different ways in to throw off anybody who might try to follow. That's what we'll be doin' when we ride out of here today. And we'll leave three or four fellas behind in these rocks for a few extra days as well. To pick off anybody who might be foolish enough to show up on our trail. Not that we usually get much of that. But Kelson wants to make damn sure nobody gets too close."

Craddock arched an eyebrow. "Kelson's a mighty careful hombre, ain't he?"

"Careful and smart. That's what's kept us runnin' clear and pilin' up plunder the way we have. Losin' as many men as we did in that piddly little town we just came from is the biggest hitch we've run into so far. That was just a piece of freak bad luck, and we still got away with a nice haul and left the place a pile of ashes." Abruptly, Pride straightened up. “Come on. Let’s go get us some of those biscuits. All this talk is makin’ me hungry.”

CHAPTER 21

"I'll be damned," Tom Burnett exclaimed from his horse. "You mean he rode right into the path of the Legion of Fire?"

"That's the way it reads." Luke stood on the ground where he'd dismounted to examine sign.

The other men sat their horses. The posse was halted in the draw where the Legion raiders had overtaken Craddock and Millie. Overhead, the sun was climbing toward its noon zenith.

"So what does it mean?" Russell Quaid said, his forehead puckering anxiously. "Did the raiders . . . harm them?"

Luke shook his head. "Doesn't look that way. There's no sign of any kind of struggle, no trace of blood that I can see. Appears they palavered here a bit and then all just rode on together."

"You mean Craddock *joined* them?" Burnett asked.

Luke frowned for a moment, considering the question before answering. "I'd be inclined to think so, yeah. Either that or they took him prisoner. But that doesn't make much sense. What use would they have for him as their prisoner? From what you've told me, anybody who's of no use to them pretty quickly ends up dead. Since there's no sign of that, most likely they signed Craddock on as a new member of their gang. With his background, it would make a certain amount of sense for both parties."

"So what does that mean for my daughter?" Burnett said, a trace of hoarseness creeping into his voice as he made the inquiry.

"I imagine it means she got tossed in with the rest of the women hostages the Legion took," Luke responded. He wished he could have stated it less bluntly, but there was no sense sugar-coating it. The answer should have been obvious enough to begin with. Still, he tried to soften it some by adding, "Could be that works in her favor — being part of a group rather than left strictly in the hands of Craddock. I doubt, him being a new recruit and all, he'd rate laying claim to a woman all his own."

Russell scowled. "I don't care much for

the callous manner in which you discuss Millie and the other women. You make them sound like soulless objects to be passed around by this pack of scum as if they're . . . they're —"

"Those are your words, kid, not mine," Luke cut him off. "If your sensibilities are too tender for the picture you're conjuring up, then don't go there. And if you haven't got it in your head by now that the hombres we're on the trail of are as harsh and lowdown as they come, then maybe you'd better go back home."

"I'm not stopping until I'm dead or have rescued Millie!"

"Have it your way," Luke said, "but don't waste any more of my time objecting to the way I say things!"

"Jensen's right, Russell," Marshal Burnett said. "I don't like hearing or thinking about the plight of our women, either. But what we say or don't say means little compared to what we do and how fast we're able to do it. That's why we need to quit jawing and get to riding hard again, especially now that we've got a single trail to follow."

"I'm all for getting a move on," Luke said, "but it might be best to hold off for a spell on that riding hard part. We've pushed our horses at a pretty good clip ever since leaving town. I'd suggest walking them for a ways, letting them cool off, then watering them and ourselves before we saddle up again. We're still a full day behind the Legion with no chance of catching up any time soon, no matter how hard we ride. No sense burning out our mounts the first day."

It was true they'd worked their horses steady all morning, following the wide loop Craddock had made to the east upon first leaving town, before curling back to aim due north and eventually reach the draw where he'd encountered the Legion of Fire. The posse horses, even though they'd been halted for a few minutes, were still blowing fairly hard.

"I guess you're right," Burnett said, his expression a bit sour at having his command questioned. Nevertheless, he was savvy enough to see the wisdom in Luke's suggestion. "Everybody climb down. Let's walk for a ways, give our horses a breather."

They set out in a somewhat ragged single file with Luke leading the way, continuing to study ground sign. The trail of the Legion gang, from every indication with Craddock and Millie in their midst, could have been followed by anybody short of a blind man. A score of horses pounding hard across the prairie tended to chew the ground pretty thoroughly and mark their passage plain.

Still, Luke continued to scan the marks closely. Not so much to determine their obvious direction, but rather to pick out any oddity or distinction in any particular hoofprint that might mean something or could perhaps be useful later on.

After they'd been walking for several minutes, Burnett moved up beside him. It turned out that the tracks were on his mind, too. "Now that they're all in a jumble, is there any way of picking out the marks of Craddock's horse as for sure being one of them?"

Luke shook his head. "Not by me. I've known a couple of trackers who might be good enough for that." He was thinking mostly of Preacher, the old mountain man who was his brother Smoke's friend and mentor. "Unfortunately, I'm not one of them. Not even close. There was nothing distinct or special about the prints Craddock left when we were following just him. To try and pick them out of all these others . . ."

Burnett didn't say anything right away after Luke's words trailed off, then finally said, "What I'm thinking . . . what I'm worried about . . . is that if the gang splits apart like we expect them to do at some point . . .

well, I guess you can figure out the rest."

"Unless I can spot something in the tracks," Luke said, picking up the marshal's train of thought, "there'd be no way of telling who was in any one of the groups they splinter into."

"And we damn sure don't have enough men to split our own force and try to follow *each* of their smaller groups. Hell," Burnett said gruffly, "we don't even have enough men to make a decent-sized posse to begin with."

"You said back in town there's been speculation that the Legion has a hideout in the Pawnee Badlands," Luke reminded him. "Is that the way we're headed?"

"Yeah. At least in a general sense. The badlands lay to the north."

"If the gang splits and there's uncertainty about which trail to follow," Luke said, "maybe we should think about going straight on to the badlands and waiting to catch them when they converge again there."

Burnett gave him a look. "You ever been up that way?"

"No, can't say as I have."

The marshal shook his head. "Those badlands sprawl for hundreds, maybe thousands, of square miles. It'd take an army to cover all the ways in and out of there, not to mention the snake's nest of canyons and gullies and dead ends that twist all through the heart of it. Like I just pointed out, we're a long way from being an army."

"We've got what we've got," Luke said stubbornly. "Sometimes a small, quick-moving force can be surprisingly effective."

The remark didn't improve Burnett's gloomy expression any. "Not effective enough to be in more than one place at a time," he said, sounding almost bitter. No sooner had he spoken the words than he appeared to regret them. "Damn it," he quickly added. "I didn't mean for that to sound ungrateful, but I can't get out of my head what that doggone kid said. It's tearing me up inside — the thought of the two people I care about most in the world, my daughter and the woman I'm intending to marry, in the hands of those animals. When it looked like we had a decent chance of catching up with at least Millie fairly quick, I could bear it, stay hopeful. But faced with possibly failing both of them . . ."

"You only fail if you give up," Luke said sternly. "And you, especially, can't do that. You're the reason these other men signed on for this. And no matter how long it takes, the only chance those women have is this posse. We all need to keep that in mind."

Burnett grimaced. "You're right. Damn it, I've never been a whiner or a quitter. I don't know what came over me, but I guarantee you won't hear any more of it."

Luke nodded. "That's more like it. Now let's get these horses watered and then saddle up again."

The posse rode at a smart, steady pace through the balance of the day and well into the evening. They didn't stop for a midday break but rather chewed jerky and drank from their canteens as they went. Twice more they dismounted and walked their horses for stretches of rest. The trail of the Legion raiders remained plain and singular.

With darkness full upon them, Burnett and Luke agreed on a low, grassy expanse between a pair of smoothly rounded hills to make their night camp. The graze was rich and green for the animals and there was even a shallow spring-fed pool for watering them and for refilling canteens and water skins. Although Luke didn't believe they had closed the gap on the Legion anywhere near enough to worry about drawing attention, the hollow between the hills nevertheless provided good cover for a campfire to remain unseen.

While Whitey Mason and his son tended to hobbling and graining the horses, the rest of the men divided up chores such as spreading out bedrolls and scrounging for fuel to feed the fire. As soon as the latter was crackling good, Hennesy, the former cook, started preparing a meal of bacon, biscuits, and coffee. A low, cold wind was building out of the northwest, making a good fire, hot food, and some coffee very welcome indeed.

When the meal was done, the men sat close around the fire, some of them smoking, all with additional cups of coffee clutched between their palms. There wasn't a lot of conversation. Weariness had a grip on each man. It was evident in the slump of their shoulders and in their expressions displayed by the pulsing light of the flames. It wouldn't be long before the bedrolls became occupied.

Sitting slightly apart from the others, Luke studied each of them and calculated how they measured up for the job before them, the task barely underway. Their spirit and intentions were solid. These were good men out to find a measure of justice, to right a terrible wrong. He could take heart in that much.

Where he had some concerns, however,

was in the physical stamina of the group as a whole. Whitey Mason and his son Keith, the two ranchers, were used to being on horseback several hours each day. The others were town dwellers who might know their way around a horse well enough but weren't really in shape for long, grueling stretches in the saddle. Their commitment to the cause would take them a long way. Far enough, Luke hoped, but it was going to be mighty tough on some of them before it was over.

Even Burnett, who as recently as a couple of days ago had been lamenting about how stiff and sore he was after a night of chasing rustlers, had to be included in this. Although with his daughter and the woman he intended to marry somewhere out ahead, Luke pegged him as not apt to give up even if he had to drag himself across the ground.

Big, powerful Swede Norsky seemed cut from similar cloth. It was quickly apparent he was the least skilled horseman of the lot, but if Luke knew his type, he figured the blacksmith's pride in his raw strength wouldn't let him give up.

Pete Hennesy, the cook, was a little tougher for Luke to get a read on. He was also husky in build, but older than Swede. His broad, weathered, sad-looking face appeared to have a lot of hard miles on it, though, marking him as a survivor. Plus, the café where he'd been employed had been destroyed, giving him a personal ax to grind. There was something more. Luke couldn't put his finger on exactly why, but he'd somehow picked up the feeling that Hennesy was very devoted to Lucinda Davis, the café owner who'd been taken hostage. She might be Burnett's betrothed, but Luke had a pretty strong hunch that Hennesy was in love with her, too, meaning he'd push himself to the limit of his endurance in an effort to rescue her.

Harry Barlow, the bartender was another good-sized individual, broad of shoulder and thick-forearmed. He had a bushy black mustache and an intense scowl that had likely served him well when things got rowdy in the Brass Rail Saloon. What kind of fighting man he was with weapons other than his fists, Luke didn't know. But, like Hennesy, he had something of a personal stake in that his place of employment had ended up burned to the ground. All Luke knew for sure was that if he fought with anything near the intensity that showed in his eyes, then he'd be somebody to have beside you in a conflict.

Finally, there was Russell Quaid, the

young law clerk. On one hand, it would have been easy to categorize him as the weakest link in the group. Too prim, too proper, too young. Yet while all those things warranted concern, there was an undercurrent of *something* that couldn't help but curb Luke's doubts about him. Yes, he talked tough, but it was the untested bravado of youth and everybody knew what empty talk was worth. Still, it was also obvious he had feelings for Millie and was bent on making amends for being the one who got suckered by Craddock and allowed him to escape and take her with him. Were his feelings merely an infatuation or something deeper that would give him the determination to make good on his talk? Although it was too early to tell for sure, Luke suspected that maybe, just maybe, the kid had a strain of sand in him that might turn out to be surprisingly strong.

All in all, and in spite of his earlier words aimed at bolstering Burnett, Luke had to face the fact that the posse wasn't the most competent body of men he'd ever ridden with. Hardly one he would have picked for the task at hand. Nonetheless, it was what he'd agreed to be part of. And yes, on his own he could have covered ground faster and caught up with the Legion sooner. Then what? He might have even been able to spirit away one or two of the women. But unless he was able to wipe out a significant number of the Legion in the process, which was highly unlikely, all he'd accomplish would be to turn himself and whoever he took with him from pursuers into the pursued.

So it came back to the rest of what he'd told Burnett. The women were the main thing, and the best chance for getting back any or all of them lay with this posse, less than ideal in its members though it might be. And the best chance for the posse was for Luke to stick with them, leading part of the way and pushing the rest, if that's what it came down to.

Burnett disengaged from the others and walked over to where Luke sat. "You think it'd be a good idea to post somebody on watch tonight?" the marshal asked.

A corner of Luke's mouth lifted. "I think it's never a *bad* idea to post somebody on watch. I admit the chance for any kind of trouble seems remote, but I try not to take unnecessary chances. Even remote ones."

"Makes sense to me," Burnett said. "I'll let the men know, set up a schedule for them to take turns."

"It's going to be a mighty short night at

best," Luke said. "With a day's lead on us and no sign of pursuit right away, I'm thinking we might figure the Legion isn't working quite as hard to cover distance as we are. Could be they're stopping for noonings and not pushing so far after sundown before making night camp. Plus we know some of the men are riding double with the women they took, so that will slow them a certain amount, too. We need to hope for all those things to give us our best chance for closing the gap on them. In order to take full advantage, we'll have to keep riding straight through the days and longer into the nights, like we just got done doing."

"Okay. I got no argument with that." Burnett frowned. "So what are you getting at?"

"What I'm getting at is, with the exception of the Masons and me, who are used to long hours in a saddle, there are some mighty exhausted men in this posse after just one day. It's not the kind of thing they're used to. That includes you, Tom. I'm suggesting the rest of you grab every minute of sleep you can get and leave the watches to us three."

Burnett bridled. "Now wait just a minute, mister. I'm the doggone marshal here and I can hold up as good as any —"

"I'm not talking about just holding up," Luke cut him off. "I'm talking about not getting worn to a frazzle, about staying as sharp as possible for when we *do* catch up with the Legion."

Burnett started to say something more but abruptly bit it off. He just glared instead. Then slowly the heat left his eyes. "You're right. Again. I'm getting a little sick of that . . . but not too sick and not too stubborn to refuse a good idea when I hear one and know it's for the best. Go ahead and work out your watches with the Masons, then. Me and the others will grab some shut-eye."

Chapter 22

As Elmer Pride had predicted, when the Legion broke camp and rode away from the wedge of high rocks, they did split into two separate groups. Pride and Wymer, Kelson's two lieutenants, took seven men with them. Kelson took the remainder. Three raiders were left behind, assigned to hold positions of concealment for a minimum of three days in order to watch for anyone who showed up on the trail of the gang. In that event, their job was to ambush the pursuers and stop them permanently from continuing their chase.

The day had dawned clear and bright, but the low wind that had come in the night was still up and the air was chilly. The group headed by Pride and Wymer veered off in a swing to the west; Kelson and those riding with him continued on due north, though on a somewhat serpentine route.

As part of all this, Millie Burnett found

herself included with Kelson's group, once again riding with Ben Craddock. To her shock, she found herself strangely relieved by this. Much as she loathed the outlaw for his initial abduction of her and the way he'd savagely, possibly fatally beaten Russell Quaid and Jules Mycroft, she somehow felt better off in his presence than she would have if they'd been separated.

Some of these feelings, she knew, were due to the leader, Sam Kelson. Back in the draw, she hadn't missed the way his eyes had devoured her from the very first. Not to mention the numerous times she'd caught him looking at her since. Craddock made her skin crawl, it was true. With him, it was nothing but raw, crude lust. With Kelson, she sensed something deeper, more sinister. It chilled her blood. The look in his eyes said he would want a woman for more than just her body. He wouldn't be satisfied, Millie somehow knew, until he possessed her, body *and* soul.

Craddock might stand as a barrier to that. Millie guessed that was why she felt marginally safer in his presence. But, God, what a desperately small amount of solace there was in that. Her only real chance was to escape both of them, to break away from the whole nightmarish ordeal. With all her might, she wanted to believe her father was on his way at the head of a posse, riding to save her and the other women and deliver retribution to the Legion of Fire. She wanted that, but with a heart-aching stab of reality, her mind's eye kept replaying what she had last seen as she and Craddock rode away from Arapaho Springs — the town in flames, the street filled with shooting and killing. Who would be left out of that hellfire and devastation to form a posse? Was her father even still alive to lead them?

Such thoughts could have crushed Millie's spirit if she'd let them, but she refused to allow that. She would hold out hope that help was on the way, but she wouldn't cling futilely to merely waiting. She would look for her own chance to *make* something happen and seize any opportunity that presented itself.

Her mind drifted to conversation she'd had during the night while huddled with the other abducted women.

In hushed whispers, she had some chances to discuss her thoughts on dealing with their captors. Unfortunately, she got very little in the way of encouraging responses. Some of the women were widows who'd watched their men savagely cut down by the raiders. Two of them were girls even younger than her, not yet out of their teens. In a state of shock, all were still stunned, moving about woodenly and staring with dull, defeated eyes as she urged them to stay strong and work together to resist as much as possible rather than meekly accepting their fate.

Only Lucinda Davis, her father's betrothed, showed the kind of response Millie was hoping for. "I'll resist, all right," she said with a fierceness to match her flaming red hair. "I'll scratch the eyes out of any foul-smelling bastard who tries to haul me off 'for a romp' — to use the words of their black-hearted leader. I have faith that it's just a matter of time, lass, before your own father comes riding in to save us and put a bullet in that black heart, along with those of all the rest."

Millie didn't share her reservations about that possibility. She fought hard to keep believing it herself, but at the same time she vowed internally not to hold out only for precarious hope. If the rest wouldn't join her, she'd still make her move at the first chance she got.

Millie was glad to see Lucinda Davis was among those who remained in the group Millie was part of. Being at least peripherally in the presence of someone she knew and liked made these wretched circumstances somehow more bearable. What was more, if the rest of the women remained too cowed to try and save themselves, at least she would have one ally thinking the same as her, willing to join in an escape attempt. If it came to leaving the others behind because they refused to be involved, Millie knew she would feel some measure of guilt, but she was ready to accept that rather than curb her intentions to find a way to make a break for it.

It was those determined thoughts and constant vigilance for something that might give her a chance for escape that helped her endure another day. When night came once again, her brave front was strained by anticipation of what treatment she and the other women might receive.

Once again, however, Kelson ordered them to be kept separate and left untouched by all. The difference on the second night was that, recognizing he had fewer men to stand guard over them, Kelson ordered their feet and hands bound inside their bedrolls and he himself slept close enough to make sure no one bothered them. That not only inhibited the two women from talking freely and possibly doing further plotting, it also kept Millie extremely ill at ease and allowed her just fitful snatches of sleep as she imagined she could *feel* Kelson's eyes on her all during the dark hours.

Throughout the long, cold day and the murky, nearly sleepless span of night, one other thought kept winding in and out of Millie's mind. She kept remembering the icy, calm resolve on the face of the bounty hunter, Luke Jensen, as he'd quit the jail building to circle around and deal with the shooters who were keeping him and her father pinned down. He'd succeeded in that much, she knew, because the two men had then gone on to work their way up the street toward the main body of raiders who were attacking the town. She was convinced that if any man — even more so than her own father — had survived the encounter with the Legion, it would be Luke Jensen.

If she was right about that, it meant *he* would be coming in pursuit of the raiders. It made her feel ashamed to admit having more faith in him than in her father or the other townsmen, but thinking Luke Jensen possibly was part of a posse on their trail gave Millie an additional small measure of hope and comfort that she sorely needed.

The problem was, it might require an army of Luke Jensens to defeat the Legion of Fire.

CHAPTER 23

The posse started out at the first grayish wash of light in the eastern sky, taking no time for a campfire or coffee or any breakfast other than leftover biscuits and jerky that they ate once underway. The few hours of sleep were helpful, but those unaccustomed to long hours in the saddle still moved stiffly and with obvious discomfort as they'd climbed out of their bedrolls and onto the backs of their horses. Nevertheless, grim-faced and aching though they were, none complained as they fell in line behind Luke's distance-eating pace.

Despite a bright sun in a mostly clear sky, the air remained chilly and a low, steady wind bit into the riders as they moved along. The landscape changed, hills growing steeper and choppier, irregular rock outcroppings thrusting up with increased frequency. As the trail passed near some of them, Luke eyed them warily, thinking how they would make good spots from which to spring an ambush.

He reminded himself of the Legion of Fire's reputation for leaving the towns they hit so devastated that in many cases there weren't enough able-bodied, willing men to form a posse to go after them. In a town as small as Arapaho Springs, especially, they might have good reason to expect that. And if the raiders hadn't made the mistake of taking women as part of their plunder, it very possibly could have gone that way.

Still, it was a common enough tactic for an outlaw gang to peel off some men and leave them positioned to guard their back trail against pursuit, aiming to turn away a posse via an ambush intended to cut down enough of its members to discourage the rest from continuing on.

With an outfit as large, well organized, and successful as the Legion of Fire, Luke told himself it didn't seem unreasonable to think they might take such a precaution. Though he said nothing to the others, he continued to cautiously regard each of the rocky outcrops as they approached them.

It was past noon when the posse approached a wedge of high, ragged rocks. A heightened sense of precaution bordering on alarm suddenly coursed through Luke.

For one thing, the Legion's trail led directly toward the rocks, where previously it had skirted past other outcrops. Also, it was the largest of the formations they'd come to so far. Two flat-faced, jagged-topped buttes rose between thirty and forty feet high, angled together like the open pages of a book standing on end, with each side stretching out roughly fifty yards. The gap between the inner edges of the two halves looked only a few feet wide.

Luke slowed his horse to a near halt.

Moving up alongside him, Burnett said, "What's wrong?"

Luke gestured. "Those rocks up ahead, the way the trail leads straight into them . . . it gives me an itchy feeling right between my shoulder blades."

"How so?" Burnett said. Then after only a moment's consideration, he added, "You thinking it's a good spot for an ambush?"

"That's exactly what I'm thinking."

Burnett frowned. "With the big lead they've got on us, you think the Legion might still resort to something like that?"

"You tell me. You know more about them than I do. What do you think?"

Burnett's frown deepened. "There've been so few posses who ever got close to 'em . . . I don't know. If they *were* going to set up an ambush, this would be a damn good spot for one, no denying that."

"It would also be a good spot for a night camp, using those walls of rock for a windbreak," Luke mused. "That would be good news, meaning we've narrowed the gap on their lead considerably."

The other men had caught up and were gathering around them.

"So what do you suggest?" Burnett asked. "We could circle wide around, pick up the trail on the other side."

"But if this is where they spent the night," Luke said, "they might have left sign that could be worthwhile for us to pick up. I say we fan out and go on in. Everybody stay sharp, keep an eye on the high rocks."

"You heard him, men," Burnett said to the others. "Fan out and keep your eyes peeled for any sign of movement in those rocks."

The posse did as instructed, settling into a wedge formation of their own and advancing slowly. Luke rode at the point, with Burnett to his right and Whitey Mason to his left. Strung out to one side and slightly behind Burnett came Russell, then Harry Barlow the bartender, then Pete Hennesy the cook. On Whitey Mason's wing was his son Keith followed by Swede Norsky.

Luke slipped the keeper thongs off the hammers of his Remingtons and checked to make sure his Winchester was riding loose in its scabbard. His eyes were in constant motion, scanning high and low and sweeping along the base of the rocks. As they got closer, the wind passing over the jagged peaks made a low moaning sound.

Closer still, Luke could see where the spacing of the Legion's tracks grew tighter, indicating the riders had slowed their horses to a walk and then a complete halt. Soon he could see boot prints mingled with those of the horses as men had dismounted and began walking around and then the circles of gray ash where the campfires had been.

Yes, the Legion *had* made their night camp there. Luke felt a measure of satisfaction at the confirmation that the grueling pace and short night he'd held the posse to had paid off by closing the gap on their quarry by maybe as much as a third of a day.

A moment later, however, his satisfied feeling was shattered by the sudden roar of rifle blasts issuing from high up in the rocks.

CHAPTER 24

"Take cover!" Burnett bellowed.

"The rocks! Get in the rocks!" Luke shouted as he heeled his horse hard, urging the animal forward so he could follow his own advice. A moment later he was springing from his saddle, taking time to grab his Winchester, and then making a running dive in behind some toppled boulders.

The rifle blasts continued in rapid succession. Bullets filled the air, whining menacingly close, kicking up spouts of dust and spanging off rocks. A horse screamed somewhere behind Luke. Somebody hurled a curse and then there was the sound of a body — horse or man, Luke couldn't be sure — thudding heavily to the ground.

The black-clad bounty hunter squirmed in behind the boulders and rolled onto his back so that he was facing up toward where the ambushers were firing from. He spotted a telltale haze of smoke that marked where shots had recently been taken and, a dozen yards to the left of that, a rifle barrel poked into view as the man behind it was getting ready to lay down some more lead.

Luke beat him to it, triggering his Winchester and sending a bullet digging into a rim of rock just inches from the exposed barrel. The latter jerked back instantly, but Luke rapidly levered another round into the chamber and fired again and then once more. Following that, he swung his sights to the smoke that marked where the other shooter had been and sent a pair of slugs sizzling to that spot for good measure.

The other posse members were firing back, too, as they dismounted and clambered in behind various-sized boulders that had fallen and tumbled away from the butte faces. Rifles cracked, pistols popped. Bullets sizzled back and forth from on high and from the hastily acquired low cover.

Luke righted himself and scrambled inward, finding a deep, rough-edged seam at the base of the easternmost butte into which he was able to squeeze himself. A couple of bullets chased him, but the closer he got to the base the more the shooters higher up had to lean out and expose themselves in order to aim down at him. Cover fire from the other posse members as well as Luke himself helped restrain them from doing that.

Once in place, Luke took a second to assess the situation as far as the men riding with him. To his dismay he saw the bodies of both Harry Barlow and his horse lying dead about twenty yards out. Off to the west, to Luke's right as he faced out from his present position, another horse lay dead. Luke recognized it as the one Swede Norsky had been riding; he was somewhat relieved not to also see the sprawled body of the big Swede, but the fact he couldn't see any sign of him at all was worrisome.

It appeared that the rest of the men — except for the fallen Barlow and the missing Swede — were giving a good account of themselves and doing okay so far. The remaining horses, including Luke's own mount, were scattered and on the run. Trouble was, the boulders and piles of broken rocks the men had been forced to take shelter behind were several yards out away from the buttes, making the men still dangerously exposed to the elevated shooters. And the latter continued to pour it on thick and hot.

Luke shifted his gaze, sweeping it along the ragged rim of the rocks over his head. He was quickly able to determine there were three riflemen at work up there. Two fairly close together atop the eastern butte; a third quite a ways off, alone on the ragged rim of the western one. Three against eight — seven now, with Barlow down. Luke and the men riding with him had the advantage in numbers, but not in position. The rest of the posse, as far as he could tell, were at high risk where they were and unable to move to better spots without exposing themselves even more. If they stayed where they were, though, they stood a good chance of getting picked off one by one. As long as the ambushers had ammunition, that was — and the way they were burning it up they didn't seem too worried about running out any time soon.

Demonstrating how his thoughts were running along those same lines, Burnett called out from where he squatted low behind a flat-topped boulder. "This is getting to be a miserable damned habit, Jensen. Every time I'm involved in a shoot-out with you, I find myself pinned down."

A wry grin tugged at Luke's mouth. "Maybe Doc Whitney will show up to help us out with another distraction," he called back.

"If he did, I —" the marshal started to say. But his words were cut off by a pair of slugs slamming down onto the top of the boulder he was behind, splattering dust and rock chips. Bellowing a curse, Burnett popped up momentarily and returned fire with two wildly aimed shots from his handgun. Then, dropping back down, he finished his statement, saying somewhat breathily, "If Doc Whitney showed up about now, I sure wouldn't scold him for not staying put. Unfortunately, I'm afraid we can't count very much on that happening again."

There was an abrupt lull in the shooting. Men reloading, Luke guessed.

Before he had time to contemplate on it at any length, Keith Mason called out from somewhere over to the west. "We could use Doc Whitney more than you know, Marshal. My pa's taken a bullet and it's bleeding pretty bad."

As he spoke, Luke was able to identify he was nestled in behind a low spine of jagged rocks eighteen to twenty yards out.

"Is he there with you?" Burnett responded.

"Yeah, he's right here beside me." Keith's voice cracked a little, even though he was clearly trying to hold it steady.

"You be sure and keep your head down and stay calm. You've got to put pressure on that wound and slow the bleeding as much as you can," Burnett called back. "Tear off a piece of your shirt or something if you have to, and tie it tight over the bullet hole."

"For cryin' out loud," came a new voice, that of Whitey Mason. "We know how to stop bleedin', Marshal. You don't have to worry about me drainin' out on you. I didn't ride clear the hell out here for that. We'll take care of this blasted pumper. You just concentrate on returnin' the favor to those dry-gulchin' skunks that plugged me!"

"You damn betcha we will, Whitey," Burnett told him. "You just hang on."

His reply drew another slug pounding down onto Burnett's boulder, followed by a crowing taunt from one of the ambushers. "Well, go ahead and get to it then, Marshal! If you're gonna back up your big talk and do something about us dry-gulchin' skunks, you're gonna have to do more than just keep hidin' behind that big ol' rock!"

Luke could see Burnett reddening with rage and frustration. Luke felt it, too. No matter how badly the marshal wanted to make a move or how badly Luke wanted to help him, right at the moment the lawman had little choice but to hold tight to the cover of his boulder. There was simply too much open space between where he was and the base of the high rocks for him to attempt getting in any closer. To try would be suicide.

If that wasn't enough, another taunting voice called down. It came from the ambusher located off to the west. "Hey, Marshal! That kid with the wounded daddy ain't telling you the whole story! Ask him about your other posse man over that way — the big fella whose horse I shot out from under him. Either I got him, too, or maybe he busted his leg or something in the fall. He did an awful lot of flopping around to get in behind a boulder and then he ain't done much of nothing since."

"What's he talking about, Keith?" Burnett called to young Mason. "Is Swede okay? Can you see him?"

"I can see him, yeah. It looks like he's hurt, but I . . . I can't tell how bad," Keith called back. "I can make out he's breathing, but he's not moving. I don't see no blood or nothing, though."

"Whooee, Mister Marshal," crowed the first ambusher, calling down again. "Things are really goin' to hell for you, ain't they? What's left of your horses all scattered to Hades and gone, three of your men down — one plumb dead, two others on the way . . . Oh yeah, and the town you're supposed to protect? Robbed clean and left behind in a pile of ashes. Appears to me, Mister Marshal, sir, you ain't worth a damn at your job."

"You cowardly scum! You wouldn't dare talk so bold if you had the courage to come out and face us!"

This response came not from Burnett, but rather from Russell Quaid. And then, to the shock and surprise of everyone, he followed it up a moment later by bursting out from behind his boulder and racing full out toward the base of the eastern butte. He leaned forward as he ran, his head and shoulders hunched down, Henry rifle clutched in his left hand while his right arm was raised high as he triggered shots blindly up in the direction of the ambushers. Stunned into only a fraction of a second's hesitation, Burnett, Luke, Hennesy, and Keith Mason began providing him cover by unloosing a rapid-fire barrage at the raiders on the jagged rim who were trying to fix their sights on Russell's daring dash.

The ambushers managed to get off just a handful of shots before they were driven back from the rim by the fierce hail of lead pouring up at them. One of the men on the eastern butte held his ground a moment too long, however, and paid for it by taking a slug at an upward angle just above his

Adam's apple. This caused his head to snap back like it was on a hinge, even as his knees buckled and the rest of his body sagged forward. With the bullet exiting the top of his head and his hat sailing in a spray of gore and skull fragments, he dropped over the edge and fell limply, soundlessly to the rubble below.

The stricken raider hit the ground at nearly the same second Russell reached the base of the butte, throwing himself safely in behind a fingerlike extension of rock fifteen yards to the west of Luke's position.

The latter recognized the accomplishment of the young man, especially combined with the elimination of one of the ambushers, as a tide-turning development. Though all he could do was fire blindly up at the rim where he saw powder smoke, blasting away chunks of rock to make it hot for the shooters there, Luke lacked even a glimpse of a true target. It was time, he decided, to move to a spot where he *would* have a chance at an actual target.

Motioning for Burnett and the others, including Russell, to cover him during another brief lull in the gunfire as the ambushers took time to reload and possibly reconsider how to proceed in light of losing one of their number, Luke darted out of the seam into which he was lodged and ran west toward the gap between the two buttes. He stayed tight against the flat face of rock, clambering over fallen rubble. In order to move faster and quieter, he left behind his somewhat cumbersome rifle, making his left hand free to grab and help balance while he brandished a Remington in his right.

The gunfire started up again, lead burning the air, flying back and forth between the ambushers and the posse men. The rider up on the western butte was in the best position to spot and try to halt the break Luke was making. But he still had to lean out and dangerously expose himself in order to do so. In desperation, he made one attempt, his hurried shot smacking nothing but rock a foot above Luke's head before cover fire from Russell and Keith Mason drove the man back. A second later, Luke was ducking into the gap between the two buttes.

Higher up, the opening was maybe ten or twelve feet across. But at ground level it was barely wide enough to accommodate the span of Luke's shoulders, largely because it was filled with gravel and pieces of rock fallen from above. For a second, Luke feared that his plan to pass through the gap and work his way up one of the buttes from the back side might be blocked. But he was determined. He might make it through by climbing and shoving aside some of the smaller toppled boulders.

The challenge then became the speed with which he would be able to do so. Since at least one of the ambushers, the man on the western rim, knew he had made it to the gap, there wasn't much doubt the man would shift his position to make good on his attempt to stop whatever Luke was up to. If the gunman made it to the lip of the gap, back away from the front face of the butte, he would be out of sight of Burnett and the others, making it near impossible for them to threaten him with cover fire for Luke. If the outlaw got in position before Luke made it all the way through the gap, the black-clad bounty hunter would be trapped like a fish in a barrel.

Realizing this, Luke clambered and scrambled frantically over the jumble of rocks that blocked his way. He'd pouched his Remington and was clawing and pitching aside broken, ragged-edged chunks with both hands as he fought his way forward. Sweat stung his eyes and dust filled his mouth with bitter grit.

He didn't take time to look upward. If one of the ambushers appeared above him, he'd know it soon enough by the bullet plowing into him. That itch he'd felt between his shoulder blades upon first sighting the wedge of rocks was there again, stronger than ever. But he didn't allow himself to worry about it. He concentrated everything on clawing his way over the rubble and through the gap.

Not far ahead he could see the opening start to widen as the back sides of the buttes tapered off in contrast to their high, flat faces. The lack of tall sides signaled a diminished amount of fallen rubble. The pieces of rock Luke was shoving away were becoming smaller and the heap of gravel his feet were churning over began to slope away and down. He was almost through! Only a few more feet . . .

A dribble of small stones and fresh gravel dropping from above was Luke's only warning. He knew he had little or no chance. Those falling pebbles could only mean an ambusher was on the rim above, leaning over, taking aim.

Luke Jensen wasn't about to go down without a fight. He shoved himself back and to the right, twisting his upper body onto his shoulders as his left hand clawed for the Remington holstered on that side. His fingers wrapped around the grips, but before he could perform one of the lightning draws that seldom failed him, a rifle crack filled the gap and a slug punched down and struck Luke's shoulder. His fingers spasmed, losing their grip on the Remington.

And then, only a second later, a rifle cracked again, the sharp report interrupting the flat, dull echo of the first.

Luke flinched, expecting the impact of another bullet, truer this time, probably fatal. But none came. What came instead was a Winchester rifle falling as if from the sky and clattering onto the rocks only a couple of feet from where Luke lay.

For the first time, he got a clear look upward. He saw the head and limp arm of a man dangling over the butte edge directly above him.

Swinging his gaze back down, his eyes came to rest on a second shape — Russell Quaid — kneeling in a shooter's crouch at the mouth of the gap. Russell's Henry rifle was angled upward in the direction of the dead man on the rim above, a haze of bluish powder smoke still encircling his lean face and the anxious expression it wore.

Chapter 25

"When I realized what you were up to," Russell said in a rush, as soon as he'd worked his way in to where Luke was, "I also realized that if one of the ambushers got above you before you made it through the gap, you could be in serious trouble. So I hurried low across the face of the butte, just as you'd done, and tried to get here in time to cover you. I'm sorry I didn't quite make it before that snake got off his shot."

"No need to apologize, kid. You saved my bacon," Luke told him. By then the black-clad bounty hunter had pushed himself to a sitting position, slightly favoring his left arm.

"How bad are you hurt?" Russell wanted to know.

"Not very," Luke answered. "The slug only creased the corner of my shoulder. Tore through some meat, but missed the bone. I'll be sore and stiff for a couple of days, nothing worse."

"You're losing blood, though."

"Not enough to worry about right now. First things first, and that means circling around on that remaining ambusher before he shows up while we're still in this box. From the sound of it, he's still busy with the fellas out front and maybe hasn't even realized he lost another partner."

While they'd been talking, sporadic gunfire had continued between the raider up on the eastern butte and Burnett and the others down behind the outlying boulders.

"Come on. Follow me," Luke said, shoving once more into motion. "Keep a few yards' distance between us, though. And listen for a change in the pattern of the gunfire from above that might signal the varmint up there is turning his attention our way."

Russell nodded silently and fell in step behind Luke. In a matter of minutes, they were out of the gap and circling around to the sloping back side of the eastern butte. As they paused there momentarily, scanning the rocky slope for a good point of ascension, the lone ambusher's shooting faltered and they heard him call out, "Palmer! Where you at, Palmer? You hurt?"

It was clear that the lone remaining raider had realized there were no more shots coming from atop the western butte. The slight crack in his voice as he issued the last of his words indicated recognition was also setting in that he might suddenly be on his own.

Motioning for Russell to find cover and crouch down, even as he did so himself, Luke craned his neck and called up in a loud voice, "You're damned right he's hurt. Your partner's hurt permanentlike. You're on your own and you're surrounded! Your only chance is to give it up or end up like the other two skunks who started out with you!"

"To hell with you!" came the voice from above. "I ain't givin' up to no bunch of posse hounds. You'll just plug me the minute I step in the clear anyway — so I might as well go out takin' a couple more of you with me!"

"Have it your way," Luke responded. "We'll be happy to burn the cartridges on you, but if you've got a lick of sense and you stop to think a minute, you ought to see you've got a bargaining chip that could help keep you alive."

"To hell with you!" the lone raider hollered again. "I don't make bargains with posse hounds. How crazy would it make me to ever consider trustin' you?"

Faintly, from the front side of the butte,

came Burnett's voice. "Let the stubborn bastard do what he wants, Jensen! I got no stomach for bargaining with the likes of him in the first place. But I've got a powerful appetite for burnin' him down in his tracks!"

Luke couldn't be sure, but he suspected the marshal was going along with his ploy and trying to add pressure on the raider by pretending *not* to be willing to make some kind of deal. Either way, it was time to make it clear to everybody just what Luke had in mind as far as a bargain that could prove beneficial.

"What I'm thinking," he called loudly, "is that if we take this owlhoot alive, he might be willing to save his skin by telling us where the rest of the Legion of Fire is headed and how we can get there."

Before Burnett could say anything, the raider responded. "Oh yeah, that's a deal I'm really gonna jump at," he said sarcastically. "I tell you where to find Kelson and the Legion and *then* you burn me down in my tracks! Here's what I'll tell you instead — how far up you can stick an offer like that!"

"There's your answer, Jensen," Burnett called. "I say we give the mouthy piece of vermin exactly what he's asking for — nothing but lead and plenty of it!"

"You're the marshal," Luke replied, wanting to reinforce that fact with the raider. "You make the decision, the rest of us will be obliged to follow your lead."

Abruptly, the raider showed signs of changing his tune a little. "Wait a minute . . . just wait a minute." Then, addressing strictly Burnett, he said, "If you're a for-real marshal, you can't allow nobody goin' against the law by shootin' another body down in cold blood. Ain't that right?"

"That's the way it's supposed to work," Burnett allowed. "But you've got to remember that I'm a long way out of my jurisdiction. Way I see it, that sort of leaves me quite a bit of leeway."

Luke smiled wryly. He was certain Burnett saw the value in trying to take this skunk alive but was playing his part just to add pressure and make the man squirm.

"Now hold on a minute!" the raider protested. "You swore an oath or some such, didn't you? Don't that make you bound to it, no matter where you're at?"

"Way I remember it, what I swore an oath to was to rid the state of scum and lowlifes like you," Burnett told him. "But that was quite a while ago. Thinking back, I'm sorta fuzzy on all the rules and particulars I'm supposed to follow."

"Aw, come on now! That can't be so," the raider said, his voice growing more desperate. "If I was to consider a bargain like this other fella — Jensen, is it? — was suggestin', you'd be bound to not only spare me but to protect me from Sam Kelson. Ain't that right? Anybody crosses Sam Kelson, they're markin' themselves for a terrible death as payback, and that's for certain. I'd have to have a promise of protection from that if I was to consider takin' a deal."

Burnett's voice took on a hard edge that was no part of any act. "Where I intend to send Sam Kelson when I catch up with him, he'll be long past delivering payback to anybody."

A long, tense quiet followed, except for the low moan of the wind that had turned inconsequential during all the gunfire but reaffirmed its presence like a cold sigh passing over the jagged rocks.

Finally, the raider spoke again. "If I just *tell* you where to find Kelson and the rest of the Legion, I ain't convinced I can trust you not to kill me after you get what you want. And neither could you be sure I was tellin' you straight. But if you spare me and let me *lead* you to 'em, then I'll know you'll have to keep me alive and you'll know I'm not steering you false. Is that a bargain you're willin' to make?"

Luke gave a faint, involuntarily nod, grudgingly acknowledging the man's craftiness. Fact was, the terms he was suggesting made the most sense for both sides. But Luke made no comment, leaving the final say up to Burnett.

After some consideration, however, the marshal tossed it right back. "What do you think, Jensen? You want to give it a try that way?"

Luke made no pretense of having to think it over. "Sounds reasonable to me. I say yes. All he needs to do to seal the deal is throw down his guns and then show himself with raised hands. Russell and I have his way down covered here on the back side. We'll have two guns trained on him the whole way."

"You heard it plain, hombre," Burnett called. "If you're ready to go through with it, just do like the man said. And make sure you do *exactly* like he said. You heard the part about the two guns that'll be trained on you. Any funny business, guaranteed they'll do more than just point at you."

"I got the message clear, Marshal," replied the man atop the butte. "Here come my guns . . ."

There was a moment of silence, at least

from where Luke and Russell were positioned.

Than Burnett called, "Okay, he's thrown his rifle and handgun over the edge on this side. He's turning and heading your way."

Out the corner of his mouth, Luke said, "Stay sharp and behind some cover, kid. As soon as he shows, set your gunsights on him and never take 'em off. Watch for any tricks."

Following his own advice, Luke resumed his crouch behind a large split boulder. Both Remingtons were drawn and held at the ready. Ten yards to his left, Russell crouched in a similar fashion with his Henry angled expectantly upward.

It took a minute, but then the lone ambusher appeared at the top of the slope and began making his way down from the crown of the butte. He was a sandy-haired man of medium height and build, thirtyish, dressed in standard trail clothes showing the dust and wear of considerable miles. For the most part he held his hands at shoulder height but, as he ascended the rugged, uneven slope, now and then he had to suddenly thrust out one arm or the other in order to balance himself when his feet skidded on loose gravel. Each time this happened, his hand quickly snapped back to its raised position as soon as he'd righted himself. The gun muzzles of Luke and Russell never wavered as the man steadily, carefully worked his way down.

When he had only a few yards to go, the ambusher's feet hit a jumble of melon-sized rocks that suddenly broke loose from the bed of soft, sandy soil into which they'd been shallowly lodged. The man's feet went out from under him and he landed on his rump. At the same time, the loosened rocks spilled down, taking more rocks with them and creating a minor slide that carried the ambusher with it for six or eight feet. Some of the rocks from the slide bounded out ahead and came clattering close to Luke and Russell. For a moment, as they were being pelted by these bits of debris, their attention was diverted from staying strictly focused on the skidding, struggling ambusher.

Even in his plight, the man saw it as a sliver of an opening he opted to take advantage of. Though still on his backside and not yet at a complete stop, his right hand darted to the back of his neck and from where it was tucked behind the knot of his neckerchief yanked a short-barreled, small-caliber five-shot revolver. He swung the hideaway gun forward and down, extending his arm to take aim at Luke.

The bounty hunter's reflexes, even though he was bullet-creased and momentarily distracted, were too keen, too fast. Before the ambusher could trigger his little sneak shooter, both of Luke's Remingtons roared and the slugs they discharged pounded into the center of their target's chest. The man was dead before his body had completely ceased its downward skid.

Chapter 26

"So the lying dog meant to double-cross us all along. He never intended to honor any kind of bargain at all," Marshal Burnett said through gritted teeth. "If that unexpected rock slide hadn't offered him what he saw as a quicker opportunity, he'd have waited until we were on the trail or bunched up, and then gone to work with that hideaway peashooter to put down as many as he could."

"Could be that was the way he saw it," Luke allowed. "Then again, maybe he wasn't such a liar after all."

"How so?" Burnett demanded.

"He said right at the beginning that he didn't figure he had a chance, so he might as well go out taking some of us with him," Luke pointed out.

"But we *gave* him a chance. We offered him a bargain."

"Uh-huh. A chance to cross Kelson and

the rest of the Legion." Luke's mouth pulled into a tight, thin line. "I'm thinking he likely was more scared of that — crossing Kelson — than he was of anything we might do to him. So he decided to play it the way he did."

"And I'm thinking you're giving the varmint more credit than he deserves," Burnett said, scowling. "But it's all dust in the wind now. He's one less Legion raider and good riddance for that, says I."

The two men were standing on the front side of the wedge of high rocks, Luke having made his way back through the gap after dispatching the final ambusher. Russell was returning via a slower route, coming around the end of the western butte, leading the bushwhackers' three horses that he and Luke had discovered hobbled in some scrub trees not far from the rear slope. Since two of their horses had been killed and the others were last seen fleeing from the gunfire, the posse was going to need replacement mounts as well as the means to chase down the scattered animals.

And given the way things stood, they were going to need all their horses more than ever. While they'd won this battle, the cost to the posse had been significant. Harry Barlow was dead. Whitey Mason's leg wound wasn't necessarily life threatening, not unless they couldn't get the bleeding stopped, which was proving difficult to do. And Swede Norsky had, from all appearances, broken his back when he was pitched from the saddle after his horse got shot out from under him; he couldn't move anything below the neck, and while he seemed basically pain free while lying still, any attempt to move him caused considerable discomfort. Luke's shoulder wound was barely serious enough to bother with. Despite it having stopped bleeding on its own, Burnett still insisted on cleaning it and cutting a strip of bedroll blanket to tie over it under his shirt.

In short, the ambush had left things in a mess. And while Luke couldn't argue that it was indeed "good riddance" for all of the ambushers responsible to have paid with their lives, at the same time he couldn't help thinking how valuable it could have been if they'd first been able to squeeze some information out of at least one of them.

But, like Burnett had said, that was dust in the wind. They had a lot more pressing issues to deal with than fretting over what might have been.

As if reading Luke's thoughts, Burnett said, "No matter if we *had* kept that skunk alive, I don't see how we could have got much use out of him as far as leading us anywhere. Not now. We've got one man dead and two others badly in need of a doctor. Much as it galls me to say or even think it, it seems to me our days of giving chase as a posse are done with. We've got to get these injured men, as well as Barlow's corpse, back to town."

Before Luke could make any response, Whitey Mason spoke up from where he'd been laid out on a bedroll blanket near the boulder he'd been behind earlier. "Shovel that kind of talk with the rest of the horse flop. You can't call this posse off now, Marshal. I sure as hell don't want you doin' it on account of me! There's still those women to think of. You been sayin' all along how this posse is the onliest chance they got." He was propped on one elbow, his son kneeling beside him, and his right leg was heavily bandaged by what looked like somebody's shirt. A spreading oval of blood had already seeped through it, however.

Burnett turned to him, his expression one of exasperation. "I appreciate what you're saying, Whitey. But come on, you've got to see this changes everything. There's no way you're fit to saddle up and keep riding with us. You'll bleed to death for certain. And what about Swede? He can't even move, let alone sit a horse."

"I ain't talkin' about me or Swede stickin' with you," Mason insisted. "I know we're out of it. But that don't mean the rest of you can't continue on. All you need to do is build a drag litter for Swede and hitch it to a horse. Then put me on the horse and I'll ride the both of us back to town while the rest of you go on with the chase. Poor ol' Barlow can wait here covered in rocks until somebody can come back later to fetch him for a proper burial in the Arapaho Springs cemetery."

"Pa, you're talking loco," his son said. "There's no way I'm leaving you to fend for yourself with a bullet hole in you."

"Blast it, boy! Don't you argue with me."

"I'm not arguing with you," Keith said stubbornly. "I'm just telling you how it *ain't* gonna be."

Luke spoke up. "I admire your grit, Mason. But your son's right — you're talking loco. You plant yourself upright in a saddle and try riding any distance, let alone all the way back to town, that bleeding will never stop. You'll drain out before you make it halfway and you and Swede will both end up dead."

"I can't let you do it, Whitey. I just can't,"

added Burnett.

Mason cut his narrowed eyes back and forth between Burnett and Luke. "I'm an old man. Plenty damn old enough to say what's best for me. I've had my years and they was mostly good ones. I buried a wife, God rest her soul, but for the time she was with me no man ever had a better woman by his side. She gave me three strong sons who are more than fit to take over and carry on the ranch I built up for them. They'll make it bigger and better than ever.

"What I'm gettin' at is that the sand in my hourglass is runnin' low already. But those gals out there, they got a lot left to do. A couple of them are mothers with young ones yet to raise. A couple more are widows with families already missin' a father. And then there's the young ones — like your daughter, Marshal — with their whole lives still ahead of them. If I don't make it back to town, then I've had my time and I got no kick. But those gals deserve more. And this posse continuin' on is their only chance to get it."

Unexpectedly, from where he still lay belly down as he'd fallen, his face turned to one side but otherwise unmoved, Swede Norsky spoke up. "I say with Mason. My life is already done. I know what becomes of a man who's busted up like me. So if me and him try to make it and end up dying somewhere back on the trail . . . Hell, it won't be that much of a loss. But those stolen women left to the treatment they'll get at the hands of the Legion . . . that not only would be a terrible loss, it would be an unforgivable shame."

An uneasy silence gripped the scene for several heartbeats. It was broken by the appearance of Russell, coming around the end of the west butte, leading the ambushers' three horses. His eyes scanned the grim faces and he sensed the tension in the air. "What's going on?" he asked no one in particular.

Burnett answered him, giving a quick rundown of the situation and what they were faced with regarding the injured men. A range of emotions passed openly over Russell's face.

Before he could say anything, Luke took a step toward him and the horses whose reins he was holding. "No matter how we proceed, we're going to need to round up our scattered horses. I suggest Keith and I take a couple of these mounts and tend to that. It shouldn't take too long. I doubt they ran that far. The rest of you might want to keep trying to get Mason's bleeding stopped.

And, to go back to one thing the old man said that *did* make sense, you might also consider burying Barlow here in some rocks. Be a lot more convenient for somebody to come back for him later on than to haul him with us right now."

"What about the rest of these dead men?" asked Pete Hennesy.

Luke gave him a look. "I don't see them as being worth the time or the sweat. But that should be the marshal's call."

Burnett scowled at him. "Seems to me you have a strange way of deciding what *is* my call. But I don't disagree. Rounding up those horses and working on Whitey's wound is important. Bothering with the remains of those bushwhacking skunks sure as hell ain't."

As Luke reached for the reins of two of the horses, Russell set his jaw firmly and swept his gaze from Luke to Burnett and back again. "You two can make all the calls you want. But I'll tell you one thing right now. I'm continuing on after Millie and the rest of those women even if I have to go it alone. I have all the respect and sympathy in the world for the two injured men, but one man more or less isn't crucial to getting them back to town. I can appreciate the rest of you wanting to turn back for their sake, but I won't. I can't."

Luke paused with two sets of reins gripped in his right hand. He held the young law clerk's eyes for long moment and then cut his gaze to Burnett. "The kid might have hit on something. We can't let Mason and Swede try to make it back to town alone, no. But neither is it necessary for all of us to accompany them. Two riders pulling drag litters could travel just as fast and have just as much chance to get them to Doc Whitney's care in time. That would leave three men to continue on after the Legion."

Burnett's eyes widened and his expression instantly showed acceptance for the idea. "By God, you're right. That would meet both needs."

Hennesy wasn't so quick to buy in. "But a three-man posse?" he said in a doubtful tone. "We were spread too thin as it was, Marshal. Look how badly we got cut down by running into just a handful of those heathens. For three men to go after the fifteen or so that are still out there, that's . . . that's . . ."

"You don't have to worry, Pete," Burnett told him in a tolerant voice. "You can be one of the riders who go back. It stands to reason that Keith will want to accompany his father, so you can pull Swede's litter."

Hennesy's face took on a tortured expression. "Oh God, Marshal, you know how much I think of Miss Lucinda, how beholden I am to her for giving me a chance when everybody else thought I was nothing but a no-account drunk. But I . . . I . . ."

"It's okay, Pete," Burnett said. "You showed your sand and your devotion to Lucinda by coming as far as you did. And you're right, three against the rest of the Legion is mighty poor odds. But Swede and Whitey don't have the best odds neither, so there's where you can do the most good. Get 'em back to Doc and help 'em beat the chips that are stacked against 'em."

Keith Mason straightened up from where he'd been kneeling beside his father. "I don't much cotton to turning back from the trail of those murderous coyotes. But you said it right, Marshal. My first duty has to be looking out for my pa."

Burnett nodded. "You got nothing to explain, son. I understand."

The marshal turned to look once more at Luke. "Russell made it plain where he stands. And me, it goes without saying. Since you're the one who advanced the notion, I take it that makes you our third man?"

A corner of Luke's mouth quirked upward. "Wouldn't have it any other way."

CHAPTER 27

It was well into the afternoon before they rode away from the wedge of high rocks. Luke, Burnett, and Russell would continue on north or wherever the trail of the Legion raiders led them. Keith Mason and Pete Hennesy headed back south, each pulling a drag litter loaded respectively with Whitey Mason and Swede Norsky.

The parting of the two groups was somber and rather abrupt. Each knew the other had a difficult task ahead of them, with no precious time to waste. Other than an exchange of "good-byes" and "good lucks," there wasn't much more to say.

The elderly Mason's bleeding had been slowed considerably but not completely stopped. If it didn't get worse again during the trip, he had a fair chance of making it. If it did get worse, things could be dicey. As for the Swede, they had cupped the underside of a saddle around his back and lashed it there to brace him as rigidly as possible before loading him faceup onto his litter. Doing the necessary positioning was excruciating for the big man, though once he was secure on the litter he seemed relatively comfortable.

In the time it had taken Luke and Keith Mason to round up the scattered horses, which was longer than anticipated because the frightened beasts had bolted a considerable distance in every direction imaginable, Burnett and Hennesy had covered Harry Barlow in rocks. While they were doing that, Russell had returned to the stand of trees on the back side of the buttes where he'd cut and trimmed six sturdy, wrist-thick saplings to serve for the drag litter poles. Only four were necessary at the start, two for each litter, with blankets secured between them to function as beds for the injured men; the additional saplings were spares in case one of the initial poles broke being pulled over the largely treeless prairie.

Riding away from the wedge of high rocks, Keith Mason and Pete Hennesy headed back south, each pulling a drag litter loaded respectively with Whitey Mason and Swede Norsky. Luke, Burnett, and Russell continued north or wherever the trail of the Legion raiders led them.

Within minutes of circling around the buttes and again picking up the trail of the Legion raiders, Luke spotted what they had been expecting yet hoping against . . . the tracks of the outlaws had split into two different sets. Nine riders continued on north; nine others swung out to the west. There were no distinguishing marks in any of the tracks to give Luke a clue as to who was riding in any particular bunch.

"So what do we do? Which set of tracks do we follow?" Russell said, his tone tinged with anxiety and frustration.

"Every reason to think they're all headed to the same spot eventually," Luke replied. "It's just a matter of what route they take and how hard they work at fogging their trail. If we continue into more broken terrain ahead of the actual badlands, that will make it easier for them to do and harder for us to follow."

"And once they're *in* the badlands," Burnett said glumly, "tracking them there will be damn near impossible."

"Damn near isn't all the way," Russell stated firmly. "The harder it gets, the harder we'll have to work at it, that's all."

Luke smiled fleetingly, liking the young man's determination more and more all the time. "One thing for sure," he said, "is that we can't afford to waste time speculating on it. For the time being, we have tracks to follow. We just need to pick a set and get moving again."

Burnett nodded. "Since we got nothing solid to go on as far as which bunch Millie or Lucinda might be in, our chances are equal with either one. So I say we stick with due north. I know that to be the general direction of the badlands and it's the way everything has been pointing up to now, so why change?"

"Works for me," Luke agreed. "No reason I can see to favor one or the other. Let's ride!"

CHAPTER 28

With another evening closing in, Millie Burnett was feeling increasingly desperate. At first, when the raiders broke into two groups, she'd seen it as a hopeful thing. With fewer men to be on the lookout, she reasoned that ought to provide a better chance to escape. There were just two other women included in her group, and she further viewed it as a lucky break that one of them was Lucinda Davis, the only other captive who'd previously expressed a willingness to join in an attempt to try and break free.

But, as the day progressed, other considerations began to trouble Millie. For one, there was the fact that three of the raiders had been left behind at the wedge of high rocks to serve as a deterrent to anyone who came after the outlaws. That meant if her father was still alive and *had* managed to form a posse to follow on the trail of the raiders, they could end up riding straight into an ambush. That was a possibility too crushing to dwell on. All along, in spite of her doubts and her determination not to wait for rescue but rather to attempt an escape on her own if presented any chance, she had naturally wanted to believe her father had survived the slaughter back in town and was coming for her and Lucinda and the others. But if he'd survived initially only to be cut down later for her sake, that would be unbearable.

Furthermore, the realization had also sunk in that having fewer raiders around her gained little as far as improving her odds for getting away. Fewer eyes watching, true — but still nine sets and all of them watching, all of the time. And none more constant or hungrier than those of Sam Kelson, even throughout the night when they'd stopped and camped for a second time.

If that wasn't unsettling enough, Millie's growing sense of dependability and comfort drawn from the nearness of Ben Craddock disturbed her and made her feel ashamed. She kept telling herself that she loathed him, yet every time either the cold wind or the cold eyes of Kelson bit into her, she caught herself involuntarily pressing back against the warmth and solidness of Craddock directly behind her in the saddle. And when his hands roamed a little too freely, as they did from time to time when he thought no one was looking, she didn't shudder or jerk away quite as readily as she had in the beginning.

As the day wore on, what at first was a thin trickle of a thought grew into a steadily strengthening flow of an idea. Though in the beginning just the vague outlines of the notion repulsed her, Millie nevertheless wasn't able to dismiss it from her mind. As her dismay over the possible fate of her father and her feeling of desperation grew, so did the outrageous idea she could not suppress. It kept taking clearer shape and form no matter how hard she tried to will herself not to think about it.

The whole thing stemmed from her troubling sense of dependence on Craddock mixed with her recognition of an undercurrent of friction between him and Kelson. It had been there almost from the beginning, right from that moment back in the draw when Kelson's eyes had openly devoured Millie. Initially, Craddock's overriding and understandable instinct had been for survival. To eagerly agree to join the Legion, to accept the command of Kelson, to do whatever it took not to end up another victim of the ruthless gang.

To tell the truth, Millie's feelings had been pretty much the same. The terror she'd felt at the sight of that wave of horsemen coming over the crest of the grassy hill had been so relieved by not being slaughtered on the spot that any clear thought or fear of what would come next, what being spared might lead to instead, had not entered her mind until sometime later.

By the time it did, by the time fresh realizations and fears were kicking in, she was also noticing other things. In addition to the cold chill she got every time Kelson looked her way and the strange sense of contrasting comfort, for lack of a better word, furnished by Craddock's nearness, she had a vague awareness of a kind of tension building between the two men. She didn't feel it fully, though, until Kelson issued his order for all the women, including Millie, to be grouped together and kept separate from the men that first night in camp. Even though he masked his reaction from anyone else, she was too close not to notice the way Craddock's eyes narrowed and his body went rigid at the command. In that moment, she found herself enjoying his response and the fact she was being taken out of his hands. To hell with him; she wasn't his damn property, she told herself. And the only reason he cared at all what Kelson did or didn't do to her was because he wanted her for himself.

It wasn't until the following morning when they were leaving that first camp and she discovered her surprising appreciation for again being partnered on horseback with Craddock that Millie also began to pick up a heightened awareness of the tension she'd noted only faintly before. It went back, of course, to the concept of her as a piece of property that each man wanted to possess strictly for himself. It wasn't a matter of vanity to recognize this; it was just the way it was. She knew she was attractive to men, and suddenly she was caught between two ruthless sorts in the habit of simply taking what they wanted.

The fact one of them held a position of leadership might or might not affect the outcome, but for the time being it did nothing to ease the tension. Most of the time when Millie caught Kelson looking at her, she would simply avert her eyes. On more than one occasion, however, she was positioned in such a manner that, when she looked away, Craddock would come into view and it was evident that he too had seen Kelson looking at her. He never averted his eyes, at least not right away. He would meet Kelson's gaze and hold it long enough to become dangerously close to a challenge. Millie couldn't help but feel it was just a matter of time before one of them — most likely Kelson — forced the issue. Then it would very suddenly be up to the other to hold his ground or back down.

If and when it came to that, she had a strong suspicion that, no matter how much he lusted after her and in spite of his bold stare-downs, Craddock would ultimately fold. Especially with the whole rest of the Legion backing Kelson. Not that either outcome was desirable, far from it, but the thought of being Sam Kelson's "possession" was unimaginable. The phrase *fate worse than death* that so often appeared in the lurid romance tales she and her friends used to thrill to when she was younger pulsed through Millie's mind with chilling impact.

When they'd stopped to make camp for a second night, she feared it might come to a head in the event Kelson made some new demand where she was concerned. But he hadn't.

In the morning when they'd resumed riding, she was again motioned into a saddle with Craddock. Kelson's eyes continued to linger on her more openly and for increasing lengths of time, almost like he was taunting Craddock.

All of that gave impetus to the stubborn thought, that shamefully bold idea that refused to stop running through Millie's mind. *What if Craddock* didn't *fold in the event of an open conflict with Kelson over her*? It surely would result in violence, the consequences of which would just as surely leave one of the men dead. If it was Kelson who lived, that would be the worst possible outcome.

But if Kelson died and Craddock logically sought to take over the leadership of the Legion, Millie would be marginally better off, even if it went no further than that. The ultimate aim of her idea was to create, out of the violence and initial turmoil bound to follow Kelson's death, a chance for her and Lucinda to use the chaos in order to make good their escape.

The key to any or all of it was Craddock . . . building on the tension that already existed between him and the gang leader. Making sure he *would* be willing to take a stand against Kelson. Instilling in him the idea that he could become the leader of the Legion of Fire. Strengthening his desire to have her all to himself . . . and allowing him to believe that she might be ready and willing to accept it.

Millie didn't know if she had the wiles to actually sway a man's behavior in such a manner, let alone the courage to go through with it, but what she did know was that she was determined to survive her ordeal. If not completely unscathed or untarnished, then as much as possible. She would not only survive, but she would do so knowing she had fought every inch of the way and with every weapon at her disposal — even her body, if necessary.

During the night, she had half hoped for a chance to discuss her scheme with Lucinda. Even if there'd been the opportunity, she wasn't sure she could have brought herself to admit to another woman she was considering such a brazen ploy, especially not to her father's betrothed. In the end it became a moot point because their watchers stayed so alert and so close, no chance for any kind of private discussion ever presented itself.

Ultimately, Millie was faced with making her own decision on whether or not to proceed with her scheme. And, with time running out, she also had to face the fact she no longer had much time to set it in motion if she expected any chance for it to pay off.

Taking a deep breath, exhaling part of it

out against the crisp late afternoon wind that passed across her face, she leaned slowly back against Ben Craddock, very purposely pressing her shoulders to his chest and scooting her bottom slightly, pushing it tighter to him.

Chapter 29

Lucas Grogan was angry. Angry at the weather for the cold wind it sent biting into his bones. Angry at the stupid packhorse who'd stumbled and broken its leg. Angry at the two imbeciles he'd been assigned to travel with. Angry at his weakness for liquor and other things he'd let himself be tempted with. And angry at the onset of another bitter night he would be spending on the bare, empty prairie in the company of that homely damn woman and those two simpletons, Rooster and Turkey Grimes.

Now that the liquor was all gone and his head was starting to clear except for a terrible pounding inside it, Grogan could see how bad he'd fouled up. First by allowing the Grimes cousins to talk him into letting them bring the Delmonte daughter along for "company" instead of putting a bullet in her head and leaving her back at the Split D Ranch like Kelson had told them to do and like they did with her mother. Second, and worst of all, by letting them hang on to the stash of whiskey they'd found in the well house but kept secret from everybody else until the rest of the gang had ridden off for Arapaho Springs, leaving Grogan and the cousins tasked with getting the loaded packhorses to winter quarters.

It was easy for Grogan to control his liquor appetite when he was in the stern presence of Sam Kelson; he'd made the mistake of telling himself he could also control it on his own and it wouldn't be a bad idea to have a couple of bottles along for the trip to warm a body's insides when the chilly wind kicked up. Trouble was, once he started warming himself he hadn't been able to stop tipping up the bottle. Nor had the Grimes cousins, with bottles of their own. And once the drinking was in full swing, the homely daughter started looking more and more fetching. To the point where maintaining a steady pace with the packhorses and supplies became secondary to swilling whiskey and stopping frequently so that one or the other of them could take a turn with the girl.

And so it had gone for two days and nights. With the last of the whiskey swallowed and the third day coming to a close,

Grogan was faced with the consequences of his foolishness. They were at least a half day behind schedule as far as the distance they should have covered already. Whether or not the Grimes cousins realized or cared about that, Grogan couldn't say. Not that it mattered, he was the one Kelson and Elmer Pride had put in charge of this undertaking, so he'd be the one held to account for any shortcomings.

It didn't help any that one of the horses had stepped wrong and busted its leg earlier in the day. Having to shoot it and redistribute its load to the other animals meant they were moving even slower under the added weight. There was also the added burden of the girl — a burden Grogan had decided it was time to get rid of. A decision he fully expected an argument from the cousins over.

Nor did it help that a bloated, ugly gray cloud cover had rolled in during the afternoon, blocking out the sun, making it colder still and causing the increased wind to sting all the more. They'd be forced to make camp early, as soon as they found a suitable spot. Another unhelpful fact was that Grogan didn't know the area. He'd never approached the hideout from this way before. He wanted to believe they would come within sight of the badlands sometime tomorrow, but he wasn't even certain of that. All he knew for sure was that if it took too much longer and Kelson and the rest of the gang ended up getting there well ahead of them, he'd have some tall explaining to do.

As Grogan was pondering all of this and trying to ignore the pounding inside his head, Turkey Grimes, leading two of the packhorses, moved up to ride alongside him.

"I hope you're keepin' an eye peeled for someplace to make night camp," Grimes said.

"I am," Grogan responded.

"They's bad weather in the air. I can feel it certain. Rain for sure, and considerin' how cold that blamed wind is gettin', maybe even a touch of snow."

"I doubt we'll see snow."

"This time of year, you can never tell. Either way, we'll be needin' some shelter."

Grogan cringed at the thought of being huddled in a close shelter with the Grimes cousins. They were notoriously unwashed and about as foul-smelling as a couple of penned-up old boar hogs. Even out in open fresh air it was a common practice among other Legion members to never get caught riding downwind of either of them.

On a couple of occasions over the past months, Sam Kelson had ordered them to find a lake or river to soak in, one time declaring, "If a posse ever takes out after us when we ride away from a job, they won't need to bother trying to track ground sign. All they'll have to do is follow their noses!"

Any relief from these command soakings never seemed to last long, though. In a matter of days the cousins were right back to giving off their overripe odors. General consensus among the other gang members was that the filth and stink had long ago sunk so deep into their skin that no amount of surface scrubbing was going to keep it from seeping right back out again in short order. The only question after that was a debate over which of the cousins smelled the worst.

One good thing about the evening's bitter wind, Grogan told himself, was that they were riding straight into it, so whatever stink Turkey carried with him was being quickly blown away. The oldest of the two cousins, Turkey — which he swore was his given name, and likewise for Rooster — was a pinch-faced runt of fifty or so, with gray beard stubble, long stringy hair that constantly hung down around the sides of his face, and a twang to his Kentucky drawl that many found nearly as annoying as his smell.

Rooster, allegedly younger by a couple of years, was taller and stockier, with a faded yellow full beard, and a bucktoothed overbite that added a whistling sound to certain words when he spoke. Despite their unimpressive appearance and dull intelligence, however, both men were proven to be cold-blooded killers who possessed an almost eerie level of calm when lead was flying the thickest.

"Those hills in the distance," Grogan said in response to Turkey's comment about shelter, "look like they've got some trees in among 'em. That might be the best we're going to find."

"I sure hope so," Turkey said earnestly. "Cousin Rooster tends to take on the croup iffen he gets too cold and wet. I don't want to see him get sick. Me, I just plain don't like the misery of an early winter storm."

Grogan shot him a look. "You think anybody does? I've already got enough damn misery, storm or not."

Turkey met Grogan's hard gaze and then responded with a grin so wide it nearly split his narrow face in two. "Yeah, I can see that. You're lookin' a little green around the gills, Grogan. When ol' John Barleycorn runs out on you, he sometimes stomps a little hard in the leavin', don't he?"

Grogan didn't say anything right away. He was also a man of around fifty; he'd lost exact count over the years. He was medium height, on the heavy side — though solid, what some folks called "hard fat." He had pale blue eyes under a ledge of bristly brows, a blunt nose, and an oddly delicate-looking mouth. But there was little else delicate about him. He was strong as a bull, strong enough to crush a man's windpipe or cave in a rib cage with a single blow of his fist, and while he was no fast-draw artist, he was plenty capable with a shooting iron, too.

Right at the moment, however, with his skull threatening to crack open and his guts churning unsteadily, he felt barely capable of sitting his saddle and keeping the gaggle of misfits on the move.

"John Barleycorn," Grogan spat disgustedly. "He can go to hell, and good riddance to him. Thanks to him sticking his nose in, we've lost a lot of time — time we're going to have to push hard to make up tomorrow. We don't, you can bet Sam Kelson will add to our miseries — and rightfully so — when we finally do show up at the hideout."

"Aw, Sam'll be more understandin' than

that," Turkey argued. "Hell, we had a whole passel of miles to cover over ground we ain't never traveled before. And draggin' a heavy loaded pack train the whole way — includin' losin' one of the brainless critters when it fell and busted its leg. He can't blame us for that, can he?"

"Who the hell can say," Grogan grumbled. "You know as well as I do that Sam ain't exactly reasonable at times. If he made a good haul in that town him and the rest of the boys was going to hit, maybe he'll be in a mood to swallow a line like you're dishing out . . . but I wouldn't count on it."

Turkey frowned, looking a little worried. "But if we show up with all the supplies, that's what counts the most, ain't it? Sam shouldn't be too sore if we're runnin' a little late as long as we deliver the goods . . . should he?"

Grogan made a face. "Like I said, who the hell knows? I'll tell you one thing, though, and that is we for sure need to get shed of the damn girl before we get there. In addition to going against his orders and not leaving her dead back at the ranch to begin with, he'll figure we lost time dallying with her along the way."

Rooster Grimes, leading the other two packhorses, drew up on the other side of

Grogan. The Delmonte daughter was propped in the saddle in front of him. She slumped loosely and never would have been able to remain upright on her own if Rooster's thick left arm wasn't wrapped around her middle. Her appearance was bruised, battered, and bedraggled. Her heavy-lidded eyes gazed blankly down from her forward-tipped face and a string of drool hung from her blood-encrusted lips. Grogan looked at her not with any measure of sympathy but rather with revulsion at the thought that he had lain with such a sorry specimen, and, even worse, that he'd shared her with the cousins. It was nearly enough to cause his already roiling stomach to upchuck.

"Say now," Rooster said gruffly. "Is that our little sweetie here you're talkin' about so careless and rough? By God, I ain't *ready* to be shed of her. Not anytime soon! I got me a lot more ruttin' in mind!"

"If you know what's good for you," Grogan replied, "what you'd better set your mind on is getting finished with her."

Rooster's lips peeled back in a sneer. "What if I ain't so inclined? Who's gonna tell me what's good for me? You, Grogan?"

Grogan's pale blue eyes took on a deeper shade. "If I have to. If not me, you can bet your ass Sam Kelson will. You really ready to explain to him how you figure your rutting urges are more important than following his orders?"

"Now simmer down! Both of you back up a row or two," Turkey interjected. Then, looking past Grogan and focusing strictly on Rooster, he added, "I ain't keen on givin' up the girl neither, Cuz. She's been real entertainin' for all of us. But Grogan's right. Sam Kelson's mighty prickly about havin' his orders followed, and you know it. We show up with that gal after he said for us not to have any truck with her, it'll be all our asses. She was fun while it lasted, but she ain't nohow worth gettin' crossways of Sam and those who'll back him."

Rooster scowled. "Damn it all. I don't mind takin' Sam's orders on some things — things that got to do with where we rob and how we go about it and such. But there's other things that ought not be any of his doggone business."

"Maybe so. But that ain't the way Sam sees it," Turkey insisted. "You ride in his gang, you do things his way. It was made clear to us right from the git-go, and it's what we agreed to. And, I'll remind you, doin' things Sam's way has made our share of the money from the jobs we've pulled a helluva lot more than we ever scored elsewise in our lives."

Rooster's scowl shifted, turned less stubborn and more thoughtful. "Yeah, I guess I can't argue that part . . . but dang it, I still don't cotton to givin' up this sweetie."

"Elmer Pride told everybody that Sam figures on making some women part of the haul they take out of that town they rode off to hit," Grogan reminded the cousins. "That means they'll be available at winter quarters once we get settled in. It seems a sure bet to me that anything they bring is bound to be an improvement over this one you're so all-fired anxious to hang on to."

"That's ungrateful talk," Rooster huffed. "This sweetie has been servin' us right fine, ain't she? I seem to recall you takin' plenty of turns with her."

"Only because I was dog-ass drunk," Grogan said. "Look, arguing about this is wasting even more time we can't afford. We've got to get a move on and we've got to get rid of that damned girl before we get to the hideout. That's all there is to it."

Turkey heaved a big sigh and once more pinned Rooster with a direct gaze. "He's right, Cuz. We got to get shed of the gal. She's done us some good, but not enough to make her worth bracin' Sam Kelson over."

Rooster glared defiantly for several seconds. Then, gradually, the defiance went out of his eyes and his shoulders sagged. "All right," he finally said. "But it can by God wait until mornin'. Bad enough we're out of whiskey. I want this sweetie around for what's shapin' up to be a mighty cold night."

CHAPTER 30

In order to regain some of the time lost due to the ambush, Luke had hoped to forge well into the night. Upon broaching the notion to Burnett and Russell, both were quick to agree.

Unfortunately, the weather turned out not to be so agreeable. In spite of a lasting chill in the air, most of the day had been clear and bright. But late afternoon brought dark clouds out of the northwest and by the onset of evening the sky was overcast with a heavy layer of gray. When full dark set in, the moonless night cut visibility to a thick, nearly impenetrable blackness. At the same time, the ground the three men were covering grew steadily rockier and more broken, making the tracks of the raiders more difficult to read.

Finally, a frustrated Luke called a halt and suggested they stop and make camp for the night.

"I can probably hold a northerly course and pick out enough sign to keep us from wandering too far off course," Luke told the others, "but it would be slow and painstaking and I don't know that it would advance us enough to be worth the effort. I'm thinking the best thing for us is to stop, get some rest, and then hit it fresh in the morning as soon as we have light to see."

Once again Burnett and Russell agreed, albeit reluctantly.

They went a ways farther until they found a shallow arroyo with some scruffy graze along its bottom for the horses and a flat side to the northwest that would break the wind. While Luke stripped, hobbled, and watered the animals, Burnett and Russell scrounged enough fuel to make a small fire over which they cooked some coffee to wash down a meal of jerky and hardtack.

After that, they spread their bedrolls snug against the arroyo wall and crawled into them for some sleep. There was a brief discussion about posting a lookout, but all things considered, it was deemed unnecessary. Once that was decided, the long, exhausting day assured that slumber came quickly and deeply.

At first light, Luke woke to find a thin dusting of snow covering his blankets and the floor of the arroyo. He shook off the powdery coating and pushed to his feet, thankful to note that the pale gray sky appeared clear and the rim of the eastern horizon glowed with a sun that would soon be thrusting above it. Before rousting the others, he started a fire and got a fresh pot of coffee brewing.

When Marshal Burnett poked his head out of his blankets he was met with a sprinkling of fluffy flakes that spilled out of the brim of the hat he'd had cocked over his face. "What the hell?" he sputtered, suddenly sitting up the rest of the way.

Luke grinned. "It's a mite too cool for that place, Marshal. Welcome to a nice, bracing wake-up call from Mother Nature."

Burnett pulled up a corner of blanket to wipe his face. "No wonder my feet are freezing."

"Pull your boots on and stomp around some. That'll warm 'em up. Be some coffee ready in a minute."

Russell was also sitting up, his blankets still pulled tight under his chin. He was looking around, frowning as if he'd somehow been betrayed. "Snow!" he exclaimed. "Did either of you see this coming?"

"Not exactly," Luke allowed. "But this

time of year, anything can happen. We were bound to get our first taste sooner or later. Won't be much of one, though. Once the sun pokes all the way out, it will be gone quick enough."

Russell's frown deepened. "But what will it do to your ability to be able to track the outlaws?"

"It's not heavy enough to bother much," Luke told him. "Like I said, it won't last long. When it's gone, any ground sign I'm able to pick up will still be there."

Anticipating another day of pushing hard, except for stretches of walking to rest the horses, they took time to fry slices of bacon to go with the coffee and some more of the "tooth duller" hardtack, softened slightly in the bacon grease. Then, before the sun had fully risen above the horizon, they carried their bedrolls to the horses and got ready to saddle up.

It was just before they stepped into their stirrups that they heard the sound of the shot — a single flat, dull, distant report that rolled across the white-dusted terrain and reached into the shallow arroyo.

Three faces snapped toward the northeast, the direction from which the sound seemed to have originated.

"Was that a gunshot?" Russell said.

"Sure enough," Burnett responded.

"A big-bore pistol, I'd say," Luke added.

They kept quiet for a long minute, ears straining for any follow-up to the single report. None came. The air was very still, everything so quiet they could hear the soft whisper of the snow settling into the ground.

At length, Luke said, "Judging by the way we all turned, it seems like each of us heard it coming from off to the east. Not necessarily in line with any of the tracks we've been following."

"Sound coming from a distance and rolling over these hills could be a little tricky," Burnett pointed out. "It also sounded like it came some from the north, too. Could be the trail we're on veers that way up ahead."

"Could be," Luke allowed.

"In any event, we should go check it out, shouldn't we?" Russell said. "I mean, since it's so close, we can't risk that it's *not* connected somehow to the outlaws. Can we?"

Burnett grimaced. "Damn. I hate to lose more time if it turns out to be just a lone hunter or some such. But I reckon you're right, kid. We can't risk ignoring it. Don't you agree, Jensen?"

"Hunters don't usually do their shooting with a handgun," Luke said. "I don't think we have much choice."

They mounted up and heeled their horses out of the arroyo.

"How do we proceed?" Burnett said. "Just aim to the northeast and see what we come in sight of?"

Without acknowledging it in any way, and maybe without even realizing it, the marshal had come to rely on Luke's say-so in most matters. While he'd chafed a bit in the beginning when the black-clad bounty hunter showed a tendency toward taking charge, he'd since grown to recognize and accept a voice of greater experience and sharply honed instincts.

In response to the marshal's questions, Luke inclined his head in the direction of due east. "See the string of hills that rise up over that way and then reach on up to the north? Might be a good idea to cut straight over and then work our way north in amongst them. Give us some cover down in the low spots, and some high ground to scan ahead from."

Burnett nodded. "Good idea."

"When we make the swing north," Luke added, "let me take the point a dozen or so yards ahead. You two fan out and flank me. With luck, maybe we can time it so at least one of us is always topping the crown of a hill."

Glancing over at Russell, the marshal said, "Keep your eyes peeled sharp and your guns leathered loose. If you spot something, don't be too hasty to shoot . . . but don't be too slow, either."

They reached the hillier terrain quickly, their horses' hooves kicking up clouds of pure white. Some of the fine, crisp flakes within those clouds caught glints of early sunlight that made them flash like sparks.

Turning north, Luke slowed their pace, and Burnett and Russell fanned out behind him as instructed. The sun, fully risen above the horizon, cast long shadows from the slowly moving shapes. As they advanced, each man's expression was somber, eyes sweeping restlessly, alertly. The memory of the recent ambush they had ridden into was all too fresh in their minds.

Twice Luke signaled a halt from the knob of a hill. Each time he paused to listen and scan the surrounding landscape with added intensity. Neither sound nor sight of anything that might be related to the gunshot presented itself until, at last, a faint curl of smoke rising from within a low-lying cluster of distant trees became visible. Had it not been for the background of the closely grouped trunks, the wisp would have been invisible against the surrounding snow-covered hills or the clear, bright sky.

Once Luke had stopped for a third time and reached back to withdraw his binoculars from his saddlebags, Burnett and Russell came forward and reined up on either side of him.

"What is it?" Russell asked anxiously.

"A trace of smoke," Luke said, sighting through the glass. "A recent fire, part of a campsite down in those trees."

"Anybody still there?" Burnett wanted to know.

Luke took time to focus and scan with the glass before answering, "Not that I can see. Not anymore. But I can see tracks leading away through the snow — meaning they weren't made very long ago."

It was the marshal whose tone then became anxious. "How many? The riders we followed away from those ambush buttes?"

"Can't tell for sure from this far back, but it could be. They're the tracks of several horses. I can make out that much," Luke said.

Burnett swore under his breath.

"We can tell more when we reach the camp and examine it closer. If it looks right, we'll continue after whoever spent the night there. They can't have gotten far." Luke collapsed the spyglass and dropped it back into his saddlebags. "Come on. Let's go have a look."

CHAPTER 31

The fear that the body might belong to one of the women abducted from town was an immediate and understandable reaction.

"Oh, my God . . . God no," Burnett groaned, momentarily frozen in his saddle as he gazed down in horror at the still form sprawled beside the ashes of the recent campfire. The shape was clearly female, though its face was obscured by being pressed flat to the ground. It was the hair — flaming red hair stained with the darker, duller red of wet, relatively fresh blood that had spouted from a bullet hole in the back of the woman's head — that yanked the anguished reaction out of the marshal. *His beloved Lucinda had hair exactly that color and length!*

Before Luke could say or do anything to steady the lawman, Burnett suddenly broke from his shocked immobility and sprang out of the saddle. He raced to the body and dropped to his knees beside it. Luke quickly followed, only to stand uncertainly by and watch as Burnett, with trembling hands, gently lifted the head and turned it so he could see the face.

The sound that escaped the marshal was half a choked sob and half a startled cry. He released the head, spreading his hands wide, and rocked back on his heels as if he'd touched something unexpectedly hot.

Luke stepped forward and placed a hand on Burnett's shoulder. "Take it easy. Do you know this woman?"

"No . . . no, I don't." The marshal seemed short of breath, his words coming out in ragged gasps. "But the red hair . . . the shape and size of her . . . Jesus, for a minute I thought it was my Lucinda."

Luke winced, understanding the reaction he had witnessed. "So you don't recognize her at all? She's not one of the women from town?"

Burnett shook his head. "I never saw this woman before in my life."

Luke turned to Russell, who had dismounted but was hanging back reluctantly, a distraught look on his face. "How about you? Any chance you know her?"

Russell shook his head. "If the marshal doesn't recognize her, I don't see where there's much chance I —"

"Come over here and take a look to make certain." Luke could see the young man was unnerved by the dead woman and he regretted forcing the examination on him, but it was important to know for sure.

Russell came closer, leaned over to peer down at the face, then turned quickly away. "No. No, I have no idea who that . . . that poor creature is . . . was."

"Poor creature, all right," Luke echoed, his tone grim. "It's obvious she saw considerable abuse before somebody put that bullet in her head. Beaten. Choked, by the looks of those marks on her neck. And the way her clothes are disheveled . . . well, you can imagine the rest. The bullet likely came as a blessing."

Burnett stood up, his earlier distress turning into a visible display of anger. "Anybody who'd do a woman that way deserves . . . I don't know what. Even hanging would be too good for scum like that."

"What manner of filth *would* do such a thing?" Russell said, his eyes returning against his will to the fallen woman.

Luke cut him a sidelong glance, saying, "Hate to remind you, kid, but exactly the kind of filth we're on the trail of."

Burnett frowned. "So, in spite of us not

recognizing the woman, are you saying this is the work of the Legion of Fire?"

Luke didn't answer right away. He walked a few steps out from the others and paused, staring down at the hoofprints. He'd taken a cursory look earlier, upon first reaching the camp, before all attention had focused on the dead woman, but now he studied the marks more closely. Burnett and Russell watched him, waiting quietly though impatiently for his response.

Finally turning back to them, Luke said, "I don't think so. At least no part of the Legion we've been following up until now." He made a gesture with one hand. "I count the prints of seven horses here. After Craddock joined the Legion, there were twenty-one riders. Then they left three behind at the ambush buttes and split into two groups of nine. That's the number we've been trailing right up until we stopped last night."

After considering this, Burnett said, "Could it be that a couple of them separated from the nine for some reason? Maybe we didn't notice it in the dark or hadn't yet reached the spot where they split off."

Luke shook his head. "For one thing, the ones we're on the trail of are bound to be a lot farther along than this. For another, these prints don't match up with any I've previously seen. There's seven horses, true, but I make it as only three of them carrying riders. The other four are weighted down much heavier. Packhorses hauling full loads, I'd say."

Russell looked back and forth between Luke and Burnett. "So what does this mean, then, as far as the main business we're about — tracking down the raiders who hit our town and took Millie and the other women?"

Burnett's brows pinched together and his forehead filled with deep horizontal seams. "Much as it sticks in my craw, the idea of *not* going after the vermin who did this and wiping them off the face of the earth, the time it would take for that would mean precious minutes diverted from the other. And the thought of what those minutes might mean to our women . . ."

"But the idea of going after the killers who rode away from here might not necessarily mean abandoning the trail of the Legion of Fire." Luke paused, letting the puzzled looks of Burnett and Russell bore into him. "What I said was that I didn't think these tracks belonged to any part of the Legion *we've been following.* That doesn't automatically mean they don't belong to men who are still *a part* of the Legion, though."

The seams in Burnett's forehead puckered even deeper. "We don't have time for riddles, Jensen. What the hell are you driving at?"

"Look at the way these tracks are headed," Luke said, gesturing once more. "North and west, toward the same badlands we've been aiming for and where the Legion reportedly has a hideout and their winter quarters. Is it so far-fetched to think that maybe three proven killers — prime Legion material, any way you slice it — could be on their way separately to that hideout, loaded down with supplies for the upcoming winter? The main part of the gang would hardly take a slow-moving pack train on the kind of fast, smash-rob-burn raid like they're notorious for staging. Why else would anybody lead a heavily loaded pack train out here to the middle of nowhere, especially so close to the suspected stomping grounds of the Legion?"

By the time Luke was finished, Burnett and Russell had lost their puzzled expressions and were looking thoughtful if not all the way convinced.

"Just might be you're on to something," the marshal allowed. "It not only could tie together like you say, it really doesn't fit any other way."

"Plus," Luke pointed out, "following these tracks basically wouldn't change the course we were on already. And if we could manage to take one of these hombres alive — like we tried but failed to do last time — he might prove valuable for leading us to the badlands hideout."

"I see your point," Burnett said, making a sour face as his eyes went once more to the dead girl. "But I gotta say that, for me, leaving alive any of the varmints responsible for this ain't exactly the first thing that comes to mind."

Russell's gaze followed that of Burnett. In a somewhat thickened voice, he said, "Whatever else we do, we surely are going to take time to give this poor unfortunate girl a decent burial . . . aren't we?"

"You're damn right we are," Luke was quick to say, his own voice carrying a trace of huskiness. "Lord knows she suffered enough when she was alive. Her remains at least deserve to find some peace and not be left as pickings for the scavengers."

CHAPTER 32

The dusting of snow that greeted them when they woke after their third night's camp seemed to send a ripple of urgency through all of the Legion raiders who were part of Sam Kelson's group. None more so than Kelson himself. From the minute he crawled out of his bedroll, he began tromping throughout the campsite, snarling and barking orders more harshly than ever before. During the preparation and consumption of a hurry-up breakfast he was particularly relentless.

"Get your asses in gear. Eat up and get mounted so we can be on our way! This snow won't last, but I don't intend to spend one more cold night out here where we risk getting another taste of it. I mean to make the warmth and comfort of our hideout by this afternoon and I'll burn the ass of anybody who lags!"

Hearing this sent a deep, disheartening

pang through Millie Burnett. Her plan to work her wiles on Ben Craddock, to encourage him into a confrontation with Kelson in order to create a chance for her to escape, had barely gotten underway during the late hours of the previous day.

In that time, she'd snuggled closer against Craddock after finally making up her mind to proceed with the bold, desperate plan. And she'd also taken the chance to murmur a few remarks aimed at getting him thinking in the right direction.

"I know you can see the way Kelson looks at me. I know you're bothered by it, just like I am. When we get to this mysterious hideout, I don't think I'll be safe from him. And I don't think he's the kind of man a woman survives — not after he's done with her . . ."

"I want to hate you for getting me into this. But, strangely, in spite of that, I feel safer when you're around. Not like him . . ."

"When Kelson decides to take me, and we both know that time is coming, he won't let anybody stand in his way. If he thinks I mean anything to you, you may be at risk from him as well . . ."

Craddock hadn't responded to any of it in the slightest — not with words — but Millie could tell that his response to her snuggling tighter against him was certainly welcoming. And his lack of a verbal response, she told herself, was also a lack of disputing any of the things she'd said.

Trouble was, with only half a day left before they reached the badlands hideout, there might not be time left to influence Craddock enough to actually make a difference, if she ever realistically had a chance to do so in the first place.

When they made it to the hideout, Millie felt with a sinking certainty, the treatment of her and the other women was going to change drastically. And not for the better.

"Okay, then. Maybe we're not in as bad a shape as I feared." Lucas Grogan reined in his horse on the rounded crest of a hill and gazed out ahead. Some miles in the distance, their tan and brown colors showing through the light blanket of snow beginning to melt under the touch of the rising sun, the lumpy, ragged, irregular outline of the Pawnee Badlands could be seen.

Pulling up beside him, Turkey Grimes said, "Yup. There they be."

"We're still a long way off, though. Not likely to make it all the way to the hideout before another nightfall," Grogan calculated, "but we'll be there early tomorrow. Even if Sam makes it in ahead of us, it shouldn't be by much. I don't think he'll be too out of sorts over that."

"You want to worry about somebody bein' out of sorts," Rooster Grimes said, coming up alongside his cousin, "you don't have to look no farther than me. You was so hell-bent on leavin' behind our little sweetie, and now you're sayin' we'll be lookin' at another cold night out here when we could have kept her around for some more belly warmin'. What kind of crap is that, Grogan?"

"It is what it is," he snapped. "Get over that homely damn sweetie of yours, Rooster. For Christ's sake. In addition to being uglier than a mud fence, she was already half dead from you knocking her around. Probably wouldn't have lasted another night anyway."

"You don't know that. She was still breathin' when you planted that bullet in her head."

"Just barely. I did her a favor. And us, too, once we got sober enough to take a good look at what we were dragging along. You heard Kelson say they'll be bringing some fresh women from that town they set out to rob. So we'll all have some more belly warmers to share soon enough." Grogan glared at Rooster. "And if you'd keep your heavy paws from hammering 'em black and blue every time you take a turn, they might even stay worth looking at."

"I treat women the way it suits me, not nobody else," Rooster said. "And they like it just fine, too."

"Come on. Knock it off, the both of you," Turkey said. "I'm about as sick of listenin' to you two bicker as you are of each other. Especially since we guzzled down all our whiskey. *That's* the kind of belly warmin' I miss. But we ain't gonna find none, and no women, either, nor anything else of much comfort sittin' here bellyachin' about it. Let's just keep movin' on."

With a final exchange of hard looks, the other two acquiesced silently to his words. Grogan heeled his horse forward, taking the lead once again, and the two cousins fell in behind.

The air was still, motionless, warming slowly in the same sunlight that was chasing away the coating of snow on the ground. In addition to rising and falling in a series of sharper-crested hills, the terrain was growing steadily rockier. Patches of stubbled grass appeared farther apart and smaller in size. The hills were frequently cut by spine-like rock outcrops, none particularly high, running in a haphazard pattern of angles. It was as if Mother Nature had been practicing on that stretch of ground before really hitting her stride with the dizzying jumble of rock formations, twisting gullies, ragged cliffs, and blind canyons yet to come in the barren heart of the badlands.

Luke lowered his binoculars and held them out to Tom Burnett. "Have a look for yourself. If there was any doubt this bunch is on its way to join up with the ones who hit your town, I'd say those red bandannas on their sleeves pretty much settles it."

Burnett took the glasses and swung them to his eyes. It took him only a second to focus before he exclaimed, "It's Legion men wearing those red arm markers as bold as can be."

"Since they're practically on Legion home ground, wearing the red will get them welcomed by any other raiders they might run into and will cause anybody else to steer plenty clear."

"Anybody but us," Russell amended as he took the glasses for a look of his own. "Steering clear of that pack of vermin is the last thing we intend to do. Right?"

"That's the general idea, kid," agreed Luke.

"So how do you suggest we go about it?" Burnett wanted to know. "Ride straight at 'em and run the bastards down?"

A corner of Luke's mouth lifted briefly. "That might be *a* way to go about it," he allowed, "but it likely wouldn't give us our best chance for taking one of them alive. And if we break into a running shoot-out with them, all that gunfire could draw the attention of other Legion men possibly in the vicinity. Be best to get the drop on them suddenlike, put them under our guns with the least amount of trigger-pulling."

"An ambush, then," Russell said. "We circle around and ahead of them," he added eagerly, "then lay in wait behind one of those rocky spines they're bound to pass by. When the time is right, we spring out and have them under our guns."

Luke's mouth curved in a full grin. "Not bad. Sounds like a pretty slick plan to me, kid. What do you think, Marshal?"

Twisting his own mouth ruefully, Burnett said, "Don't know how much *spring* I got left in these weary old bones. But yeah, it sounds pretty good to me, too."

CHAPTER 33

It took more than an hour for Luke and the others to circle ahead of the pack train and get in position for their ambush. The snow was nearly all gone by then, but the climbing sun still had not warmed the air appreciably.

Their maneuvering took them closer to the outer fringes of the badlands and the terrain had grown accordingly more rugged. The spine of rock they chose for setting their trap was right on course for the way their prey was heading. It was fairly flat on the side the men and horses would be passing close to, about fifteen feet high at its tallest middle point, and angled almost perfectly toward the northwest.

Armed with a shotgun, Burnett hid at ground level on the far end of the spine. Luke was up in the rocks, slightly off center in a ragged notch about a dozen feet high. Also at ground level but opposite Burnett's end, Russell would emerge after the men and horses had gone by his spot. Once the posse members made their presence known, the Legion men would be blocked three ways from attempting to flee. And if they tried to make a fight of it, they'd be caught in a cross fire from above and both ends.

The outlaws proceeded exactly as anticipated, but for those awaiting them, it seemed as if they moved with agonizing slowness over the final stretch.

At last, when they were strung out along the spine with the leader near Burnett's spot, the marshal rose up out of where he'd been concealed and announced in a loud voice over the twin muzzles of his shotgun, "Hold it right there, you polecats! You're covered seven ways from Sunday. Do anything but freeze with your hands empty and in plain sight, you'll be cut to ribbons."

All horses came to an abrupt halt and the riders went rigid in their saddles, hands held in plain sight but poised only slightly above waist height.

From his elevated position, Luke jacked a cartridge into the chamber of his Winchester, the action and the sound meant to announce his presence and to back up Burnett's words. At the rear of the column, Russell moved up quietly with his Henry rifle held at the ready.

The heavyset leader's eyes, widened and somewhat alarmed, darted around for several seconds. Then they came back to rest on Burnett and the alarm turned to shrewdness. "Mister, if this is a robbery, you are making the biggest mistake of your life . . . a life that ain't going to play out very long if you continue with this."

"Seems to me," Burnett replied, "you're the one with his life on a short fuse, no longer than the distance the triggers on this gut shredder need to travel for me to blast you to hell."

"Yeah, it appears you could do that before I was able to do anything to stop you," the man admitted, his voice surprisingly calm. "But that still wouldn't improve your situation any. In fact, it would only worsen it. You see, I didn't say your life would be shortened by *me.*"

Burnett showed his teeth in a wolf's smile. "That's right. Not by you, not by one of those pieces of trash riding behind you, either."

"You damn fool," the outlaw snarled. "Don't you see these red bandannas on our sleeves? Don't you know what that means?"

"Yeah, I know exactly what it means." Burnett's words came out sounding like they were dragged across sandpaper. "It means you three piles of dog crap ride for the Legion of Fire. Is that supposed to impress or scare me? If you think that, you couldn't be more wrong. All it does is make me want to pull these triggers even more."

"Triggers don't get pulled by talk, mister," one of the other men spoke up. "You figurin' to just rob us or to kill us in the bargain? If it's both, then what've we got to lose by makin' a fight of it?"

"Your worthless damn lives, that's what," Luke said from directly above him. "But if any one of you has a morsel of a brain left in his empty skull, maybe — just maybe — there's a bargain we could strike to allow you to hang on a little longer to your miserable existence."

"We only bargain in lead," the third desperado said from farther back in line. "So what are we waitin' for? Let's get to tradin' some!"

"I'm warning you," Russell said, moving up closer behind him. "You raise that rifle one inch, I'll blow the back of your head off."

Unfortunately, in making his threat Russell had moved up foolishly close, just off the man's right flank. The outlaw made no attempt to raise the Winchester rifle he had resting directly in front of him, balanced across the pommel of his saddle. All he had to do was ram it suddenly backward and drive the buttstock as hard as he could straight into the face of the man who'd moved so obligingly close.

The impact of the vicious blow made an ugly sound as the buttstock slammed into the side of Russell's face. The young man was immediately knocked cold, his knees buckling as his upper body pitched backward. He collapsed heavily. The Henry rifle he'd been brandishing fell, too, dropped from nerveless fingers. It hit the ground in a kind of irony with its butt end striking first. The jolt caused the weapon to discharge skyward.

The sudden roar of the Henry sent the rest of the scene into instant turmoil. Horses screamed and reared up. Men spat curses.

The first outlaw to pay the price was the leader. He never had a chance. His eyes said he knew it, but he nevertheless made a grab for the gun holstered on his right hip. His hand hadn't dropped more than six inches before both barrels of Burnett's shotgun hurled smoke and flame. The double load lifted the leader out of his saddle and flung him backward and to one side, where he smashed against the flat face of the rock spine. He bounced off and dropped to the ground in a bloody heap, leaving a smeared red stain on the rocks.

The man next in line made no try for a gun as he attempted to bolt, jerking the head of his horse sharply to one side and sinking spurs deep, hoping to escape amidst the chaos of powder smoke and trampling horses. Just as his horse was beginning its lunge away from the rocks, Luke's Winchester spoke from a dozen feet above. The bullet drilled down through the top of the man's shoulder, tipping him out of his saddle and depositing him into a tumbling, rolling mass as his horse pounded away.

That left the third man. With his rifle very much raised, he snapped a pair of shots up toward Luke. They went high yet passed close enough to force the bounty hunter to duck back down into his ragged notch. The man got off a shot at Burnett but it, too, sailed high.

Bellowing, "Y'all gotta die!," the bearded outlaw slammed his heels into the sides of his horse and sent the animal charging forward, straight for Burnett. He gripped the reins in his left hand while swinging the Winchester wildly in his right, slapping it against the rump of his mount and forcing it to barge into the other wheeling, bucking horses in their way.

Burnett stood his ground. He tossed aside the spent shotgun, pulled the Colt from his holster, and extended his right arm. At the same time, up in the rocks, Luke thrust once more into view. He slammed his Winchester to his shoulder and swung its sights, tracking the charging outlaw.

Simultaneously, marshal and bounty hunter opened fire. Their bullets riddled the man's torso, raising puffs of dust from his clothing. The bearded outlaw jerked with each impact, tipping backward in the saddle until his shoulders and the back of his head were flopping loosely on the running horse's rump. He finally slid off on one side and hit the ground with thin arcs of blood still pumping from the wounds as his body skidded to a halt.

CHAPTER 34

"When I first met you a few days back," Luke said, "you were a fairly good-looking young fella. Not so good-looking, though, that you can afford to go around letting your face and head collide with hard objects. In addition to what it's apt to do to your looks, you're bound to be getting your brains scrambled some each time, too."

Russell Quaid gazed up at him through his good right eye. The left one appeared anything but good, forced closed as it was by a swollen, egg-sized lump of purplish black. Just below the damaged eye, his cheekbone bore a long, reddish abrasion.

"Thanks for the medical diagnosis," Russell replied, favoring the left side of his mouth. Then he added sarcastically, "I never would have thought any of that if you hadn't pointed it out."

Luke flashed a brief grin and spread his hands. "Hey, I'm no Doc Whitney. Just trying to offer some helpful observations based on my own experience. As you can see, I've managed to hang on to my dashing good looks."

Russell lay stretched out on a saddle blanket with another rolled blanket serving as a pillow to prop up his head. Luke knelt next to him. They were still alongside the spine of rock where they'd confronted the Legion men, not far from the spot where Russell had fallen.

An hour had passed since the shooting ended. During that time, Luke had ridden out to once again round up the scattered horses. It hadn't taken very long, since none of them, especially the pack animals, had gone very far. Still, it was enough of a chore for him to remark to Burnett, "If I'd wanted to spend this much time wrangling horses instead of outlaws, I'd have signed up to be a ranch hand a long time ago."

As for the outlaws, two of the men they'd waylaid, Grogan and Rooster, were dead. Turkey, who'd identified himself as well as the other two, had survived his bullet wound. The slug had shattered several bones in the ball of his right shoulder, rendering that arm useless and leaving him in a lot of pain. But he was still sucking air and spouting curses at his attackers.

At least he had been for a while. He was currently passed out, lying on a blanket not too far from Russell's. Luke and Burnett had tended his wound well enough to stop the bleeding and wrap the arm in a sling. They'd also cuffed his wrists and put him in leg irons, much to his wailing objections before he finally ran out of steam. His two comrades, who made no complaints whatsoever about their treatment, had been piled together close to the rocks and hastily covered over with loose rubble — better accommodations than they deserved.

Russell raised his head slightly and cast a glance from his good eye over to the pile of rubble and then to the still form of Turkey. He settled his head back and said, "It didn't go as smoothly as we'd hoped, but at least you got the live prisoner you wanted. How bad is his wound?"

"He'll make it okay," Luke answered, "unless he does something stupid to stir up some infection in that bullet hole."

Russell's mouth turned down at the corners. "Speaking of doing something stupid, I guess I managed a pretty good job of that when I moved in too close behind that bearded fellow. He was talking so loud and bold, I . . . I just wanted to make sure I'd be in position to stop him if he tried something."

"Don't worry about it. Things turned out all right."

Russell shook his head. "I'm just thankful neither you nor Marshal Burnett got hurt as a result of my foolish—"

"I said don't worry about it," Luke cut him off. "Just move on past it and learn so you'll know better next time."

Tom Burnett walked over from where he'd been examining the bundles of supplies loaded on the now hobbled packhorses and looked down at Russell. "Well now. I see you're getting a little color back, and I don't mean just that doozy of a black eye you're sporting. A little while ago your face was pale as a bowl of milk."

"I don't know about that," Russell replied, "but I can tell you I'd gladly take being pale over the way my head is feeling right about now."

"I figured as much. That's why I brought you this," Burnett said, holding out a dented silver flask.

"What's in there?" Russell wanted to know.

"Medicine. Some of the finest whiskey I ever confiscated."

Russell's forehead puckered. "Thank you.

But I . . . I never touch the stuff."

"Don't want you to touch it. Want you to swallow down a couple of swigs," Burnett told him. "We need to get back on the trail as soon as we can, and this will help dull your bustin' head and make it easier for you to feel like crawling back in the saddle."

Russell held up a hand, palm out. "I'll manage. I started this excursion with an aching head, remember? I figure I can bear some more."

"Go ahead and take a drink," Luke encouraged him. "It'll do you good."

Continuing to look doubtful, Russell pushed to a sitting position and reached out to take the flask Burnett was still holding out to him. He undid the cap, wincing when he got his first whiff of the contents. "Good Lord! Are you sure this won't numb my whole body?"

"Been known to do that for a good many over-imbibers," Burnett said. "But we're not fixing to go to that extreme. In moderation, whiskey is a blessed cure-all."

"Cure or kill, might be more like it," Russell murmured. But then, taking a deep breath and expelling part of it, he tipped the flask high and poured some of the contents down. When he lowered his arm, his mouth rapidly and silently opened and closed several times, like a fish out of water, until he managed to gasp, "You're right. I'm suddenly not noticing my aching head anymore, because I'm thinking about my throat being on fire!"

Burnett and Luke had a good chuckle over that.

Then Burnett said, "Okay. You've lost your whiskey virginity. So taking one more slug will be easier, and that should be enough to set you up pretty good."

Russell cocked the brow over his good eye, saying, "Set me up or flatten me out entirely. But if you insist." After he'd taken his second drink, he handed the flask back to Burnett.

"Since it's not polite to let a fella drink alone, I'll join you in a nip," the marshal said. After doing so, he held the flask out to Luke. "You, Jensen?"

Luke took his turn. "Mighty prime," he said, handing the flask back. "You find that among the supplies we recently inherited?"

"Not at all. This is out of my saddlebags," Burnett replied, slipping the flask back into a vest pocket. "Oddly enough, I didn't spot any liquor at all in those supplies. Nary a drop."

Luke frowned. "From the breath on the one who's still alive and from the stink soaked into the clothes of the two dead ones, I'd have to say they haven't been separated from some kind of booze for very long."

"That may be." Burnett shrugged. "They must have guzzled everything they had, then."

"So what *do* they have in the way of supplies on those horses?" Russell asked.

"Just about anything you can name, they've got," Burnett answered. "From grain for the horses to salt pork and canned goods to needles and thread, these boys were doing their part to help make for a well-stocked outfit. Hell, I even ran across half a case of dynamite."

"Dynamite," echoed Luke.

"That's right." Burnett made a sour face. "As if the Legion doesn't already raise enough hell when they raid a place, think how much worse it could be if they added explosives to their bag of tricks."

"You damn betcha you'd better be thinkin' how much hell can come from the Legion of Fire!" That statement, carried in a harsh Kentucky twang, was suddenly issued by Turkey Grimes from where he lay in chains just a few feet away.

The faces of Luke, Burnett, and Russell all snapped in his direction. The wounded outlaw had obviously regained consciousness in time to hear part of the three men's conversation. As their eyes swept to him, he struggled to shove himself up on the elbow of his good arm, returning their looks with a hard glare and a sneering twist to his mouth.

"Go ahead and gawk. Take a good look," he said. "Everything you've done to me and my pards is gonna be paid back to you tenfold when Sam Kelson and the rest of the Legion catches up with y'all. They'll rip out your black hearts and hold 'em up for you to see before they're ever done pumpin'!"

Luke rose to his feet. He and Burnett drifted closer to the sneering outlaw. Slowly, gingerly, Russell also got to his feet and walked over to stand with them.

Turkey glared up at all three with hatred brimming in his eyes. "Go ahead and gawp. I ain't scared of you three nor twenty more just like you. I know you're gonna kill me. What I don't know is why you didn't finish the job after you planted that first pill in me. But it don't matter none. I'll be watchin' from the windows of Hell when you sorry sons get your payback and I want you to be sure and remember that the laughter you hear echoin' from out of the flames down there will be me!"

"The only truth that spilled out of that festering pie hole of yours," Burnett grated, "is the part about one day having a smoky view from the depths of Hell. That's a guarantee."

Turkey's lips peeled back, displaying a row of twisted yellow teeth. "Damn. Tell me something I ain't knowed since I was a towhead. But don't think you're discouragin' me none. Fact is, ain't no place I'd rather be. Already got plenty of friends there waitin', and plenty more who'll be showin' up by and by. So go ahead. Which one of you circlin' buzzards is gonna be the one to send me on my way?"

Luke snorted derisively. "Boy, when they were passing out smarts you must have stepped out of line too early. That about right? How else to explain you thinking we'd go to all the trouble of dressing your wound and slapping cuffs on you if all we intended was to shoot you?"

Turkey's sneer turned into a puzzled scowl. "I already told you, I can't feature why you didn't finish the job on me right off. What are you up to, anyhow?"

"Are you in such a hurry to die that you don't bother to listen?" Burnett said. "Or is it that your grimy, unwashed ears are so full of dust from tearing around playing desperado that you plain can't hear?"

Turkey's sneer returned. "Me and the rest of the Legion ain't *playin'* desperado, mister — we're the real deal. And all the law dogs and all the fine citizens throughout the state ain't been able to do a damn thing to stop us."

"Up until now, that is," Luke said. "Maybe the whole gang isn't stopped. Not yet. But in case you haven't noticed, you sure are. Your two pals permanentlike, and you well on your way . . . unless you're willing to show some better sense than any you've demonstrated so far."

"What's that supposed to mean?" Turkey growled. "You keep hintin' around like you're talkin' in, what ya call riddles or some such. How about *you* start makin' some damn sense?"

Chapter 35

"So that's how things stand," Luke said, summing up. "We know the Legion has a hideout up in the Pawnee Badlands. We figure that's where they're headed to hole up for the winter, now that they've hit Arapaho Springs. All these supplies you and your pals were on your way to deliver are further proof of that. We've stopped you and the supplies. Now all that's left is putting a stop to the rest."

"Just the three of you?" Turkey rolled his eyes. "You fellas must be smokin' Indian weed to make you think so loco. A damn army couldn't root Kelson and the boys out of those badlands. In the first place, they couldn't even find 'em."

"It wouldn't take an army," Luke said in a level tone that matched the gaze he pinned Turkey with, "if the right team of men had the right person to lead them in."

Turkey's eyes stopped rolling and bugged

with disbelief. "Me? You think *I'm* gonna lead you to the Legion hideout?"

"Depends," Luke said. "How serious were you a minute ago about being ready to die?"

"Rather than cross the Legion? Hell, it's the same difference." Turkey thrust out his chin defiantly. "So go ahead, if you got the guts. Gun me down in cold blood."

Luke turned his head slowly from side to side. "Oh, I'm not going to burn another cartridge on the likes of you. You're not worth it. There's only one thing that gives you any worth at all — and if you're not willing to cooperate, you got nothing to offer as far as we're concerned. We'll be on our way, and you'll be on your own."

Turkey scowled. "What's that supposed to mean?"

"Are we back to you having dirt in your ears?" Burnett said, joining in the whipsawing. "The man couldn't have made it any plainer. We're not inclined to waste time any more than we are bullets. So you can help us out and save your skin, or we'll ride off and leave your sorry ass to fend for yourself."

"What do you mean 'fend for myself'?" Turkey was beginning to look uncertain, worried.

Luke sighed. "Once again, I don't know

how it could be said any plainer. We ride away and you'll be on your own . . . just exactly the way you are."

"Like I am? Still in chains, you mean?" Turkey wailed.

"Now you're starting to get the picture," Burnett said. "Chained. No water. No food. No horse. No gun. On your own."

Turkey edged toward panic. "That ain't human! This is the middle of nowhere. I got no chance to make it no place, not hurt and in chains like I am. Not before I freeze or starve or get et by wild critters!"

"Oh, you'll make it somewhere eventually," Luke told him. "That place you said you'd rather be than any other. Where all your pals will be waiting for you. Remember?"

Burnett added, "In other words, in case that's something else that wasn't plain enough . . . *Hell.*"

Turkey struggled in an attempt to get to his feet but lost his balance and fell back, jarring his injured shoulder. After emitting a shriek of pain, he hissed out between gulps of ragged breathing, "You can't treat a body that way. It's worse than Injun torture. Nobody deserves to be done like that!"

Burnett suddenly lunged forward and leaned down, grabbing Turkey by the front of his shirt and shaking him. "You listen to me, you disgusting piece of filth," the marshal growled over Turkey's squeals of pain. "We saw what you and your two friends did to that girl you left dead back in your last camp. What's more, we saw what the rest of your gang did to the town of Arapaho Springs — not just the robbing and burning and killing, but the women they carried off with them to be used the same way you did that poor dead girl. Don't you dare talk to me about what you deserve, damn your vermin-ridden hide!"

Luke stepped forward and put a hand on the marshal's shoulder. "Take it easy, Tom. He's not worth it. We probably couldn't have trusted him, anyway. Come on. If we're going to do those gals any good, we need to get moving again."

Burnett remained hunched over, holding Turkey in his grip for several more heartbeats before abruptly flinging him away. Straightening up, he turned toward the horses and, without a backward glance, said, "You're right. Let's saddle up and get headed into those badlands."

In a matter of minutes, the horses were unhobbled and Luke, Burnett, and Russell were in their saddles. The packhorses and the three former mounts of Grogan and the

Grimes cousins were strung on tethers behind them. Turkey remained sprawled on the rocky ground, unmoved from where Burnett had flung him. As the others made their preparations to depart, he watched them with alternating expressions of hate and near-panic playing across his dirt-streaked face. They, in turn, gave no further acknowledgment of his presence. No glance in his direction, no word spoken.

Luke rode out in the lead. Burnett and Russell and the horse string fell in behind him.

They hadn't gone more than a dozen yards before Turkey called out in a desperate voice, "Wait! For God's sake, hold up! Give me another chance. I'll take your deal."

Luke reined in, as did those behind him. The bounty hunter sat his saddle very still for a long moment as if considering. Then he wheeled his horse and, with just a quick sidelong glance at Burnett, trotted back to the wounded man. He walked his horse up very close, making Turkey crab awkwardly backward so he didn't get stepped on.

Looming over the trembling outlaw, Luke slowly pulled the little sneak shooter out of his pocket — the hideaway gun the ambusher back at the wedge buttes had tried to kill him with. He held it up for Turkey to see. "I took this off the body of another Legion skunk we ran into a while back. Not really a man stopper, as you can see, but an emergency popper meant for squeezing out of a tight spot. A pill from this in your belly wouldn't kill you. Not right away. But I shouldn't have to tell you what a small-caliber gut shot would lead to way out here in the wild with no proper care close by. Maybe it wouldn't be quite as slow and miserable as being left behind in your present condition, but you can bet it wouldn't be pleasant. You'd either bleed out or die from lead poisoning, and neither would come very fast."

Turkey licked his lips. "W-why are you tellin' me this? I said I'd cooperate, that I'd take your deal. What more do you want?"

"What I want," Luke grated, "is to make sure you understand one false move, one slightest sign of a trick by you — no matter what else happens — I won't hesitate to plant a pill from this peashooter in your gut and leave your miserable hide to suffer the consequences. Is that plain enough for you?"

Chapter 36

When they finally reached it, Ben Craddock had to admit that the Legion of Fire's hideout and winter quarters was a mighty impressive setup. Located in the heart of the Pawnee Badlands, accessible only after winding through a maze of twisting gullies and canyons amidst weather-beaten, often grotesquely shaped rock outcroppings, it was revealed to be a deep, high-ceilinged cave gained by passing through a narrow, hidden crevice between massive, inward-sloping cliffs. Negotiating the passage meant everyone had to dismount and lead their horses through in single file.

Inside, the enormous central room of the cave was outfitted with three large fire pits each surrounded by a scattering of cooking utensils; numerous blankets and pelts were spread all around for sitting or lying on; a mound of canned goods, flour, coffee, beans, burlap-wrapped smoked meats, and a variety of other foods was piled between the fire pits; and a half dozen rough-hewn tables and chairs were available for eating or playing cards on. For illumination, coal oil lanterns were placed at regular intervals.

Off one end of the supply pile sat a large box, four feet high and wide, five feet long. It was made of smooth, mortar-seamed logs with a leather-hinged lid of the same. Holding the lid in place was a crisscross of heavy chains fastened by a fist-sized padlock. One look at that box, the way it was constructed and chained, was enough to tell Craddock that it held something mighty valuable.

Had there been the slightest doubt, it was promptly removed when Kelson, immediately upon their arrival in the cave, marched over to the box and unlocked it so he could pour in the contents of the money bag he'd been carrying with him ever since the Arapaho Springs bank robbery. Craddock watched the bundles of fresh bills tumble down over those already contained in the box and realized he was catching a glimpse of more money than he'd ever seen in one place before. Almost more than he could imagine.

As Kelson rechained and relocked the strongbox, Craddock managed to tear his gaze away so he wouldn't appear quite as awestruck as he felt.

Damn, that was a lot of money!

With effort, he returned to examining the rest of the hideout's features. Some soot-fringed seams high up in the ceiling indicated a spiderweb of thin openings that evidently served as natural chimneys for smoke from the lanterns and fire pits. Far to the rear, the ceiling sloped down to less than ten feet in height and the area had been sectioned off by a gated barricade of saplings and branches where the horses were kept corralled. A dozen yards to one side of this corral, Craddock could see a rock-rimmed pool of clear water, a natural tank, fed by the steady runoff of a seep trickling down from a crack in the low, sloping ceiling. The tank's overflow was channeled into a man-made trench that ran over to a wide depression in the floor of the corral.

Around the edges of the central room, the rock walls were pocked with half a dozen irregularly shaped, concave natural chambers big enough to be entered into for anyone perhaps seeking a modicum of privacy. The largest of these, the size to accommodate six to eight average-sized people, had also been barricaded by a construction of saplings and branches. In this case, the barricade had been built even sturdier than the corral, with its uprights and cross members secured much closer together.

As Craddock absorbed the full scene, he helped Millie down out of the saddle and held on to her by one arm, keeping her close to him as he stripped his bedroll from their horse with his other hand. He turned the animal over to a man who'd stepped forward saying he would take it to the corral. While he absently watched the gent lead away a couple other horses, he glanced at the barricaded chamber, thinking it resembled an army post stockade. As someone who'd spent his adult life trying to avoid jails of all kinds, the sight of it gave him an uneasy feeling.

A moment later, he saw the faces of three women suddenly appear between the wooden bars, gazing out with frightened and forlorn expressions, and he realized more clearly what the barricaded chamber actually was. And that realization was somehow even more unsettling.

It *was* a stockade — a holding pen for women the Legion periodically abducted to keep on hand for "entertainment" during extended periods such as the winter months ahead when the gang planned on laying low for a while.

His final thought — that Millie Burnett was among those destined to be kept in that stockade and made available as part of that entertainment — jolted Craddock. More than he ever would have expected and more than he wanted to admit to himself.

What was it about the girl that got under his skin the way it did?

In the beginning it had been about strictly one thing . . . or had it ever been that basic? From the start, his yearning for her and his inability to stop thinking about her had been stronger than the way he usually felt about any woman. And then, when he was able to make his escape from the town jail and she happened to be right there, the decision to take her with him had more or less made itself, even to the point of failing to take hardly anything else into consideration.

The next indication she was getting to him had come right after being swept into the ranks of the Legion of Fire and he saw Sam Kelson's reaction to Millie. Why the hell had that bothered him so much? As long as he got what he wanted, why did he care if he had to share with Kelson or anybody else? Especially after Millie and her sassy mouth had made it clear how she felt about Craddock, saying that merely having him look at her made her want to gag.

But it did bother him. He didn't like the thought of other men having their way with Millie. Not out of jealousy or what might be mistaken for fondness. It was just that she belonged to *him,* damn it . . . like a new saddle or a fancy watch, a personal possession he didn't want others to handle. There likely would come a time when he wouldn't care about Millie being passed around. But that time wasn't now, not yet. And he particularly didn't want her to fall into the hands of the smirking, cold-eyed Kelson.

No matter how he felt, Craddock didn't see where he could realistically do much to change the situation. A confrontation with Kelson would be futile, what with a score of other guns backing him. Guns in the hands of men not only loyal to the gang leader but men sure to be thinking about their own chances at Millie. The idea of fleeing and taking Millie with him, especially now that he'd not only been accepted into the Legion but had seen the location of their hideout, amounted to contemplating suicide. He'd be hunted down and killed for certain, and Millie would likely end up being treated harsher than ever.

No woman — or girl, for that's all she really was — was worth *that.* No matter how much she'd gotten under his skin. As far as the things she'd recently begun whispering to him, confiding in him how scared she was of Kelson, telling Craddock how she felt safer in his presence, warning him that Kelson wouldn't hesitate to remove him if he got in the way . . . what the hell was that all about? She was angling for something, that was plain enough. Did she really think he was a big enough fool to actually believe that somebody who'd threatened to gag merely from the way he looked at her would all at once turn so cuddly and dependent and willing? It was intriguing to think how far he might get with her if he played along, but —

Craddock's reverie, the flood of thoughts that had poured over him so suddenly after he'd sighted the stockade for the women captives, was broken more suddenly than it had come upon him. A furious outburst came from Sam Kelson, who stood only a few feet away.

They'd barely had time for their full group to file into the cave and get dismounted. Craddock had helped Millie down out of the saddle and was holding on to her by one arm, keeping her close to him as he'd stripped his bedroll from their horse with his other hand. He'd turned the animal over to a man who'd stepped forward saying he would take it to the corral. While he'd absently watched the gent lead a couple of other horses, Craddock had taken a few moments to scan their surroundings and in the process allow his mind to wander some.

"What the hell do you mean we lost another man?" Kelson ranted. "And Pride got seriously hurt in the bargain? How could the two of you let a simple diversionary maneuver go so badly wrong? What happened?"

The man he was addressing, right in the middle of everything for everyone to see and hear, was Henry Wymer, one of his chief lieutenants. The latter stood ramrod straight, chin up, almost as if at military attention, with Kelson's face shoved within inches of his.

"It was a dispute between two of the men — Eames and Browne," Wymer responded calmly, flatly. "Neither Pride nor I knew anything was building until it came to a head yesterday morning when we were breaking camp. It was over one of the women. They began fighting about who she was going to ride with. Eames pulled a knife. Pride tried to separate them, made the mistake of stepping in between, and got slashed pretty badly. That's when I shot Eames dead."

"Where was this?" Kelson said.

"Little over a day's ride to the south and west. When I saw how bad Pride was hurt, I shortened the wider loop we were making and came here in the most direct way possible."

Some of the heat left Kelson's face. "Where is Pride?" he asked in a quiet voice.

Wymer inclined his head toward one of the side chambers. "Over yonder. He's hanging on, but he lost a lot of blood on the trail. Crowley's been tending him the best he can ever since we got here."

Crowley, Craddock had learned, was a game-legged old man who stayed behind and guarded the lair while the rest of the Legion was out doing their raiding.

"In case you're wondering," Wymer added, "I've ordered Browne stripped of his guns and kept tied up. I figured you'd want to deal with him yourself. No Nation Smith is keeping a close eye on him until then."

Kelson gave a sharp nod. "Good. I'll get to him in time. But first, I want to see Pride." He turned toward the side chamber Wymer had indicated. Men parted out of the way ahead of him.

He'd only taken a couple of steps when, after his gaze happened to pass over Millie, he paused. Raising his voice again, addressing no one in particular yet raking his eyes over everybody, he said, "Before anything else, I want the rest of these damn women put in the stockade. And hear this, every one of you randy curs — there will be no putting your paws on 'em until I give the word.

"We've already lost at least one man because somebody got too overheated and eager. That's the trouble with having women around. I allowed half a dozen of them to be gathered up and brought here so we'd have some company for the upcoming winter. That breaks down to only six for twenty." Kelson's eyes narrowed as they continued to sweep the faces before him. "So that means none of you fools have the luxury of thinking you've fallen in love and that any one of these women is special to just you. That's how jealousies and trouble starts in an outfit like ours. And I will be *damned* if I let that set in! You all know we lost nearly a third of our force in that raid a few days ago. We can't afford to lose any more. Certainly not due to squabbling among ourselves over a bunch of throwaway women. You'd better pray each and every one of you believes and understands what I'm saying . . . because before I allow that kind of rot to set in, I will take a shotgun into the stockade and get rid of the problem by getting rid of the women!" His words hung heavy in the air for a long count.

Hearing them, Craddock thought *The crazy bastard would do it, too. He'd do it and never blink an eye.*

He felt Millie tremble in his grasp, signaling her fear and sense of desperation. Craddock had enough feeling for her to wish he could say something to soothe her, but before he had any chance, two burly raiders, acting on a signal from Wymer, stepped forward to take Millie and the other two women who'd arrived with their group over to the stockade where the rest were already penned up. Watching her being led away, Craddock couldn't help thinking what a loss it would be if anything happened to her. More than ever, he didn't see where he had much chance to do anything about it. Above all else, he had to think of his own neck.

Kelson wasn't done. He made a final statement. "Until I announce an orderly procedure for consorting with those women, the stockade will remain off limits except for those assigned to guard it. In the meantime, I'd advise everyone to put your minds on other things and go about getting settled in."

Craddock's eyes went back to Millie as

she was being shoved behind the barricade of the stockade. It tugged at him some to see her treated in such a way. At the same time, he felt a sense of relief for her being spared, at least temporarily, from whatever was in store for her and the other women.

Hopefully, if Kelson could keep his temper, it wouldn't involve a shotgun.

Kelson's next display of anger came within minutes of concluding his visit with Elmer Pride. The gang leader emerged from the chamber clearly troubled by the wounded man's condition. He appeared saddened and somewhat subdued, but it didn't take long for a new rage to build in him. He ordered Wymer to have Browne brought before him.

As all the men gathered round, the half-breed No Nation Smith trotted out Browne. The latter was a heavyset individual with thinning hair and contrastingly shaggy brows above dark eyes that darted anxiously from side to side as he was shoved roughly in front of Kelson. With his wrists bound at the small of his back, Browne staggered slightly from the shove, then caught his balance and drew himself up straight. His eyes quit darting around and settled into an unflinching gaze that met Kelson's glare.

"I don't deserve this treatment," Browne protested. "Eames was the one with the knife. All I did was defend myself. I never —"

"Shut up!" Kelson cut him off. "You were a participant in a fight over a lousy damn woman. A fight that ended up getting one man killed and left another, a man worth ten of you on the best day you ever had, with his gut sliced open. What do you think you deserve for that? Praise?"

"It was that damn Eames, I tell you," Browne insisted. "He kept needling me about a gal he stole away from me down in Arizona a few years back. Saying how I didn't know how to satisfy a woman. Asking if I wanted to watch so he could show me —"

"I don't give a damn about that kind of foolishness!" Kelson cut him off again. "It may be that Eames got what he had coming. And if it wasn't that we've recently lost so many men, I likely would see to it you got the same. If Elmer Pride dies, I'll still see to that, and will handle it personally."

"But I never laid a finger on Pride!"

"No matter! It was the fight you were involved in that led to him getting stabbed." Kelson sneered in disdain. "You and Eames, two grown men taunting each other and fighting over a girl like a couple of schoolboys. Well, you know what they do with schoolboys to punish them and set them straight, don't you? They get a whipping!"

Browne's mouth dropped open, half in disbelief. "No! No, you're not going to whip me!"

Kelson's own mouth went from a sneer to a cruel smile. "You're right. *I'm* not going to whip you. But you're damn sure going to get one." He made a gesture. "Smith and a couple of you other men, drag him over to the women's stockade. Strip off his shirt and tie him to the barricade. I want those damn women to see what their flaunting ways cause, and I want Browne to have a good look at what he's getting his fool hide shredded over!"

Had his hands not been tied behind his back, the husky Browne might have made a good fight of it. Even as it was, before he was subdued he got in a couple of solid kicks and a teeth-rattling shoulder slam to the jaw of one of the men who converged to grab hold of him. No Nation Smith finally took the starch out of him with a kick of his own to the big man's solar plexus. After that it was easy enough for the half-breed and his two accomplices to drag Browne over to the barricade where they stripped off his shirt and then retied his wrists high and wide to the rugged latticework.

All the other men, including Craddock, had formed a loose semicircle and stood looking on. No one spoke.

Old Man Crowley, the caretaker, came limping over from the corral area with a coiled bullwhip in one gnarled hand. He silently handed it to Kelson.

The gang leader held the whip in front of him for a long moment, glaring down at it. Then he looked up and swept his glare across the faces of the onlookers.

His eyes came to rest on Craddock. "You," he said flatly. "You haven't done hardly anything to earn your way into our ranks yet. But you're a friend of Elmer Pride. It was thanks to him speaking up for you that you got invited in to begin with. So I think it only fitting that you start earning your keep and at the same time do a little something to repay Elmer." Kelson extended his arm, holding the whip out to Craddock. "Twenty lashes. Make 'em pop, and make 'em bite in good and deep."

CHAPTER 37

Luke and the others made it within the boundaries of the badlands by the time night fell. Despite a clear sky and a wash of bright starlight, Turkey Grimes claimed conditions were too murky for him to negotiate an accurate course through the twisting arroyos and increasingly erratic pattern of rock formations so they stopped to make camp in a narrow, sandy-bottomed gap between two high, flat rock faces.

Luke suspected their captive probably *could* have gone farther if pushed, but he had no way of being certain. He also had to consider that the darkness might lend itself to some attempt at trickery by Grimes, so he agreed to stop.

They kept the camp cold. No fire for warmth or coffee or a hot meal. Without knowing how close they actually were to the Legion's hideout, the risk of exposing themselves via a campfire could not be afforded. Recognizing the necessity for making this sacrifice, however, did not make it a welcome decision. Although all traces of snow had disappeared during the course of the day, the air had remained chilled. With the sun down, it rapidly grew more so.

"Christ Almighty," Grimes grumbled. "If I knew you were gonna freeze me and starve me anyway, I might as well had you leave me back there where you killed my cousin and Grogan."

"You've got a blanket to cover up with and some jerky to eat, don't you?" Burnett responded. "If you really want to see how it would have been if we'd left you back there, I can show you real quick by taking those things away. So shut up with your complaining."

Turkey pulled his blanket tighter around him, muttering and mumbling a few more indecipherable things, then was quiet.

Draped in his own blanket where he sat with Luke and Russell a short distance removed from Turkey, Burnett did some muttering of his own. "Much as I hate to agree with that miserable skunk about anything, I have to go along that this is kind of lousy. Freezing and gnawing on another damn meal of jerky and hardtack, especially considering all that food and other supplies we had at our disposal only a short time ago."

Before entering the barren badlands, they'd decided to leave behind the pack animals and spare horses they had acquired after their ambush. Luke had pointed out that keeping the pack train with them and leading it into the twisting sprawl of rocks would make their passage noisier and much more awkward should they find themselves in a situation where they'd need to fight or flee. The practicality of it couldn't be argued, so they'd left the animals picketed in a decent-sized patch of graze, one of the last to be found before rocks and bare ground dominated the landscape.

If they returned relatively soon, the animals would still be there; if things worked out where they were gone too long, maybe permanently, the restraints weren't so strong that the horses wouldn't be able to break them when prodded by thirst and the need to find additional graze.

Responding to Burnett's reference to the abandoned supplies, Luke said, "Without a fire to cook them over, not much of what we left behind would increase our comfort significantly. Maybe a can of peaches or some such. Hard to argue something like that wouldn't go pretty good right about now."

"Yeah, I guess you're right," Burnett allowed. "A pot of coffee, which we do have the makings for, would go a long way toward fixing most everything, if we could risk a fire."

"Talking about what we don't have only makes it worse," Russell said. "Think about what Millie and the other women are probably going without, the sacrifices they're having to make. That's what we have to stay focused on, what needs to keep driving us no matter how uncomfortable we are."

"Goes without saying, kid," Luke told him.

"That's right. No need preaching to the choir," Burnett added. "None of us has to be reminded about our purpose for being here."

"No, of course not," Russell said. "I'm sorry. I didn't mean for it to sound like I was . . . preaching. It's just that I can't help thinking about what those women might be going through."

"None of us can. But you've got to put it out of your mind," Luke advised. "Like you said a minute ago as far as too much talk about what we don't have. Same thing when it comes to thinking. Thinking and making careful plans is good — too much thinking about what you can't control can bog you down, make you start second-guessing yourself. Not good to let that happen."

"Tomorrow will come," Burnett said somberly. "It will come after yet another mighty cold and slow night. But it'll get here . . . And when it does, that's when we'll finally get our chance to face those heathen raiders again and set things right for our women."

Inside the stockade within the Legion cave, Millie was discovering how difficult it was to gauge the passage of time with no view of the sky or sense of day from night. She knew they had first arrived about midday. How many hours had gone by since then she could only guess. At first there was a flurry of activity, getting inside, getting dismounted, and then being herded in behind the barricade.

Then there had been Kelson's rant upon hearing about the fight and the stabbing that took place. Following that came the horror of seeing the man named Browne get tied down and whipped. Since that took place right against the latticework of the barricade that imprisoned her and the other women in their chamber, it was impossible not to hear the savage crack of the whip striking bare flesh and the cries that resulted each time it did.

Almost as bad as watching that was the sight of Craddock being the one to administer the whipping.

At first he'd shown some reluctance, though he had little choice but to carry out Kelson's cruel order. But then, after he'd commenced and the beating was underway, something strange and troubling had occurred. A kind of wild gleam had formed in Craddock's eyes, growing brighter with each swing of his arm and each groan of pain from Browne. By the time all twenty lashes had been administered, his eyes were devilish and the expression on his sweat-slicked face appeared to be one of . . . satisfaction . . . or maybe even pleasure.

Millie couldn't decide which.

Either one was frightening to her. He was the man she'd allowed herself to believe — in a tentative, desperate kind of way — she might somehow be able to manipulate and depend on to help her facilitate an escape. Abruptly, she saw him in a different kind of light. Or perhaps more accurately, she was reminded once again of how she had originally seen him, before her desperation clouded her thinking.

Craddock was every bit as violent and vicious as the rest of the Legion raiders. Maybe even as bad as Kelson himself. Millie shuddered at ever duping herself into believing otherwise.

In the unknowable length of time — hours, to be sure — that followed the whipping, the women in the stockade were more thoroughly searched than at any time previous. They were stripped of shoes, belts, rings, bracelets — anything that might serve as a weapon.

Once that was done, they were left without anyone standing guard over the stockade. Apparently it was accepted that the barricade alone was fully adequate to restrain them. Though that wasn't to say no one kept an eye on them. At all times, Millie and the others were very aware of hungry, longing gazes being cast their way by one or more of the men.

A pail of fairly fresh drinking water and another for washing with was placed inside the stockade. At one point, Old Man Crowley, the caretaker of the cave, showed up with a pot of stew and gourd cups for them to partake of what Millie assumed was their evening meal. For the time it took the old man to enter and then leave again, two raiders with Winchesters stood close by. The stew, as it turned out, was actually quite good.

While the women were taking their meal, the men gathered around the large central fire pit and ate as well. After the pot and gourds were removed from the women's quarters, the men split into two or three smaller bunches and sat playing cards or just visiting.

Craddock and a couple of others kept to themselves. Kelson was nowhere to be seen, but Millie had a hunch he was in with the wounded Elmer Pride. Every once in a while, she sensed that he was casting his cold gaze her way, even though she couldn't see him.

Eventually, the men drifted off to their bedrolls and crawled in them to sleep. From this, Millie was able to judge that night had descended.

From the time he'd been beaten, Browne was left to hang by his wrists on the outside of the barricade latticework. If he placed his feet flat on the ground, he could stand. But if he relaxed or passed out, his weight would collapse and put a painful strain on his chafed, bleeding wrists. He groaned frequently, sometimes sobbing, and at regular intervals asked for water. No one brought him any. When Millie and Lucinda attempted to give him a drink from their pail, Old Man Crowley appeared as if from nowhere and warned them that if Kelson saw them doing that, their own water would be removed.

It was the beginning of a long, restless night. Millie lay wrapped tight in her blankets and listened to Browne groan and sob from time to time.

For the first time since being abducted, it took all of her willpower not to join in.

CHAPTER 38

"Cut him down. I trust I've made my point." Sam Kelson stood a dozen feet from Browne's sagging form, letting his fresh-poured cup of coffee cool some before he drank from it. He looked on indifferently as No Nation Smith and two other men moved to follow his order, putting their knives to the bonds that secured the whipping victim. Once his wrists were free, Browne's arms dropped limply. He tried to stand, but his knees buckled almost immediately. The men on either side grabbed him and held him up, taking a certain amount of care not to bump against his ravaged back.

"Take him to one of the side chambers," Kelson said, gesturing, "and lay him out so Crowley can dress those wounds. Tell the old man to get some food and water in him. Maybe a couple of swallows of wine when he's able to hold it down. He needs to get started on healing."

As the men took Browne away, Henry Wymer edged up beside Kelson. "You want my opinion, you'd better consider growing a set of eyes in the back of your head for when he *does* get healed up."

Kelson glanced over at him. "You really think Browne's got it in him to be the vengeful sort?"

"You never can tell," Wymer said. "All I know is that few men come back the same after a whipping. Some, it cows into obedient little pups. Others it fills full of humiliation that festers into hate and rage. I don't see Browne as the sort who'll come out of this all that cowed."

"His choice. Should he decide to be difficult, he can always meet the same fate as Eames. If Pride doesn't make it, that's a guarantee."

"Uh-huh. I'm half thinking that after Elmer got cut, I maybe should have gone ahead and handled it that way right then and there."

The mention of Pride caused the eyes of both men to swing involuntarily toward the side chamber inside of which the wounded man lay.

All around them, the other men inside the cave were stirring and rising to a new day. Flames were crackling high in the central fire pit and on its edge a pair of huge coffeepots were bubbling and sending out a strong aroma.

"Speaking of Elmer, how is he?" Wymer wanted to know.

"Holding his own. That's about all anybody can say," Kelson responded grimly. "I stayed close by all through the night. So did Crowley. Elmer doesn't seem to be in a lot of pain, at least none he's showing. But you know how tough and damn stubborn he can be. He's so weak, though, from blood loss. When he breathes, you can hardly see his chest rise and fall."

The muscles at the hinges of Wymer's jaw bulged visibly. "Like you said, he's tough and stubborn. If anybody can make it, he can."

Kelson took a sip of his coffee. Lowering the cup, his gaze drifted to the main fire pit and hung there as if he were trying to see something deep within the writhing flames. "Damn that no-account pissant of a town. Arapaho Springs," he muttered bitterly. "I wish we never would have set foot there. It's almost like it was a jinx to us. All the men who fell in the raid itself, more than we lost in the previous seven or eight towns combined. Then you having to shoot Eames. Elmer laid up bad the way he is. Browne maybe due to get his next . . ." The gang leader let his words trail off, wagging his head slowly.

"Just between me and you, Wymer, I've got a bad feeling. It weighed on me all night. We've had awful good luck up until now. The law, the Pinks — nobody's ever been able to run us down or lay a hand on us. Never even close.

"But sometimes the cards start running cold for no reason. Not because you make a mistake or run into a player who's more skillful. Nothing like that, nothing you can pin down. When the jinx decides to sink its claws in you, you can't always make sense of the reason why. You think Elmer's stubborn? When the jinx lands on you, nothing can be more stubborn. And if you try to outlast it, it'll grind you down every time."

Wymer frowned. "Come on, Sam. I never heard you carry on that way before. It's not like you."

"Like I said, those were words between just me and you. But whether I say it out loud or hold it in, it doesn't change the feeling gnawing at me."

"That'll pass. You're just worried about Elmer, that's all. Other than his injury and us getting stung worse than usual in that last raid, just look around. Things ain't so bad otherwise. We're burrowed snug in for the winter, we got a pile of supplies to last us, we've got money stashed away that adds up to more than any bank in the state. All that's pretty good, ain't it? Come spring, we'll add on some new men and go back to raiding right where we left off. And Elmer will be right there in the thick of it with us. You watch and see."

Kelson drank some more of his coffee. "Maybe you're right. Hope to hell so. But speaking of supplies, in case you haven't noticed, Grogan and those stinkin' Grimes cousins haven't made it here yet. That's something else bothering me. They should have gotten in well ahead of us, yet still no sign of them."

"Yeah, I was thinking the same myself," Wymer admitted. "Seems like they should have made it in before this. Still, in the meantime, it's not like we're running short of supplies."

"Doesn't change that them not being here could be one more sign of some damn thing gone wrong."

"Maybe, but not necessarily. Most likely there's a simple explanation. Probably nothing more than one of the horses pulling up lame going over rugged country. As heavily loaded as they were, that would slow them considerable. Plus there was that freak snowfall we got caught in, remember. Maybe they got hit harder than we did. Something like that could explain it, too."

"The fact remains," Kelson said, "that they aren't here but they should be. Makes it one more thing gnawing at me."

Wymer sighed. "You want me to take a few men and go out looking for them? Would that make you feel better? Surely they can't be more than a half day or so out."

Kelson had started to raise his coffee for another drink, but paused with the cup short of his mouth. "That's not a bad idea. I'd appreciate you doing that, Henry. It'd ease my worry a fair amount to have those fools here among us, even with the stink of the Grimes cousins. And to know they haven't run into some kind of trouble."

"I wish you wouldn't have reminded me about that — the way those Grimeses smell, I mean," Wymer said, making a sour face. "Sort of takes the edge off wanting to succeed in what we're going out for."

A ghost of a smile passed across Kelson's stern expression. "Look on the bright side. Catch the wind right, it ought to make finding them easy. Just follow the smell."

■ ■ ■ ■

Millie was relieved to see them finally take Browne down. What was more, observing how they used at least a little bit of care when it came to his wounds and then overhearing Kelson say to give him some food and water gave her hope that the poor devil was past his worst treatment.

In the deepest part of the night, when the fire pits were all burnt down to reddish coals with only a few small flames licking up through them, Millie had slipped slowly through the shadows within the stockade and risked giving Browne a drink of water. Finding it impossible to fit the dipper through the openings between the wooden bars made it difficult, but she'd nevertheless managed to pour part of the contents over his upturned face and into his mouth. It was pitiful little solace for what he'd been through, but it was enough to ease his suffering somewhat and he repeatedly whispered his gratitude in a hoarse voice.

When she returned to her blankets afterward, she'd experienced a wave of fear that her actions had somehow been spotted and Kelson would suddenly appear outside the barricade flanked by riflemen he would order to drag her out and punish her in some unspeakable way. But the minutes ticked by and nothing happened. Eventually she was able to slip into a shallow, troubled sleep.

When she woke in the morning, her night fears didn't awaken with her. But it wouldn't be long, Millie thought dejectedly, before Kelson was certain to find a way of introducing some new ones.

Across the cave, as Ben Craddock opened his eyes to the new day, his thoughts returned to his unsettled night.

The way he saw it, he hadn't had much choice but to comply with Kelson's command to whip the man Browne. But in the hours that followed, before everybody settled into their bedrolls, the number of hard looks he got from some of the other men — friends of Browne, he surmised — sent a pretty clear message his actions didn't set well with them. They didn't register any of the same toward Kelson, at least none they displayed openly, but Craddock was a different story. After all, he was a new addition to their ranks and he'd beaten hell out of one the veterans.

Up to a point, he could understand their feelings toward him. But it still came down to him only following orders. If he'd refused, would any of the same men so quick to cast glares his way have come to his defense against Kelson's wrath? You damn well bet they wouldn't.

He conceded the fact that he had conducted the whipping with more zeal than probably had been necessary. At first, he'd actually been a bit reluctant. But after only a few swings of the whip, the memory of being a lad growing up back in Ohio and all the hickory switch beatings he had endured at the hand of his father suddenly flashed through his mind. The next thing he knew it felt like he was striking back against his father and that dreaded hickory switch. By the time he'd finished administering the beating he'd been bathed in sweat, breathing hard, and for a few seconds had actually felt good . . . until he'd noticed the way the other men were looking at him. Even Kelson.

To hell with them all. He'd done what he'd been told to do.

Only after most everyone else had turned in did he go over to the stew pot hanging over the main fire pit and scrape out something to eat, along with a cup of overcooked coffee. Returning to his bedroll he felt baleful eyes following him even in the dark.

To hell with them, he thought again. He hadn't asked for any of it. He was only trying to get by, to survive.

With the stew lumped heavily in his gut and the bitter aftertaste of the coffee filling his mouth, he lay awake, realizing more and more that the situation wasn't for him. He'd known from the beginning he wasn't cut out to be a follower in a gang. The one link that held the promise of making it bearable, possibly workable, was Elmer Pride, but from all reports, he was hovering at death's door.

It seemed just a matter of time before the rest of it stood a good chance of falling apart. And if he waited to see what happened, he'd likely end up dead.

At some timeless point in the middle of the bleak night, he decided he was going to have to do something more than just wait. The lousy odds against him would only stack up more unfavorably if all he did was hang around and hope for things to get better.

He was going to shoot for the works, not settle for simply riding clear of the Legion of Fire. There was the girl . . . and there was the strongbox full of money — each separated from his reach by a mere few yards.

He'd already tried hard to convince himself he was willing to be shed of conniving little Millie, but he still wanted her. As much or more than since first laying eyes on her.

Additionally, he yearned for some of the

money the Legion had accumulated. It sat right in the middle of the cave with only that damnable log box in the way to becoming wealthier than the richest cattle baron. Wealthier than a damn king!

Craddock rose and rolled up his bedroll. *The money and the girl . . .*

He didn't know exactly how, but he meant to get his hands on both. And when he did, all those narrow-eyed bastards who were giving him the cold shoulder would be left aiming their glares at nothing but the dust of his departure.

CHAPTER 39

"You mean you're nothing but a damn law dog? That's what you've been all this time?" Turkey Grimes looked mortified, scarcely able to believe his eyes and ears.

"By God," marveled Tom Burnett, "you must be getting smarter just by hanging around with us. Look how much faster you're catching on to things."

"How could I catch on to something you never gave a clue to before this, you damn sneak?" Turkey wailed. "I thought all you stinkin' law dogs had your tin stars pinned on you! What's the big idea not showin' yours before this?"

"Would it have done any good except to give you and your pals a bright, shiny target to shoot at?"

"You're damn right about that! Not many things us boys like better than pluggin' holes through badges and those we find 'em pinned on."

"That's exactly the kind of attitude we'd expect from the likes of you," Luke said. "That's why, if you're lying about Kelson not having any lookouts posted around the Legion hideout, you might be in a touchy situation."

Turkey scowled. "What's that supposed to mean? In the first place, I ain't lyin'. But even if I was, what difference would a lousy tin star make to me?"

"Because," Burnett told him, "for all your friendliness and willing assistance, I'm about to make you an honorary special deputy. And that means you get to wear your very own shiny tin star. As a matter of fact, I'm going to go so far as to loan you mine."

When Burnett held up the marshal's badge he'd only recently removed from his shirt pocket and extended it toward Turkey, the outlaw recoiled as if a snake was being waved in his face. "What's the big idea? Are you crazy? Get that thing away from me!"

The sun wasn't fully above the ragged horizon of the badlands. As the group was making ready to ride away from their night camp Burnett had revealed his badge for the first time. It had come on the heels of a brief consultation between the marshal and Luke following a dawn grilling of Turkey about how far away from the Legion hideout they were and what they could expect in the way of lookouts or guards as they drew nearer. Turkey had assured them repeatedly that the hideout was so cleverly concealed the gang never felt the need for such measures.

"No, no, I insist," Burnett said, his tone patient and soothing to an exaggerated degree as he reached out and pinned the badge to the front of Turkey's shirt.

The recipient tried to twist away but, with his wounded arm in a sling and his wrists handcuffed to the saddle horn, his elusive movements were too limited to be effective.

"We want to make sure you feel like a welcome part of our little group," Luke added, adopting the same tone as the marshal.

"I don't want to be welcomed to your damn group!" Turkey protested. "Ain't like I'm here by choice, you loco varmints. Get that stinkin' piece of tin offa me!"

"Consider it a trade. Here's the item we'll remove instead." Burnett undid the knot on the red bandanna tied around Turkey's arm, then pulled the piece of cloth loose and flung it away.

"Fetch that back, damn you!" Turkey wailed. "It *means* something."

"Yeah. And everything it means is evil and lowdown," Russell said, joining in on pressuring the outlaw.

"To you, maybe. To me, it means a helluva lot more than your stupid badge. I hate it and want nothing to do with it. Can't you understand that?"

"What I understand," Luke said, suddenly leaning close and dropping the phony tone from his voice, "is that if you're lying about there being no lookouts posted around the Legion hideout and we ride up with you in the lead — like we're fixing to do from here on — the first thing a lookout is going to spot when they see us coming is that nice bright target on your shirt. You know, the kind of thing you and the boys like nothing better than plugging holes in. Remember?"

Turkey's eyes bugged. "Here now! You can't do a thing like that. You're law dogs — er, I mean, you're officers of the law. You gotta do things legal. You can't plop me in front and make a target out of me that way."

"If there aren't any lookouts, like you claim," Russell reminded him, "how would that make you a target? What are you so worried about?"

Turkey's wide eyes were whipping from one face to the other of those drawn up in a semi-circle around him. "B-but you never know," he stammered. "Kelson might not have lookouts posted regularlike, but that don't mean there still ain't men who go out and sorta patrol once in a while. If we ran into somebody like that and they saw me with this damn star stuck on me, I . . . I . . ."

"You'd get your ass shot off," Burnett bluntly finished for him. "But just so you know, we'd be grateful to you for drawing attention that way and giving us an opening to return fire."

"You go to hell!" Turkey's eyes suddenly quit whipping around and blazed with defiance. "You might think that sounds like a real cute trick, but it wouldn't fool my boys. They'd recognize me in time to hold off pluggin' me."

"They might recognize your smell," Luke said. "But if they see that star, that's all that will matter to them."

"Says you," Turkey sneered. "All the cheap tricks you can think to try ain't gonna put you over on the Legion. The only slim chance you got is to turn and make a run for it right now. Otherwise your bones will be stayin' in these badlands forever."

"Maybe so. But they won't be the only ones," Luke said. "Either courtesy of your trigger-happy friends or if you keep annoying me, yours could be among the first to start bleaching out. Now lead on, you pile of rodent guts. And you'd better get us somewhere pretty quick or I can't make any promises about holding my annoyance level in check."

As it turned out, Turkey indeed led them "somewhere" pretty quick. Albeit quite inadvertently, he led them into a direct confrontation with Henry Wymer and the four men accompanying him who were looking for sign of the overdue supply train.

It happened suddenly and unexpectedly about halfway through a narrow, twisty arroyo into which Luke and the others had followed Turkey. As they rounded a leftward bend between moderately high sides with jagged rims, the arroyo flared out wider for the next thirty-odd yards, its walls tapering back to sloping, weather-worn shoulders. Directly in the center of the widened section were Wymer and the other raiders.

Riding at the head of his own group, Turkey was naturally the first to see them. Unable to lift his hands and motion in any way, he still didn't hesitate to hail his fellow outlaws and put the spurs to his horse, causing the animal to lunge forward with a startled yelp. "Don't shoot, boys! It's me! It's good ol' —"

That was as far as he got before he was hammered by a hail of bullets. Had he kept his mouth shut and not spurred the horse into leaping ahead, Wymer and those riding with him might not have reacted so hastily and actually taken a moment to recognize good ol' Turkey. Instead — exactly as Luke and Burnett calculated — all the Legion men saw was a badge pinned on a man shouting and appearing to charge toward them.

Whether Wymer or any of the others ever realized who it was they'd cut down, there was no way of knowing. They quickly found themselves on the receiving end of a hail of lead that did some messy cutting in return. Caught in the widened stretch of the arroyo with rounded, sloping sides that offered no cover, they were hopelessly exposed.

As soon as Turkey had shouted out and put the spurs to his horse, Luke, who was riding just half a length back from him, knew what was happening — that Turkey had spotted one or more Legion raiders just ahead around the bend. Rather than try to restrain Turkey, Luke had dived out of his saddle and scrambled for cover in the splits and seams of the arroyo wall. Directly behind him, also reading the situation and reacting accordingly, Burnett did the same, only on the opposite wall of the passage. Hearing the shots, Russell also dismounted and ran for cover.

Edging up quickly on either side of the fallen Turkey, Luke and Burnett moved forward far enough to see around the bend and into the open area where Wymer and his men were poised somewhat uncertainly with pistols and rifles still extended.

The marshal and the bounty hunter didn't waste any time in taking advantage of the moment. Without hesitation, they opened up. Burnett levered rounds from his Winchester and Luke fired first one Remington and then the other as fast as they could squeeze their triggers.

It was savage and bloody and over quickly. The arroyo was so choked with roiling blue powder smoke that visibility was almost nonexistent. Nevertheless, Luke was able to make out that four men and three horses were down. The raider who'd been riding at the head of the group had fallen without getting off a shot. The men behind him had managed to trigger a smattering of desperate rounds before they too had spilled from their saddles, but all their shots had gone high and wild, none coming anywhere close to either Luke or Burnett. A single raider, the man farthest back in the pack, had wheeled around and ridden clear, bullets chasing as his horse's hooves clattered a frantic retreat on the hardpan floor of the arroyo.

Luke and Burnett held to cover for a full minute longer, their hands automatically reloading their weapons as their eyes carefully surveyed the scene for any sign of life that might still pose a danger. Satisfied it appeared safe, they rose out of their crouches and moved forward. Russell, who hadn't been positioned to participate in any of the shooting, came from behind them, leading their horses.

All of the fallen men were dead. Two of the downed horses still had life in them but were too badly injured to leave suffering, so the marshal solemnly planted a Winchester slug in the brain of each.

"Helluva thing to say," he muttered afterward, "but I feel a lot worse about plugging those horses than I do for shooting the men we dropped here."

"Makes sense to me," Luke said. "The four-legged critters had good hearts. The two-legged ones were nothing but wastes of air that quit deserving to breathe a long time ago."

Burnett expelled some air of his own. "Well, then I reckon we cured 'em of that."

He turned his head and looked up the arroyo, the way the escaped raider had gone. "Don't expect we'll have to look much farther, though, to find more requiring some of the same medicine."

"But how will we know how to find them now?" asked Russell, looking anxious. His gaze cut back to the sprawled form of Turkey Grimes. "We've lost our guide."

"I doubt we'll need to worry very long about finding the rest of the Legion," Luke told him. "Between the raider who got away to carry word and the noise we kicked up with this little skirmish, I expect the others will bust their humps wanting to introduce themselves."

Chapter 40

"How big a posse was it? How many men?" Sam Kelson was peppering Josh Stringer, the lone raider who'd escaped the arroyo shoot-out, with rapid, demanding questions.

Stringer stood somewhat unsteadily before the gang leader, still fighting to catch his breath, dripping clammy fear-sweat and blood from the bullet gash high on his right arm. The other men present inside the cave crowded around close.

"At least half a dozen, I'd say," Stringer reported. "It was hard to tell for sure because part of them were still around the bend of that little canyon. Hell, there could have been twenty or thirty back there for all I know. Mostly all I could see was the storm of lead they were pouring on us!"

"You whittle down any of them in return?"

"The front one. The first one we saw. I can't say for sure after that."

"Seems to me there's a damn lot you're

not sure of. But all the rest of our boys bought it? Even Wymer? You saw that for certain?"

Stringer's face bunched into an anguished expression. "Oh God, they fell like stalks of corn. We was caught in the open with no chance to find cover. And Wymer was riding right in front. He never had a chance."

Kelson slammed his right fist into his left palm. "Damn! Damn it all!"

"What are we waiting for?" No Nation Smith growled. "Let's go get the bastards!"

"Why not let 'em come to us?" somebody else said. "We can hold off an army from the mouth of this cave."

Another voice said, "But if we let 'em bottle us up, that's exactly what they'll do — bring in an army!"

"Everybody be quiet! Let me think!" Kelson focused his attention back on Stringer. "No mistake about it being a posse? A pack of law dogs?"

Stringer's head bobbed up and down. "That one in front, the one we cut down, was wearing a big shiny star. He called for us not to shoot, like he expected we'd just go along and let him get the drop on us because of his star. He was a law dog right enough. But he was dead wrong about how far he thought that would get him."

"Where was this? How far out?"

"Not quite a mile. We was heading for that high ground to the southeast," Stringer explained, "where Wymer figured we'd have a chance to look out and maybe spot the pack train coming in."

"That must be it. That must be how they got in so close," Smith said. "That lousy posse must have stumbled onto Grogan and the others by accident, then forced 'em to tell where to find us."

"Take a lot to make Grogan spill," somebody stated.

"You couldn't say the same about those Grimes boys, though," somebody else replied. "I never did trust them stinkin' damn hillbillies."

"How they found us," Kelson said, "doesn't matter so much for right now. It's over and done. What matters is deciding on the smartest way to deal with them. And it sure as hell isn't going to be sitting here waiting for them to land in our laps!"

"That's the talk I want to hear!" Smith said. "We go find 'em and jump in *their* laps. Right? And make sure we finish every last one of 'em so they can't lead anybody else here."

Kelson held up a hand, palm out. "Not quite so fast. I'm all for landing on them and landing hard. But recall I said we needed to deal with them in the smartest way. Rushing out against a force of unknown size with nothing more than a notion to retaliate doesn't seem overly smart, but drawing them in closer for the sake of sizing them up, does. And as long as we're the ones pulling the strings, it's hardly allowing them to land in our laps."

Smith scowled. "Just say how you want to play it, that's all. Long as you give us the chance to put 'em in our gunsights."

"Thoughtful of him to leave us such a nice, clear trail," Burnett remarked, responding to the smear of fresh blood Luke was pointing out on a chest-high ledge of rock. "I didn't think either of us hit that runaway skunk."

"Looks like one of us must have," Luke said. "He's not bleeding too heavy, but he's spilling enough to mark the way he went."

"Ordinarily, I'd cuss myself for having shot a varmint and not put him down," the marshal said. "This time I'm glad I only grazed him."

"What makes you think it was you who grazed him?" Luke asked. "How do you know it wasn't me?"

Burnett shrugged. "Because you're a better shot than me. If you'd hit him, you *would* have put him down."

Luke's mouth twisted ruefully. "You make it hard for me to argue the point, don't you?"

"The main thing," Russell put in with a touch of impatience in his tone, "is that *one* of you hit the scoundrel and now his wound is marking his passage. That means, as long as he keeps dripping, he could lead us straight to the Legion hideout. Correct?"

"Could," Luke allowed. "If we stick with the blood trail all the way."

Having decided not to wait where they were for the expected response from other members of the Legion of Fire, they had continued on through the arroyo where the shoot-out took place. They hadn't gone far past the open space littered with the bodies of men and horses before Luke spotted the first splotch of fresh blood. More had been appearing at regular intervals ever since.

Frowning, Russell said in response to Luke's statement, "Why wouldn't we follow it all the way? I thought that was the whole idea."

"Tracking a grizzly to his den is different from charging in after him," Burnett said.

"Especially when you have reason to believe he's caught your scent and knows you're on the way," Luke added.

Russell's frowned deepened. "Now you've got me even more confused. Back there just a little bit ago we agreed not to wait for the Legion to come to us. Now it sounds like you're saying we're not going after them, either. What am I missing?"

Luke set his jaw firmly, then said, "The part where we show the grizzly we're a trickier handful of trouble than he's ready for."

Chapter 41

Sam Kelson sat on a chunk of broken boulder about ten yards outside the entrance to the hideout cave. The morning was clear and bright, the air feeling like it had the potential to warm up more than it had over the past couple of days. A faint breeze was whispering through the surrounding rocks, stirring curls of dust across the oval of open ground that flared out away from his position.

The gang leader sat unmoving, appearing quite calm. He gripped a Winchester rifle in his right hand, its butt resting on his thigh, barrel angled skyward. On the ground in front of Kelson sat a bedraggled Millie Burnett. A five-foot length of leather thong was cinched around her throat, its opposite end looped over Kelson's left wrist. Another leather thong bound the girl's wrists. Her tangled, matted hair stirred slightly in the breeze. The expression on her pretty face was defiant, unafraid, but tension and traces of fear that she couldn't suppress were evident deep in her eyes.

The pair had been sitting that way for several minutes. The balance of Kelson's men — including the recently wounded Stringer as well as Browne, the still-healing whipping victim — were dispersed at strategic points in the ragged thrusts of rock on either side of the oval area fronting the cave. Only the helpless Elmer Pride and Old Man Crowley were left inside.

Kelson's plan was simple. He meant to lure the posse in close, using the girl as bait to represent the other hostages and giving the impression there might be room for negotiation. Once he had the fools lulled and he and his men had had the chance to better gauge what they were up against, he'd give the signal to open fire. From their hidden positions, Smith and the others would hand the posse bastards a taste of what they'd done to Wymer, and blast them to hell and gone.

All they had to do was show up . . .

More minutes dragged by. The shoot-out had occurred less than a mile away by Stringer's estimate. Kelson willed himself to stay patient. The posse would naturally approach with caution and they had some mighty rugged ground to cover. It was bound to take some time.

And then, faintly at first, just barely above the low moan of the wind, he heard a sound. It gradually grew louder and closer. *Clop . . . Clop . . . Clop.* The footfalls of a single horse advancing steadily but slowly nearer.

Kelson scowled. *A single horse? What sense did that make?*

Before he had time to fret about it too much, the rider came into sight. One man. Tall in the saddle, solidly built, somber expression. Dressed all in black. Millie made as if to say — or possibly shout — something, and Kelson immediately silenced her with a sharp yank of the thong, turning whatever she was going to say into a gagging, strangled gasp.

Horse and rider paused on the far side of the open area. Then, after just a moment, the man touched his heels to the horse's sides and the animal proceeded on forward. The man's eyes touched briefly on the girl before settling on Kelson. They stayed there, looking neither to the left or right as he rode the rest of the way. A dozen yards out, he reined up.

Kelson held his eyes, trying to read something there while at the same time seeing if he could wait him out, get him to speak first. The man in black rested the heel of one hand on the pommel of his saddle and leaned forward in a relaxed manner, saying nothing.

Finally, Kelson peeled back one side of his mouth and said, "You're a mighty bold one, aren't you? Riding up here all alone, acting cool as a cucumber."

The man gave it a beat before answering. "Appearances can be deceiving."

"What's that supposed to mean?" Kelson wanted to know.

The man's shoulders lifted and fell in a faint shrug. "Maybe I'm not quite as cool as I act. Maybe I'm not all that alone."

Kelson leaned to one side and craned his neck with a bit of exaggeration to look past the rider. "If you're thinking you're not alone, there sure seems to be an awful lot of empty all around you."

"Uh-huh. And, except for the young lady, the same could be said for you. But we both know that's not true, don't we?"

"Do we?"

"Let's not waste time dancing around it. You really think I'm dumb enough to ride in here, find you waiting in plain sight, and not figure you've got gunmen squirreled up in these rocks on all sides?"

Kelson arched a brow. "But I'm supposed to believe that, if you truly figure that way, you'd still ride up all by yourself?"

"I don't recall saying I'm by myself," the man reminded him. "There are a *lot* of rocks hereabouts. Surely you don't claim to have a man behind each and every one of them, do you?"

"Meaning that you claim to have men squirreled in among them, too?" Kelson emitted a derisive snort. "That's so ridiculous it's insulting."

The stranger's eyes turned flinty. "One way to find out. Or we could try to reach some middle ground instead."

"Negotiate, you mean?"

"Isn't that why you've got the girl on display?"

"Maybe. The rest of the women are inside. But this one, after all, is the daughter of your town marshal. Assuming, that is, you're from Arapaho Springs or are at least aware of the recent trouble there?"

"I know about Arapaho Springs, but I'm not connected with the law there. Matter of fact, there *is* no law there. Not anymore. You and your men saw to that — the marshal's dead."

Millie gasped at the words.

"Wait a minute," Kelson was quick to

protest. "My man who escaped that recent shoot-out back in the arroyo reported you were being led by a man wearing a badge. How can you claim you're not connected to the law?"

The man smiled slyly. "Badges aren't all that hard to come by. Sometimes they come in handy, sometimes not so much. Turned out not to work so well for the fella your man reported on. But the truth of the matter is that the whole thing with him was a ruse. We thought having somebody out front with a badge might give us a bit of an edge. We didn't know your men were primed to open fire on the first tin star they came in sight of."

Kelson's patience with this cat-and-mouse banter and the stranger's seemingly unflappable demeanor was wearing thin. "Just what the hell is it you're after?" he demanded.

"One thing. Money. I'm a bounty hunter, and the men I rounded up to ride with me are of a like mind."

"And getting back the women is no part of it? They mean nothing to you?"

"Women have their uses. But they tend to cost money, not make it." The man's head moved from side to side. "And there's no reward that I know of riding on the heads of the ones you have."

Kelson's mouth pulled into a tight, thin line. "Like there are on me and my men. Is that it?"

There was no reply.

"And you really think you and these phantom men allegedly riding with you are up to claiming those rewards?" Kelson's voice was growing strident.

"I said we're after money. But it don't have to come from the rewards. We're reasonable sorts." The man inclined his head toward the inward sloping cliffs behind Kelson, where it seemed obvious the cave entrance must be. "I'm guessing that, somewhere in there, you must have a stash accumulated by now that more than equals the amount of the reward money being offered for you."

Kelson looked astonished. "And you expect us to part with some of it? To buy you off?"

"Like I said, we're reasonable sorts. No need making things harder than they have to be."

"You're not reasonable — you're insane! One twitch of my hand, I can have you burned out of that saddle before your heart beats one more time. Don't you realize that?"

"Truth to tell, I've been thinking quite a bit about that ever since I rode up here. But here's something you need to realize. Not to brag, but I'm pretty fast with this pair of six-guns I'm packing. Now that you've let me in close enough, you go ahead with that twitch you're threatening to make and I guarantee I'll plant a slug from one or both of them in you before I hit the ground."

Kelson's mouth hung open, the sheer audacity of this man in black leaving him speechless.

The stranger picked that moment to straighten up in his saddle and leisurely lift his hand off the pommel.

Eight seconds after that innocent-seeming movement, which was in fact a prearranged signal, all hell broke loose.

Chapter 42

Two near-simultaneous explosions, one on either side of the oval clearing, suddenly ripped apart the morning. The twin blasts, occurring high in the ragged rocks bracketing the clearing, sent clouds of black smoke and dust boiling upward and outward. Chunks of debris were hurled in every direction. The ground trembled as a great, rumbling growl filled the air and rolled across the landscape.

Barely had the initial concussions begun to ebb when two more blasts went off, also in the high rocks though about a dozen yards closer to where the slanted cliffs hovered above the cave entrance. More smoke and dust and flying debris resulted, accompanied by another ear-pounding roar of sound.

The Legion men hiding in the rocks were mercilessly battered. The ones unfortunate enough to be caught in closest proximity to the blasts became broken, twisted forms hurtling through the air. Others were crushed by large, loosened rocks tumbling down on them while still others were merely knocked flat by the force of the explosions. Only a lucky few escaped unscathed.

In the area directly in front of the cave entrance, a startled Sam Kelson shot to his feet and attempted to back away so frantically that he stumbled over the very boulder he'd been sitting on and fell to the ground. Millie, still attached by the leather thong, was dragged roughly after him.

As for Luke, since his signal was what triggered the blasts, he thought he was sufficiently braced for what would result. But it turned out he was unprepared on two counts. One, the way his horse panicked and reared up in fright, and two, the fist-sized chunk of rock the second explosion sent spinning wildly through the air to deliver a glancing blow to the back of his head. He was pitched from his saddle and sent sprawling to the ground, stunned and with most of the wind knocked out of him. It left him temporarily immobile yet with a vague, murky awareness of the events unfolding around him.

Of the ten men Kelson had sent into the high rocks to trap the posse, only four were left undamaged and still able to function. And in the immediate aftermath of the explosions, even they were disoriented and uncertain as how to respond.

"Back to the safety of the cave!" somebody shouted.

"No! Our fight is here," argued No Nation Smith.

"Fight against who?" he was asked.

The answer to that came a moment later. From their own concealment at the far end of the oval clearing, Burnett and Russell had thrown their short-fused sticks of dynamite at randomly selected spots along the high rocks in hopes of flushing out the raiders they suspected were hiding there. With more than half of the outlaws eliminated in the process, the plan had succeeded better than expected.

As far as what the remaining skunks' next move should be, the marshal and the former law clerk were quick to give them a hint. They followed their dynamite blasts by opening up with rifle blasts aimed at finishing off the indecisive and newly exposed men. As a result, one more raider bit the dust before the rest again scrambled to fresh cover and began returning fire.

In a matter of scant minutes, the scene had transformed from one of outward peace and quiet, disturbed only by the low, moaning wind, to an explosion-ripped hellbox and a pocket of screaming, ricocheting lead.

As his men exchanged bullets with the invaders on the far end of the clearing, Kelson scrambled to his feet. Running bent forward while dragging Millie viciously after him, he turned and raced for the mouth of the cave. He ducked behind a corner of the slanted cliff without a single slug sent in his direction.

At the last second, before he and his captive plunged into the cave's narrow entrance, an anguished wail somehow seemed to slice through the chatter of gunfire and reach their ears. *"Millleeee!"*

A moment after that they were wrapped in a thick, sound-muffling cocoon of rock and the wail was gone.

Out front of the cave, where he still lay sprawled, fighting to suck some air back into his lungs and at the same time clear away the thick wool of near unconsciousness filling his head, Luke heard the wailing voice, too. He recognized it as that of Tom Burnett, venting his agony at the sight of his daughter — so close and yet so far and being so abusively treated. Luke felt the man's pain and at the same time, even in his mind-blurred condition, felt a pang of shame for having misled the girl about her father's death.

Closest to the cave, and to Kelson and Millie, Luke had to move, had to do something! Yet he was unable. A raspy, rattling noise in his chest told him he was finally managing to pull in some breath but that was little solace when the rest of him still wasn't working.

No matter the growing frustration it caused to rage inside his muddled mind, what Luke was missing was the fact that his motionlessness probably saved his life. While the raiders up in the rocks continued to trade lead with Burnett and Russell, none paid any attention to Luke. They took him for already being dead.

Even Ben Craddock thought so. He suddenly came bursting out of the rocks off to one side and made a dash for the slanting cliffs and the cave opening beyond. Had he thought for a second that Luke was still alive, he surely would have taken time to spend a bullet to confirm it. As it was, he barely glanced at the fallen bounty hunter, instead focusing solely on reaching the thick-walled safety of the cave.

CHAPTER 43

Midway through the narrow passage that opened to the cave proper, Kelson encountered Old Man Crowley guarding the way. He gripped a Henry repeating rifle in his gnarled hands. Close at his side, leaning against a vertical support timber, was a double-barreled shotgun and a fully loaded Winchester. The oldster was physically unable to ride out on raids and the like, but when it came to defending home ground, there were few in the gang more tenacious or dependable.

"Sounded like things went bad out there," he said as Kelson reached him.

"Couldn't have gone much worse," Kelson affirmed. "The jinx is on us bad, just like I feared. I think it's all over. What Stringer mistook for a posse turned out to be a pack of ruthless bounty hunters. The tricky bastards made a play like they wanted to deal then started flinging around some dynamite they showed up with. Tore hell out of our boys."

"Sounds like they're still making a fight of it, though," Crowley said.

"Those who are left. But that's precious few," Kelson told him.

"I could take up a position out at the front of this passage and lend a hand to our boys."

"No," Kelson was quick to say. "I can't afford to have you picked off by a lucky shot or a freak ricochet. You hold the line right here."

"So what's our play, then?"

Kelson's expression turned hard as the stone walls around him. "We fall back on the emergency plan I put in place right at the beginning. While I make some final preparations inside, you stay on guard here. In case any of our boys make it this far, cover them so they can make it through. Anybody else tries to poke their head in, you know what to do."

"I can hold this passage till Hell freezes over."

"I know you can — and would, if asked," Kelson said earnestly. "But we're not going to take it that far. Give me a chance to do what I need to and then, once enough time has passed so we can be sure no more of our boys are going to make it, I'll come back and help you trip the dropfall. That will buy us all the rest of the time we'll need."

Millie was vaguely listening to the exchange between Kelson and Old Man Crowley. She should have been paying closer attention, especially after Kelson said he thought it was "all over." Coming on the heels of the chaos that had erupted outside, that should have stirred renewed hope for an opening to make good the escape she'd so long sought.

But she was struggling hard with the concept of hope. Only minutes ago, all hope inside her had been pretty effectively crushed when the bounty hunter Luke Jensen — the man she'd at one point harbored romantic fantasies over and then had dared hope might be in on an attempted rescue of her and the other women — coldly disclaimed any such interest after first delivering the news that her father was dead.

Yet after the explosions had gone off, the shooting had broken out, and Kelson was dragging her back into the cave, she'd heard what sounded like a voice calling her name. And she could have sworn it was the voice of her father. But how could that be? Had the bounty hunter lied? If so, for what purpose? Was she hallucinating — her mind playing cruel tricks as a result of her desperation and despair?

Millie didn't know what to think.

But she kept hearing that voice call her name. She felt certain it had been the voice of her father. But was her certainty genuine . . . or did it merely come from *wanting* it to be real, to continue having a reason for futile hope?

Craddock made it to Crowley in the entrance passage.

The first thing out of the old man's mouth was, "Are there any more behind you? Any of the rest going to make it?"

Craddock shook his head. Breathing hard, he said, "I don't know. Everything went a little crazy after they started throwin' around dynamite. My assigned position was fairly close to the cave entrance, partly to cover Kelson. When I saw him fade back in here, I thought it looked like a smart move, so I followed him the first chance I got."

"Kelson thinks the jinx is on us," Crowley said glumly. "He figures the whole thing is falling apart."

"Kinda hard to argue that notion the way things stand," Craddock said. "Those bounty hunters are really tearin' us up out there. There's only a couple of the others left — leastways only a couple of in any condition to make a fight of it. One of 'em is Smith, though, and he made it clear he's gonna fight clean to the end."

The wrinkles in Crowley's brow puckered deeper. "I ain't ever had much like for Injuns. But that 'breed Smith, he's something else. If the redskins woulda had more like him to go nose to nose against the cavalry in times past, things mighta turned out different around these parts."

"The thing I'm interested in seeing turn out different," Craddock said anxiously, "is this fix we're in the middle of. What does Kelson intend to do about it?"

"He's got a plan. Don't you worry," the old man told him. "Go ahead on in. You'll see. There'll be a part for each of us to play. Right now, mine is to hold here and cover any of our boys trying to get through — and make sure any undesirables don't."

Half a minute later, Craddock emerged from the narrow passage and stepped into the heart of the cave. Seeing the place so empty bought on an eerie feeling. Always before when he'd been present, it had been teeming with activity and other Legion members. Only if he strained hard was he able to hear the faint crack of the gunfire outside.

His gaze cut to the stockade. The women were still there, forlorn faces looking out at him. But Millie's wasn't among them. Next his eyes went to the log strongbox near the middle of the room. It appeared undisturbed, the chains and padlock intact.

It took him a minute to spot Kelson. A sound, like a choked sob, drew his attention to one of the side chambers. It was the one where Elmer Pride had been placed to recover from his wounds. As Craddock looked around, he saw Kelson backing out from the chamber very slowly. His gaze stayed locked on the space he was exiting, his expression one of deep anguish. Still tethered to him, Millie had no choice but to move along with him, her own expression impassive, her movements slow and listless.

Craddock walked over to them.

Kelson stopped backing up. He stood very still, seeming not to notice Craddock right away. When he did, he turned his head and regarded him with a flat, blank stare. "You."

Craddock thought the word sounded almost like an accusation. "That's right. I was able to follow you in here to safety. Things were going pretty bad out there in the rocks."

Kelson's eyes flared. "That's because the jinx is on us. Everything is falling apart! I started to feel it last night. Then, this morning, when that patrol got ambushed and Wymer was killed, there wasn't much doubt. Now, on top of everything else, Elmer is gone, too."

"Pride is dead?"

"That's right," Kelson said, a distinct sadness weighing down his words. "It's all over. I fear the bright-burning flame that was the Legion of Fire is all but flickered out. And at the hands of a bunch of bounty-hunting rabble, no less. I never would have thought it possible!"

"I don't know about the rest of that bunch he put together," Craddock said, "but the leader, the fella dressed all in black you were palaverin' with before the explosions, he ain't exactly rabble. His name's Luke Jensen and he's got a rep for bein' one of the best bounty men in the business. I thought we left him pickin' out lead and slappin' down flames back in Arapaho Springs. If I'd had any idea he was part of the so-called posse that hit Wymer's group this morning, I would have warned you right up front not to take him too lightly."

"I *didn't* take him lightly," Kelson insisted stubbornly.

"Okay, okay," Craddock said, holding up his hands palms out. "The point I was gonna make was that you might find a little bit of consolation in knowin' Jensen bought it plenty quick when the shootin' started out there. He's layin' not far from where you and him was talkin'. I only wish I was the one who'd gotten the chance to drop that bastard."

"And I wish that I would have paid more attention to my hunch that the jinx was taking hold of us," Kelson said bitterly. "If I would have listened to my instincts and accepted it right from the start, we could have begun making plans to pull our picket pins and light the hell out of here before it took losing Wymer and Pride and all those other good men." He stopped suddenly and pinned Craddock with a hard look. "Are any of the others going to make it?"

Craddock shook his head. "I don't know . . . I don't think so. There's only a couple of left out there in any condition to put up a fight, and they're takin' pretty heavy fire. Plus one of 'em is Smith, the half-breed, and he's hell-bent on pushin' it to the limit."

"That sounds like Smith. Crazy damn 'breed," Kelson muttered.

Craddock licked his lips. "Listen. Old Man Crowley said you had a plan for when . . . well, in case things turned out like this. I think it's pretty safe to say it's gonna come down to you, me, and Crowley as the only ones left, so if you've got some kind of plan, I'd sure be obliged to be hearin' it somewhere about now."

CHAPTER 44

Luke was able to function again. He felt the sensation coursing through him, reaching his hands and feet like water flowing to the outer extremities of an intricate piping system. The wool was gone from inside his head and his breathing, though still somewhat ragged, was reasonably level. He was ready to rise up and join the fray of the gun battle still raging between Burnett and Russell, and the remaining Legion raiders still up in the rocks.

Along with the awareness of his returning capabilities, Luke had also become keenly aware of the exposed, vulnerable position he was in. He lay on his stomach ten yards away from the boulder Kelson had been sitting on earlier. Replaying the rest of the setting in his mind, Luke visualized there was no nearer scrap of cover in any direction. If he were to suddenly rise up the way he wanted, the movement would likely draw attention and gunfire from raiders up in the rocks. Ten yards was a long way to scramble out in the open with bullets chasing you.

Still, Luke was determined to join the fight. He'd lain there long enough *not able* to take action. Now that he had his faculties about him again, he damn sure wasn't going to continue doing nothing.

He risked turning his head slowly so that he was facing into the clearing, hoping it would reveal how the different shooters were positioned. Luckily, the view he gained was fairly complete. He could see where Burnett and Russell were shooting from, down at the opposite end of the oval clearing. They were well concealed and pouring a steady stream of lead at their foes. By canting his head just a bit more and rolling his eyes upward and to his right, Luke was able to locate the raiders returning fire. It only took a minute to determine just two Legion men were still involved, and both of them, fortunately, were up in the rocks on the same side of the clearing. The other side evidently had been cleared out by the explosions.

Luke wondered why Burnett or Russell didn't employ the use of some more dynamite to remove the final two men. Before leaving behind the pack animals they'd commandeered from Grogan and the Grimes cousins, it had been Marshal Burnett's idea to take along a dozen sticks of the dynamite he'd found in one of the supply bundles. Once they'd seen how Kelson had the stage set for their arrival at the hideout cave, having the explosives at their disposal turned out to be extremely fortunate. Why neither of his comrades were opting to put more of it to use, Luke could only guess . . . and he wasn't in the mood to waste time guessing.

His appraisal of the scene quickly convinced him he was in a better position than he'd estimated. First, there were only two raiders left to deal with. Second, their attention was so focused on Burnett and Russell at the opposite end of the clearing that sudden movement by the bounty hunter, whom they'd apparently written off as already being eliminated, wasn't likely to be immediately noticed. Especially if Burnett and Russell took note of Luke rejoining the fray and poured on an extra dose of hot lead to keep the men in the rocks occupied.

Still unmoving, with his cheek pressed flat to the dirt, Luke made a final sweep with his eyes, calculating, getting himself tensed. The base of the rocks bordering the clearing to the west was between fifteen and twenty yards away. If he made it that far, there was plenty of cover for him to get behind. From there, the closest of the two raiders was another fifteen yards higher up and about twice that far down, to the south. If Luke made it into the rocks, even if his dash to get there was spotted, he could start closing in on the pair of Legion shooters. They'd be caught in a pincer between him and Burnett and Russell down at the south end of the clearing.

Luke grinned wryly at the thought. If it worked out like that, for once he and the marshal wouldn't be the ones pinned down.

All that stood in the way was him making it to those rocks.

"My brother and I first discovered this cave when we were young men," Kelson explained to Craddock. "Young enough and naïve enough to be duped into helping some men drive a herd of cattle that turned out not to belong to them. When the posse showed up, those scoundrels who hired us split for the tall and uncut and left us to fend for ourselves. Our flight took us into these badlands and to this cave. After that, even though we drifted east and south aiming to stay on the straight and narrow, we seemed to make a habit of somehow always ending up on the wrong side of the law.

"The war came along and put a stop to that for a while, even though it turned out we ended up on the wrong side in that case, too. My brother didn't live to discover as much, but I did. When the bugles stopped blowing and the shooting stopped, I found myself in Missouri. Not long after that, I found myself riding with some boys by the name of Frank and Jesse James. It was from them that I learned how useful big old deep caves could be for laying low and setting up hideouts."

Kelson paused as he stepped up and planted his feet in a wide-legged stance in front of the strongbox. In his free hand he held the key to the massive padlock. "When I decided to start my own gang out here amidst the growing cattle settlements, I remembered this cave. I brought Wymer and Elmer here with me. We explored every nook and cranny, and when we were in agreement that it was damn near perfect for a hideout and base of operations, we started stocking it with goods and gathering men to form the Legion of Fire."

"In those early explorations," Craddock said, "I take it you found another way in and out. You know, in case of trouble like we've got now?"

Kelson glared at him. "Hell, yes. That was the *first* thing we made sure of. You think I'd be stupid enough to put myself in an underground box with no back door?"

After a moment, Kelson withdrew his glare and returned his attention to the strongbox. He leaned over and unfastened the lock, then threw back the chains. Before straightening up, he lifted the lid.

Inside the cavity that yawned before them was an astonishing pile of bundled paper money with a few bits of jewelry and watches mixed in. Even Millie, who stood at the end of her tether looking on in dull subservience, drew an audible intake of breath.

"There it is," Kelson proclaimed. "More money than a man could spend in five lifetimes. Even divided among the others, though we hadn't yet figured on being done, it would have made everybody rich beyond their dreams. But now . . ." He let his words trail off.

After a moment his eyes shifted to Craddock. "You are one lucky man, mister. Just a handful of days riding with the Legion and you stand to pocket a huge share of what so many others rode hard, bled, and died for."

"You sound like you begrudge me any of it," Craddock said.

Kelson's gaze remained steady. "In a way, I guess I do. But what the hell . . . what other choice is there? I could kill you, I suppose. But to tell the truth, I've had my fill of having dead men around me. At least for the time being. Besides, there's more money here than I can carry or ever imagine being able to spend on my own. So you and the old man loading up some of it . . . Like I said, what the hell?"

"All that money is real nice," Craddock responded. "But it won't do much good if all we do is squeeze out of here and get hunted down all over again. This back door of yours — where's it gonna take us?"

Kelson smiled slyly. Then, lowering his voice so the women over in the stockade wouldn't hear, he said, "To another cave a little over a mile from where we exit. That one is quite a bit smaller, but it's already stocked with emergency supplies to last half a dozen people a week to ten days. Long enough, in other words, for any posse on the hunt for us to have long since moved on with their search before we ever come out of hiding." The smile widened. "You see, I've thought of everything."

"Sounds like," Craddock allowed. "But if

Old Man Crowley is gonna be joinin' us when we slip out the back, what's to prevent that bunch outside, once they get past Smith, from coming boilin' in here and then give chase out the back way practically right on our heels?"

Kelson's smile turned smug. "Because anybody who attempts to come boiling in here is going to find themselves slowed considerably by the blockage that will be filling a section of the entrance passage after we trigger the dropfall that's going to pour in several hundred pounds of rocks and heavy timber."

Craddock didn't say anything, but his expression displayed a clear lack of comprehension.

"Those support timbers back in the passage where the old man is waiting? They're mainly in place," Kelson further explained, "to hold up a sort of platform we built overhead. Piled on that platform is a heap of small boulders and leftover timber sections. A couple of sledgehammer whacks to a key wedge at the base of one of those support beams will collapse the whole works and fill the passage with enough rocks and wreckage to halt a team of men for a full day or more before they're able to dig through."

Craddock emitted a low whistle. "I've got to hand it to you. You do have things thought through mighty slick."

Kelson grunted. "Real touching that you approve. The thing now, as I see it, is not to waste any more time getting back to the passage and helping the old man go ahead with triggering that dropfall. Once we're assured the passage is sealed off, we can return here, load up on money, and then make tracks out the back."

"Sounds good to me." Craddock jerked a thumb toward the stockade. "What about the women?"

"What about 'em? After the bounty hunters have dug their way in, let them worry about how to handle the women . . . all except this one." Kelson pulled on the tether still cinched around Millie's neck, jerking her closer to him. "She stays with me."

"With *us,*" Craddock was quick to amend, the undertone of a challenge in his words.

Kelson regarded him. Tension between the two men weighted the air for a long moment.

Kelson finally shrugged dismissively. "Go ahead and look at it that way, if it makes you feel better. For now, anyway. There'll be time in the days ahead for us to sort it out."

Craddock dipped his chin in a curt nod. "Yeah, there will."

"In the meantime, let's go take care of blocking that passage."

Chapter 45

It was almost too easy. Luke pushed to his feet and covered the distance to the western rocks without a single shot being fired in his direction. He dropped in behind a weather-worn boulder and hunkered low, both Remingtons drawn and clutched in his fists.

The exchange of gunfire continued, but none of it involved him . . . yet.

Cautiously, he raised up and scanned the situation from his new perspective. It appeared that none of the four men trading shots had shifted their positions significantly from when he'd last looked. He could see for certain that neither of the raiders was looking his way at all. Luke had to believe that Burnett and Russell, since they were facing his general direction, must have seen him make his move. It hadn't seemed like they laid down any heavier fire to cover him, but his maneuver was so quick and unexpected there wasn't much time for them to react. Plus, with the owlhoots never even noticing, there really hadn't been any call for the added distraction.

The main thing was, Luke told himself, that he was in place to aid Burnett and Russell in finishing off the last two shooters so all three of them could turn their attention to getting inside the cave and doing whatever it took to end the Legion of Fire and rescue the women. He toyed briefly with the notion of leaving Burnett and Russell to handle things while he went ahead and plunged into the cave on his own. The idea didn't last long, though. Their force was small enough as it was; to unnecessarily split it more wasn't smart.

Luke's scan of his new location revealed a shallow, ragged-edged trough, a rain scour, running diagonally up from just above where he was crouched. It led to an even narrower but relatively flat ledge that extended toward and above the nearest shooter.

Luke reholstered his Remingtons, paused no more than a second to make sure his target was continuing to face away, then hoisted himself up and bellied through the trough. Digging with fingers and toes, he began to ascend. The incline wasn't very steep, but the confines of the trough were tight and the whole way was littered with loose chunks of rock, some of them containing sharp edges that chewed into his belly and thighs like the gnawing of small animals. He greeted several of the harder-biting critters with plenty of coarse muttering.

Other than the bit of discomfort, everything went well all the way up to the ledge. At that point, however, things took a turn. Unexpectedly, for no discernible reason other than perhaps the kind of instinctive feeling a deer sometimes gets when a hunter is on the approach, the man Luke was closing in on suddenly twisted around and looked directly at him.

Luke instantly froze. But it was already too late. The raider had clearly spotted him. Then the moment of misfortune took another turn. While Luke had ceased all motion on purpose, the man facing him did the same out of surprise and shock. When motion was again required to defend himself, the man was caught unable to react as quickly as needed.

Such was not the case for Luke.

With himself revealed and his target equally so, the bounty hunter didn't hesitate to draw both of his Remingtons and plant a slug from each scarcely a fraction of an inch apart in the man's chest. The raider slammed back against a flat slab of rock, twisted away, and then spilled forward over the lip of a sharply sloping cliff. Surprisingly, he had enough life left to emit a gargling scream for part of the way down.

It was the scream that served to alert the remaining shooter in the rocks several yards ahead. The reports from Luke's guns might not have sounded appreciably different to the second man, a copper-skinned, fierce-eyed half-breed by the look of him, if the varmint they'd cut down hadn't managed a death scream. But he did, and the half-breed took notice.

What was more, the 'breed did not allow himself to be frozen by surprise. Far from it, he spun back and away from the position he'd been maintaining and dropped out of sight from Luke as well as Burnett and Russell in positions farther down. Luke rapid-fired three shots at where the man had been, but that was as close as he got.

Thinking the lone remaining raider would likely make a run for it, try to escape from continuing a fight with the odds stacked against him, Luke went in pursuit. He pushed himself forward, scrambling past the ledge and heading for where he'd last seen the half-breed. Peripherally, he noted that

Burnett and Russell were also on the move, leaving their prior positions and moving with caution along the base of the rocks to the south, working in that direction. Keeping the pincer alive.

But the half-breed didn't act as expected. He had no intention of abandoning the fight.

A dozen feet above the spot he'd disappeared from, he thrust back into view with his rifle raised and ready. Rapidly firing and levering fresh cartridges into his Winchester, he sent two rounds sizzling toward Luke, forcing him to drop flat in order to avoid the bullets whistling mere inches above his head. Quickly, the 'breed twisted the other way and triggered three blasts down at Burnett and Russell before once again dropping out of sight.

When Luke shoved up, intending to return fire, his target had already disappeared.

Cursing under his breath, Luke quickly shifted to a different position, but he didn't continue his advance. He crouched low and still, both pistols drawn and held at the ready. Down below, Burnett and Russell had also taken to fresh cover and were gone from Luke's field of vision. He didn't take time to worry about that, though. His eyes intently scanned the rocks up ahead, trying to anticipate where the half-breed might appear next.

He didn't have long to wait.

But the remaining raider had a trick up his sleeve. Rather than shifting to an altogether new spot, the bastard popped up out of the jagged pocket where he'd been initially. It was a clever ruse, and he almost got away with it. Luke had more or less been expecting him to show still higher.

The crafty varmint made one careless mistake. Apparently still having Burnett and Russell in sight from his vantage point, he fired his first rounds down at them.

That gave Luke all the time he needed to react and adjust his aim. The Remingtons spoke twice each and three of the four rounds blazing from their muzzles pounded into the 'breed. The impacts jerked him upright, spun him partway around, and the Winchester slipped from his grasp. He teetered, supported momentarily by the rocks tight around him. Luke was poised to trigger a finishing round when, very slowly, the 'breed slipped down and tipped out of sight.

Luke felt confident the outlaw wouldn't be making a reappearance.

After double-checking to make sure the

half-breed and the first man he'd shot were dead, Luke descended to the edge of the clearing. He was somewhat surprised that Burnett and Russell didn't step out to meet him. A moment later he found out why.

"Over here, Mr. Jensen," called Russell's voice. He rose up from behind a nest of boulders, revealing himself to be bare chested. He motioned with one hand, adding, "The marshal has been hit!"

Luke hurried forward. When he got to the boulders, he found Russell kneeling beside Burnett, who was lying on the ground with his head and shoulders propped against some rocks. He was grimacing and pressing a bloodstained sleeve against his left side. The make-do bandage had been torn from Russell's shirt.

"Can you believe the damn luck?" Burnett growled. "A ricochet from the last shot that lousy half-breed got off, and it finds *me.* It passed all the way through, at least, but I'm pretty sure it busted some ribs during the trip."

"We've got the bleeding in front pretty well stopped, but it's still flowing some in back," reported Russell as he continued tearing his shirt into long strips. "We need to sit him up and get his own shirt off so we can make a tight wrap all the way around his middle."

Burnett scowled at him. "I thought you were studying law, not medicine."

"Believe it or not," Russell replied, "in either practice there's room for a bit of common sense, like direct pressure to stop a bleeding wound."

"Okay," the wounded man said. "Then here's some more common sense you can use — the two of you leave me and get on into the cave where that bastard Kelson dragged my daughter! I'm not bleeding so bad I can't hold out for a while on my own. Millie and the rest of those gals have been through enough hell already, and there's no telling what more those scurvy dogs are putting them through. Leave me and go get them!"

Luke and Russell exchanged uncertain glances.

"Get going, damn it!" Burnett urged. "I've been shot before. I know what I can stand and what I can't. I'm telling you, I'll be all right until you get back."

Luke stood up and began reloading his guns. "I think the man has a point, kid. We don't know how many are left in that cave or what they're up to. And the longer we wait to find out, the more time it gives them to plan and get set up."

Russell looked troubled, undecided. His eyes went from Luke to Burnett then back to Luke again. Then he reached for his Henry rifle and also stood up. "Okay, if you both think that's the best way, just give me a minute to reload and then —"

His statement was cut short by a sudden rumbling sound from the direction of the cave. The ground underneath them trembled. All three men looked around sharply and saw a billowing yellow-brown dust cloud come rolling out from under the slanted cliff where the cave entrance was.

Russell breathlessly blurted another half-finished exclamation. "What the —"

Burnett pushed to a sitting position, wincing at the pain it caused him. Through gritted teeth, he groaned, "No! Millie!"

CHAPTER 46

The dropfall worked to effectively seal the passage — but it came at a heavy price. To Kelson's way of thinking, it was yet another sign of the jinx still wreaking havoc, not yet being done with them.

The price was Old Man Crowley's life. It resulted from the oldster's insistence on being the one to wield the sledgehammer to knock out the wedge that released the overhead pile of boulders and timber. When the wedge gave way easier than expected, the momentum of Crowley's hard swing of the heavy hammer pulled him sharply off balance. This, combined with the limited mobility of his game leg, made it impossible for him to right himself and jerk back out of the way in time. He stumbled a stuttering step and a half forward, directly into the avalanche of crushing debris. He had no chance to scream or even let out a yelp before he disappeared under tumbling rocks and boiling dust.

Millie screamed for him as Craddock and Kelson jumped back from the sudden release, yanking her along with them. The men joined her with bitter curses, but the rumbling, roaring clatter of the falling rocks echoed through the passage and on into the cave, drowning out all other sound.

The passage promptly filled with a dense haze of dust that blurred vision and caused choking and coughing. Kelson led the way out of it, the three of them moving deeper into the cave, hacking to clear their throats as they swatted the dust from their clothing and rubbed grit out of their eyes.

The women in the stockade, not knowing what to think of the sound and dust cloud that rolled out of the cave, were in a frenzy. They clamored and howled to be freed, not left trapped. It was only Kelson's threat of silencing them with a couple of shotgun blasts that settled them down. All Millie could do was look on, agonizing for the imprisoned women yet at the same time thinking how their fate might actually be better than what seemed to be awaiting her.

Kelson and Craddock wasted no time descending on the strongbox and proceeding to fill the pouches of wide money belts that Kelson provided for each of them.

"Poor old Crowley," Craddock muttered. "I'm beginnin' to think you're right about some kind of damn jinx, Kelson. It's almost like this whole cave and the area around it is suddenly cursed. I can't wait to get the hell clear of here!"

"You think you're telling me something I don't already know?" Kelson grunted. "I just hope the jinx *is* broken by putting some distance between us and it."

"You know," Craddock said as he continued stuffing clumps of money into the pouches around his waist, "if we took a couple of spare horses so we could keep switchin' back and forth to fresh mounts, we wouldn't have to stop at that layover cave. We could just keep on ridin' until we made sure we was clear of this place and all the bad that goes with it."

"That wouldn't be a bad idea, except for one little detail," Kelson told him. "You see, we won't be taking any horses with us when we leave here. The back way out is only a tunnel for the last stretch. No horse could ever fit."

Craddock looked startled. "What the hell, man! What kind of escape plan is it without horses? How far do you expect to get that way?"

"Just as far as it pleases me," Kelson

snapped back. "These badlands don't run on forever, you know. A few more miles to the north, within walking distance, they fade off into grasslands up near the Nebraska border. Even Crowley on his bum leg could have made it that far. In that grassland are scattered a dozen or more small ranches. We'll be able to get horses from whichever one we make it to first."

"And you don't expect those ranchers will think it's fishy, us wandering in on foot out of nowhere? What if they've heard about us and are on the lookout?"

Kelson scowled. "What if they are? They're out in the middle of nowhere, too — who are they going to tell? Besides, we'll have enough money to buy their quiet. If not, we'll damn well take what want and make sure they stay quiet, permanentlike. It's not like we haven't played it that way before."

Craddock matched his scowl. "Okay. I guess we got no choice. But I'd like it a whole lot better if we had horses to make our getaway on."

"Yeah, well, there's a lot of things I'd like, too. But listening to you bellyache isn't one of them," Kelson said. "This escape plan was in place a long time before you came along to benefit from it with more money than you otherwise stood to see in your whole life. Maybe you think sticking around to talk things over with those bounty hunters when they show up is a better plan?"

Craddock glared at him. "Okay, you made your point. Forget I said anything. Let's just do whatever we have to so we can get the hell out of here."

Chapter 47

"How far back do you think this cave-in reaches?" Russell wanted to know.

Luke shook his head. "Not far, I don't think. Mainly, because I don't believe it's an actual cave-in. Not a natural one, that is."

Russell gave him a look. "What do you mean? All these fallen rocks and everything — what else would you call it?"

"That's just it. All these rocks and *everything.* See those chunks of timber mixed in the rubble" — Luke pointed — "and that support beam still partially showing along the side? I think this was rigged, done intentionally. Still a *cave-in,* for want of a better word, but a man-made one."

"For what purpose?" Burnett asked. "Was it supposed to be a booby trap? Meant to fall on us or something?"

After the rumble and dust of the falling rocks had demanded their attention, the three men — Luke and Russell supporting the marshal, one on each side — had made their way from the far edge of the clearing and as far as they could go into the passage before finding their way blocked. Burnett was leaning against the smoothly worn rock wall for support, clutching the makeshift bandage to his side as he watched Luke and Russell examine the dropfall. His mouth was stretched in a grimace, fighting back the pain he was trying not to show.

In answer to the marshal's question, Luke said, "If it was meant for that, it must have gotten triggered prematurely. But no, I've got a hunch it was supposed to do nothing more than what it's accomplished — seal off the cave and block us from getting in."

Russell's forehead puckered. "Block us for how long? You mean seal off the cave forever?"

"I doubt that," Luke said. "It would have taken explosives to bring down enough rock for that. I'd say this was rigged to hold us back for more like a matter of hours, maybe a day."

"Why go to so much bother to gain themselves no longer than that?" Russell frowned. "Maybe to buy enough time to set up a better trap, another ambush of some kind to have waiting for us once we dig our way through?"

"That don't make no sense," Burnett said. "If they wanted to make a stand and fight us off, they could have done it right here in the narrow part of this passage. A handful of men with a good supply of ammunition could hold off an army from this spot."

"Not if it was us. With the dynamite we brought along, we could have blasted our way right through them," Russell said. Then, after a moment, his expression brightened with an idea. "Hey. We've still got some sticks left, why not use a couple of them to make short work of this blockade they plunked down in front of us?"

"Speaking of that dynamite," Luke said, "why didn't you use some more of it to finish off the last of those varmints out there in the rocks? It would've saved burning up a lot of powder and likely have kept the marshal from stopping that ricochet."

It was Burnett who answered. "After we realized how close the cave entrance was and then saw Kelson dragging Millie toward it, I worried about which way the cave ran underneath and for how far it stretched. I made the decision we couldn't risk setting off any more explosives for fear of causing a collapse inside the cave and possibly endangering Millie and the other women who must also be in there."

Luke nodded. "Good to be cautious."

Russell's expression turned sour. "Making what I said just a minute ago pretty stupid. If there was risk of more dynamite possibly endangering Millie and the others before, it would be even greater if we set off something here, even closer."

"You were right about one thing, though," Luke told him. "We need to concentrate on digging through this blockage as quickly as possible. If the rest of my hunch is right, we won't have to worry about an ambush waiting on the other side. In fact, I doubt we'll find anybody waiting on the other side at all except, hopefully, the abducted women."

"How so?" Burnett said. "We saw Kelson go in there. And that Craddock skunk ducked in after him. So there's at least those two, plus maybe some other Legion men inside."

"Uh-huh," Luke allowed. "But that doesn't mean whoever was inside has to *stay* there. I'm guessing there's a back door to that cave. Kelson may be a lot of things, but he's not a fool. At least not a big enough one to bottle himself up without an escape route. I see all of this as a way to keep us busy in order to give Kelson and whoever he's got with him the time they need for using that back door and making their getaway."

"In that case," Russell said, "rather than do what he wants by wasting time here, we should circle around and find wherever the back door empties out. Stop that devil dead in his tracks."

"You make finding that back door sound mighty easy," Luke pointed out. "If we miss Kelson on his way out, you've already seen how difficult it is to track anybody over this godforsaken terrain. We could spend days trying to catch up with him again that way."

"And in the meantime," Burnett said, "what about the women we believe are still here in the cave? Our first and foremost thing all along, remember, has been to save those women."

"Of course. I never meant to imply we'd lose sight of that," Russell said defensively.

Luke's expression took on an added somberness. "The other thing, much as he's not going to want hear it or admit it, is that the marshal is clearly in no shape to continue on with any kind of chase or track down."

"Now hold on. Don't be so damn sure about that, mister," Burnett protested. "If somebody finishes patching me up and binds my middle good and tight, you just watch and see if —"

"Save it," Luke cut him off. "We'll patch and bind you, like you said. Russell and I will go to work on clearing this blockage while you rest up from your wound. Depending on what we find on the other side, *then* we'll decide on the who and how when it comes to proceeding from there."

After first tending to the marshal and making him as comfortable as possible in an out-of-the-way space along one side of the passage, Luke and Russell dug — literally — into the task at hand, working feverishly through the balance of the day.

Using a folding shovel from Luke's saddle gear and a length of split timber to serve as a pry bar, they removed rock after rock and scraped away heaps of loose dirt and gravel. For the larger, boulder-sized pieces, they tied lariats around them and used their horses to pull them free and drag them away.

When darkness fell and visibility in the passage turned impenetrable, they rigged torches and lodged them in crevices on the rock walls in order to see well enough to keep working. Through all of it, Luke and Russell maintained a punishingly steady pace. They stopped rarely and only briefly to drink from their canteens and catch a moment's breather.

At one point in the middle of the night, Burnett, moving slowly and painfully, made a fire from some pieces of broken timber over which he cooked a pot of coffee. He insisted the other two stop long enough to drink some as well as eat from the jerky and hardtack he laid out in order to sustain their strength.

Shortly after dawn broke on the outside, Luke and Russell pulled down some smaller, crumbled boulders from near the top of the heap and suddenly saw an open space with the faint illumination of firelight behind it. They had broken through. The cave lay just beyond!

They continued yanking away more rocks, and shovelfuls and handfuls of dirt, digging like groundhogs until they had an opening large enough to pass through. With difficulty, they restrained themselves from barging through right away. First they took a couple of minutes to catch their breath and trade their digging tools for their guns. Then, with Russell's Henry rifle covering him, Luke slipped through the opening and over to the other side. He next covered Russell while the young man came over. Together, they made their way cautiously through the remainder of the feeder passage and on into the cave itself.

Back on the other side of the rubble, in the outer section of the passage, Burnett waited with gnawing anxiety for what seemed like an eternity. On the brink of going after the other two, he considered dragging himself forward even in his injured condition in order to find out what was going on.

Russell suddenly reappeared in the opening atop of the rubble pile. "The cave is empty," he reported, "except for the women. They appear safe and unharmed!"

Chapter 48

While Russell was fetching Burnett, which involved widening the gap at the top of the rubble heap a bit more before assisting the marshal through, Luke took care of freeing the women from the stockade. They were naturally elated and grateful and for several minutes their reactions ranged from tears of joy to an excited babble to a flood of questions.

As Luke endured this emotional outpouring, he tried to get in some questions of his own. What could they tell him about Kelson and Craddock and any other Legion men who'd been in the cave? What was the fate of Millie Burnett, who was glaringly absent? Only one of the women, a handsome, middle-aged redhead who identified herself as Lucinda Davis, seemed to grasp the urgency of what Luke was asking and calmed herself enough to provide some answers.

Luke immediately recognized her name as that of Arapaho Springs' café owner and Burnett's betrothed. He wasn't surprised when, in the midst of their discussion, she spotted Russell arriving with the marshal and broke away to go running to them.

All of the women, in fact, were quick to huddle around Burnett and Russell. In spite of playing a part in their rescue, Luke was basically a stranger, so it was only natural they gravitated more to those who were familiar. Plus, the sight of Burnett's wounded condition also triggered their concern and an immediate desire to provide care and comfort.

To facilitate the latter, a fresh fire for light and warmth was stoked in the central fire pit and Burnett was laid out close by on a pile of thick blankets. Lucinda took primary charge of the proceedings and didn't hesitate to bark orders to the other women, who scrambled to do as instructed, preparing hot water and rummaging through the supply pile to find appropriate material for bandages and clean shirts for the marshal and Russell.

In the middle of all that, although appreciative of the attention and care, Burnett did not fail to miss the obvious absence of Millie. When he raised the question, Lucinda answered him.

Luke and Russell stepped in closer to hear what she had to say. The rest of the women also gathered tighter around, their emotions in check and very somber as they cared for the marshal.

Even as his wound continued to be treated and redressed and his ribs tightly wrapped with strips of blanket material, the women — all of them — participated in relating how things had gone since they were abducted during the raid on the town. It concluded with what they'd seen and heard of the previous day's frantic happenings, ending with the flight of Kelson and Craddock, the only two Legion men left . . . and the taking of Millie as their hostage.

When the talking was done, a heavy silence filled the cave. Burnett was a doubly wounded man, his bullet hole and resulting broken ribs, as well as the far more painful revelation that his daughter remained at the mercy of a pair of ruthless men. The women, though themselves at last in safe hands, shared a measure of his pain.

Lucinda put it into words. "None of us can feel truly rescued as long as Millie is still out there being led like a dog by the leather strap around her throat. Someone has to go after her!"

"I never figured it any other way," Luke told her and the rest of them in a low, steady voice. His eyes cut to Burnett. "Though the marshal here will argue against it, you can all see he's in no shape to continue on. He needs to get back to where Doc Whitney can take care of that wound. And you women have endured enough. You need to get home as well." His gaze shifted to Russell. "That falls to you. You need to lead them. I'll go after Kelson and Craddock and the girl."

"No!" Russell's response was so quick and sharp it was like the snap of a whip. "I said from the outset I would never turn back from going after Millie as long as I had breath left in me. Well, I'm still breathing and my vow stands as strong as ever."

"Don't be a stubborn fool," Luke said. "You're not turning back in any sense of giving up. You're being asked to make a change for the greater good — for the marshal, for the women. They need one of us to see they make it back okay. I'm the experienced tracker and man hunter, I have the best odds for running down Craddock and Kelson."

"But those odds are still two to one," Russell insisted, "and they're stacked against you by a pair of cold-blooded killers. I can even things up and improve the chances for bringing back Millie."

"But what about the marshal? The other women?" Luke pressed. "They deserve a fair chance, too."

Russell seemed uncertain for just a moment. Then said, "They can make it on their own. The marshal is hurting, but he's still alert, lucid. And the women are strong and resilient. Haven't they proven that by holding up through everything already thrown at them? With plenty of horses and supplies and the marshal to guide them, there's no reason they can't make it back to town without me. My place is to go with you after Millie . . . and you're going to have to shoot me to stop me."

"Don't tempt me," Luke said.

Lucinda stepped forward. "Russell is right," she said, chin thrust out defiantly and eyes flashing. "We gals are sturdy pioneer stock. A few hardships on the trail or wherever are nothing new to us. Especially compared to what we were faced with up until only a few hours ago. Tom is strong enough and alert enough to guide us, and if need be, we can find our own way. We'll make it back to Arapaho Springs just fine. Russell should go with you. You need all the help and all the guns you can get to go against those two killers. And Millie needs every chance you can give her."

"But that passage needs to be cleared before you'll have any hope of even getting these horses out of here. And that's just for starters."

"We'll handle whatever we have to," Lucinda said confidently. "If it takes another day or so to be on our way, there are plenty of supplies and reasonable comforts here to see us through. Unless Tom's wound takes a drastic turn for the worse, there's no terrible urgency for us now that the outlaws are gone. But you and Russell *do* have urgent business."

Luke had often said he'd rather face a pack of ornery gun wolves than a strong-willed woman with fire in her eyes. Especially a pretty redhead, he now amended.

As if he weren't already wavering enough, Burnett put a cap on it by saying, "Seems like I have a knack for surrounding myself with headstrong, outspoken gals, Jensen. And you for getting caught in the cross fire. In this case, though, I have to side with Russell and Lucinda. Much as I hate to admit it, I'm in no shape to continue chasing after the likes of those two bastards who have Millie. But I *am* fit enough to guide these other ladies back to town. I can assure you of that." He winced through a spasm of pain and then continued. "So take Russell with you. Go. Quit wasting valuable time. Find that back door out of here and use it to go after them."

"You're right about having no time to waste," Luke allowed.

Burnett's eyes took on a kind of hard-edged warmth. "One more thing I want you to hear. Both of you. It galls me more than I can put into words how much I regret being unable to go on with you. But know this. There aren't two other men on the face of this earth I'd put more faith in to bring my daughter back to me."

Chapter 49

"You sneaky, conniving bitch!"

The sound of a fist striking thinly padded flesh and bone was greatly amplified in the small, stone-walled cavity. On the receiving end of the blow, Millie Burnett was keenly aware of its impact against the side of her face. All else, including the harsh words behind the fist, came to her only through a stunned haze as she was knocked to the hard ground.

Sprawled there, the haze threatened to envelop her in complete unconsciousness, then it ebbed back and she was left with a vague awareness of Sam Kelson hovering over her with his fists still balled. Ben Craddock was pressed against him, grabbing Kelson's arm to prevent him from delivering another blow.

"What the hell's gotten into you? What was that for?" Craddock demanded.

Thrusting out a wisp of flimsy white cloth

clutched in his left fist, Kelson replied, "This! This is why. And what's gotten into me is the discovery of what this treacherous brat has been trying to do to betray us."

A puzzled scowl appeared on Craddock's face. "I don't understand. What about a scrap of cloth has you so riled and what's it got to do with the girl?"

Kelson leaned over and flipped up the skirt of Millie's dress. In her stunned state, Millie was too groggy to do anything to try and stop him. Underneath the skirt, up near the waist line of the soiled petticoat, several of the frilly bands that encircled the garment had been torn away and sections were missing.

"There!" Kelson said, pointing. "I don't know exactly how, but —" He paused to pull the skirt back down and examine it. After a moment he found a five-inch vertical rent high in the front of the material. Thrusting his hand through it, he said, "Right here! Don't you see? As we were making our way here from the other cave last evening, with her hands tied in front, our little miss was sneakily reaching through the tear in her skirt and ripping off pieces of her petticoat to drop and leave behind as trail markers for somebody to follow."

Craddock still looked confused. "But I still

don't . . . How could . . ."

Kelson made another attempt to push past him, reaching for Millie. "I aim to teach this brat a lesson and show her how her treachery is only going to fix it so things don't go so good for her."

Craddock planted a hand in Kelson's chest and shoved him back. "Now, damn it, back off a minute! What are you gonna do? Kill her? Beat her to a pulp? How is that gonna change or fix anything?"

"It'll make me feel better and teach her a lesson she won't ever forget!"

"If she survives the beating maybe. But is that why we brought her along? Do we want her all beaten and bruised to hell?"

"If she brings that bounty hunter pack down on our necks, what difference does it make?" Kelson protested. "She may have ruined the whole damn plan!"

Where she lay at the two men's feet, Millie had regained her full senses by that point. Her bloodied mouth curved into a coldly satisfied smile. From the scrap of petticoat Kelson had somehow found, he'd guessed exactly what she'd done and what she hoped to accomplish. As her despair grew over failing to escape and then hearing her father had been killed, Millie's spirit had for a time spiraled to near hopelessness.

But that voice calling her name — the voice of her father, impossible as it seemed — had reawakened her will to survive and her fierce determination to keep fighting back against these lowlifes who believed they had her worn down and helpless.

So, on the trek from the larger cavern to the temporary cave, while neither Kelson or Craddock were paying much attention to her due to her seemingly defeated behavior, she'd devised the plan to reach through her torn skirt and tear off pieces of petticoat to leave as a trail for someone to follow. It was a long shot, of course, based solely on that voice calling her name and her subsequent belief it must mean there was something more to Jensen showing up and the dreadful claims he'd made. But it was a beginning, the beginning of her once again resisting and dedicating herself to finding a way to thwart those who held her captive.

"You're not thinkin' straight," Craddock was telling Kelson forcefully. "Sure, you may have caught on to her little trick and that was mighty sharp of you. But the way you're reactin' is pullin' you off the rails. Beatin' the hell out of the girl might make you feel better, but what else is it gonna gain?"

"What else is there? What are you getting

at?" Kelson wanted to know.

"Stop and think. How did you find that scrap of cloth?"

"When I went out to reconnoiter a little bit ago. The wind is starting to pick up some and I noticed it fluttering where it was sticking out of a crack in the ground. I went a little ways farther back the way we came and there was another one. That's when it hit me — when I figured out what the little bitch was trying to pull."

Craddock nodded. "Okay. Like I said, that was sharp of you to notice and then figure out. But don't you see? So far, it doesn't really matter. It hasn't had any chance to accomplish what it was meant to."

Kelson scowled, said nothing.

"Here's the thing," Craddock went on. "We got here last evening then holed up for the night. So it's about midmorning now, right? How long did you figure it would take somebody to dig through that passage the way we left it blocked?"

Kelson's scowl relaxed a bit. "A day or so. Depending how many men worked on it, what they had in the way of tools."

"Are you startin' to see what I'm gettin' at now?" Craddock said, spreading his hands. "There's a good chance those bounty hunters ain't even dug all the way through that pile of rubble yet. Or, if they have, just barely. Either way, I'd say it's damned unlikely anybody has found their way through that escape tunnel and are tryin' to follow us yet. That means no matter how many trail markers the girl left, they got no chance to lead anybody anywhere because nobody's had the chance to find any of 'em yet."

"You know, you make a good point. Hell, I think you might be exactly right," Kelson agreed. "There hasn't been time enough for anybody to start tracking us yet."

"I don't see how," Craddock said.

"Meaning if we go out and remove those damn markers they won't lead nobody nowhere."

"One of us goin' out to remove the markers might run a risk of bein' spotted, especially back closer to that other cave, in case some of those bounty hunters have started sniffin' out our trail sooner than we're figurin'."

Kelson shook his head. "Don't matter. It's a risk worth taking. It's better than leaving those scraps of frillies in place to lead right to us. Even if some of those bounty hunters are on the prowl, nobody alive knows these badlands better than me. I guarantee I'll see them before they do me."

Craddock eyed him. "So you figure you're the one to go out?"

"That's right," Kelson stated firmly. "Like I said, I'm the one with the best chance of not getting spotted in case we've already got company roaming around out there." He returned Craddock's gaze and put a trace of flint in his. "Besides, if I was to turn you loose, you might get lost and not ever find your way back. And since you've now got a full money belt around your waist, that might not bother you very much. But it would pure annoy the hell out of me."

"Same could be said about you, couldn't it?"

Kelson gave a slow shake of his head. "Not hardly. This cave is part of my escape plan and I have no intention of abandoning it until I'm ready or am forced to. Also part of my escape plan is for my whole gang — which amounts to me and you, the way it's turned out — to stick together until I say it's time to split up. So if you get a notion to take off on me while I'm gone, you'd best remember what I said about how well I know these badlands."

CHAPTER 50

Luke and Russell were following the trail of petticoat scraps.

"That is one clever gal," Luke had muttered after they came across the second torn piece and recognized what it meant. "In this rocky, trackless terrain where picking out sign is damn near impossible, she's practically drawing us a map."

"Not many others take the time to notice it," Russell said earnestly, "but I've long been aware that Millie has a brain to match her beauty."

Luke gave him a sidelong glance. "Uh-huh. And I suppose that's what first attracted you to her, eh? Her big, beautiful brain?"

Russell blushed. "I never meant to imply . . . That is to say . . ."

"What your tongue is stumbling over," Luke told him, "is admitting you're in love with Millie. If you can't even say it to yourself, how in blazes are you ever going to get around to telling her?"

Russell suddenly looked like a sour taste had filled his mouth. "How could I ever tell her that? Practically the only time I ever work up the courage to talk to her at all is when I run into her on the street or maybe at her father's office when I'm there on some legal business for Mr. Mycroft . . . or *was,* I guess I should say. Even those times, I get so . . . well, like you just said, my tongue sort of stumbles all over itself."

"The thing you'd better get through your thick skull," Luke said, "is that those days are over."

"What do you mean?" Russell asked.

Luke showed him a tolerant smile. "What I mean is, when this thing is all done and we get Millie back to Arapaho Springs, you won't have to tell her anything about how you feel. Unless she's blind or a whole lot dumber than you make her out to be, she's going to see what everybody else can — how much you love her and what you've put yourself through to prove it."

Russell's forehead puckered. "You really think so? But there was also you and all the others who started out with us. Everybody put themselves through a lot. Why would she see something different in me?"

"It shows, kid. Trust me, she'll see the difference," Luke assured him. A second later, he suddenly threw himself to the ground and bellied flat behind a hump of weather-smoothed rock.

Russell didn't hesitate to do the same. And when Luke swept off his hat, Russell also copied that.

After several seconds, Luke cautiously lifted his head and scanned ahead over the barren, rugged landscape, looking for the source of the movement that had caught his eye and caused him to react. Flattening back down again, he turned to Russell. First he held his index finger straight up; then he tipped it and pointed in the direction he'd been looking; then he tipped it downward, extended the finger next to it, and moved them together to simulate a walking motion. Signaling: One man, straight ahead, walking in their direction.

Russell nodded his understanding.

Next, Luke pointed to himself and swirled his hand in a C-shaped motion to his left. He followed that by pointing to Russell and making the same motion off to the right. *I'll circle around this way; you do the same that way.* Again, Russell nodded his understanding, and they each slipped away as indicated. Like the approaching man, they were on foot since the escape tunnel from the cavern was too small for horses.

As Luke slowly, carefully moved over and through the badlands moonscape, he puzzled some on why the man he had spotted was moving back toward the big cavern. Assuming it must be either Craddock or Kelson, what could be their purpose? Maybe to sneak back into the cavern and try a surprise ambush on whoever they found there? If so, why only one of them? Maybe they'd had a falling-out. That wouldn't be especially surprising, considering the temperament of two such ruthless men. But if it had come to that, where did it leave Millie?

As he wrestled with those thoughts, it neither slowed Luke's progress nor dulled the intensity with which he continued to stalk the man in question. Abruptly, he again caught sight of the man and saw him clearly. It was Kelson. Luke saw what he was up to. He was gathering up the scraps of cloth, trying to erase the trail Millie had laid down.

Luke grimaced. Discovery of what the girl had done couldn't bode well for her resulting treatment. He reasoned that Craddock was probably hunkered down somewhere with Millie while Kelson undertook this mission to get rid of the markers that would lead to them. Too bad for him that his mission had put him on a "get rid of" list all his own. The trick, though, was to do it quietly so as not to alert Craddock right away. Then, after he had time to work up a nervous sweat because his partner didn't make it back, maybe he'd reach a panic point where he'd reveal himself for his own turn to be gotten rid of.

Luke looked beyond Kelson, hoping for some sign of Russell so he could signal him not to do anything too rash, but he had no luck spotting the young man. In the meantime, Kelson was on the move, increasing the risk it might take him to a position where he couldn't get at so easily. Luke made the decision to act on the opportunity while it was presenting itself.

Aiming to strike his target silently in order to avoid alerting Craddock, Luke pouched his Remingtons then edged along parallel with the outlaw for a few yards, working his way up onto a high slab of rock that came to a peak directly above where Kelson would pass. He poised, balanced, then launched himself when the man was directly below.

Luke landed on his feet, skimming down mere inches behind Kelson, slamming the edges of his fists hard against the sides of the outlaw's neck. Kelson's knees instantly buckled. He emitted a grunt of pain and surprise as he fell back against Luke. The bounty hunter hooked the crook of his right arm under Kelson's chin, simultaneously twisting and pulling, meaning to drag his foe over his hip and throw him to the ground.

At the last second, Kelson reached back and up, clawing Luke's ear and then wrapping his fingers around a thick mass of hair. When Kelson went down he also pulled Luke off his feet. Locked together, the two men rolled over and over, pummeling and kicking. Luke was momentarily disconcerted that the outlaw hadn't been stunned more by the twin blows to his neck, but he couldn't afford to wonder about the why of that. He had to focus everything on the fight he was embroiled in.

Bumping up against a low, spinelike thrust of jagged rock, the two men suddenly stopped rolling. Before Kelson could take advantage of being on top, Luke slipped an arm free and shot a hard right uppercut straight to the point of the outlaw's chin. As Kelson's head snapped back, Luke used the same hand he had thrown the punch with and clamped hard onto the outlaw's throat, digging his fingers in deep. Kelson made a squawking sound and stopped pummeling and punching with his own two hands in order to grab Luke's wrist and try to break the hold.

Luke suddenly arched his back and twisted his body, rolling both of them away from the rock spine and shifting himself to the top position. He released his throat hold. Kelson's hands stayed locked on his wrist and jerked his right arm away. Luke immediately brought his left arm up and around and slammed the edge of the forearm down across Kelson's throat. Another squawking sound came out, but much weaker. Knowing the outlaw hadn't been able to catch a breath for some time and that it was taking its toll, Luke ground down harder, working his shoulder and more of his body weight into the pressure.

Kelson threw some desperate, ineffective punches to the sides of Luke's head, but he tucked his chin and let them bounce off. He sensed Kelson was nearly out of gas, growing incapable of fighting back. Then somehow he managed to get a knee in under the bounty hunter's hip and made a frantic thrust with his leg that lifted Luke's body and hurled it to one side.

Luke rolled away, separating them. Luke scrambled to his feet first but got too eager to close in again and missed with a whooshing roundhouse right that almost certainly would have ended the fight.

Kelson ducked under it, dropping to his knees. Thrusting upward and into Luke's forward momentum, the outlaw landed a punishing uppercut that jolted Luke hard and knocked him to one side where he stumbled over the low spine of rock he had been jammed against just a minute earlier. Unable to keep his balance, the bounty hunter toppled to the ground, the jagged points of the rocks chewing painfully into his legs, his body landing in such a way that his left arm was pinned under it.

Kicking and scrambling frantically to get clear of the rocks and regain his footing, Luke looked up to see Kelson take a hurried step forward and come to a jerky halt, looming over him. The outlaw's right hand was stabbing downward, clawing for the gun on his hip.

Few men across the frontier were faster on the draw than Luke Jensen. But in his present position — sprawled with his feet and legs tangled in sharp rocks, his body twisted awkwardly, one arm pinned underneath him — while Kelson was already reaching to clear leather, meant impossible odds for Luke to beat, even with the quickness of his draw. Never one to back down or give up, no matter how bad the odds against him, Luke's right hand went ahead and blurred into motion . . .

A rifle shot blasted.

Sam Kelson's eyes bugged in surprise, his mouth fell open, and a bullet exited. After passing through the back of his head, it carried with it a comet's tail of blood and tissue fragments as the dull report of the shot rolled through the air in its wake. Kelson's body seemed to fold in on itself like an accordion being pressed shut, collapsing straight down until it came to rest in a lumpy heap.

Looking over his gunsight, past the fallen man he'd been swinging his aim toward, Luke saw Russell standing a little short of twenty yards away lowering the Henry rifle from his shoulder. His face was a grim mask blurred faintly by the haze of powder smoke hanging in the air in front of him.

Chapter 51

"A gunshot!" Craddock exclaimed, his body tensing as his face snapped toward the narrow, vertical slash that was the mouth of the cave. Muttering, he added, "Damn, that can't be good. That can't be good at all."

The new layover cave was a bubblelike cavity within a conical mound of rock. It was barely twenty feet in diameter and only half that at the highest point of its domed top. A pile of meager supplies — blankets, candles, canteens, beef jerky, hardtack — were pushed to the back side. Millie sat on a blanket spread on the hard, cold ground next to them.

The tether previously cinched around her neck had been removed, but her hands were still bound tightly in front of her. At the sound of the rifle shot, she also had gone tense, although with anticipation, not alarm. If Kelson had run into something that resulted in gunfire, it could mean only one thing.

Somebody else was out there, too. Somebody, Millie chose to believe, following the markers she'd dropped. Anybody on the trail of the evil curs who were holding her captive represented a thread of hope for her rescue!

Sidling closer to the cave's slice of an opening, Craddock was still muttering worriedly to himself. "That fool Kelson. Supposed to know this leftover piece of Hell so good, be so good at findin' his way . . . What did he find that would've caused shootin'?"

"Maybe," Millie said, wanting to calm Craddock so he wouldn't do anything too wild or unpredictable, "he saw a jackrabbit or possibly an antelope and shot it so we'd have some fresh meat."

Craddock turned his head to glare at her. "Don't be stupid! Kelson went out there to get rid of anything that would lead to us. He wouldn't draw attention by takin' a potshot at a damn jackrabbit!"

"Maybe a rattlesnake," Millie suggested. "Maybe he *had* to shoot. You know, to keep from getting bitten."

Scowling, Craddock said, "That might be possible, I guess . . . but it seems awful thin."

"Still" — Millie pushed off her blanket

and slipped closer to Craddock, feigning concern — "if he *did* get bitten, he might be out there needing your help."

"Oh, you'd like that, wouldn't you?" Craddock sneered. "Havin' me leave to go check on him? As if you give a damn if Kelson got snakebit or not and like you wouldn't bolt out of here the second you was left alone. How big a fool do you take me for?"

"Where would I bolt to?" Millie argued. "I've been dragged out here to this leftover corner of Hell, to use your own words, where I have no clue which way to turn, not even to get back to that other cave. I won't pretend to like the way things are, but I'm not ready to trade them for wandering off and ending up freezing or starving to death!"

"Well, you ain't gonna end up doin' either one. 'Cause you ain't goin' nowhere, and neither am I," Craddock said firmly. "We're gonna sit right here and wait this out. Kelson's been gone long enough so's he must have picked up most of those trick markers you dropped — leastways the ones anywhere close to here. If he ran into those bounty hunters and got his wick trimmed tight, there ain't nothing left to bring 'em the rest of the way. Hell, with the money they'd find around his waist on top of what we left back in the big cave, the greedy sonsabitches oughta be satisfied enough to call it a day and ride off. So, like I said, if we stay right here and keep quiet, we still got a chance of gettin' through this."

With a sinking feeling, Millie realized he could be right. Even if Kelson had fallen prey to somebody who would continue searching through the badlands' endless sprawl of rocks and twisting gullies, they might very possibly never discover that godforsaken hole in the ground.

Something must have shown in her eyes. Suddenly Craddock reached out and grabbed her by the throat with his right hand. Shoving his face close to hers, he hissed out through clenched teeth, "And if you're thinkin' of screamin' out or makin' a ruckus to give away this position, you'd better get it out of your pretty little head. I ain't ever yet got what I've been wantin' so bad from you but, by God, I'll throttle you right here and now and settle for never gettin' it before I let you betray me again!"

He'd gotten too close and made the mistake of believing he was too intimidating for Millie to put up any resistance. He couldn't have fathomed all the humiliation and rage and determination that had been building in her. When he shoved against her, choking and threatening, and his body pressed close enough for her hands, even though bound at the wrists, to touch the revolver on his hip, there was no fear or hesitation when it came to what she did next.

Tugging on the gun to lift it out of its holster just far enough for her to slip a finger through the trigger guard and wrap a thumb over the hammer, Millie cocked and fired. Twice.

The roar of the discharges was deafening in the small cave. Craddock's scream of pain and surprise only added to it. The first shot passed close to his leg, burning a bullet gash the length of his thigh. The second slug was angled more inward and tore a large chunk out of the same thigh, just above the knee.

Craddock hurled Millie violently away, sending her crashing hard against the wall of the cave as he rolled in the opposite direction, grabbing at his injured leg and cursing. "Damn you! Damn you, you *did* betray me again!"

He struggled to his feet and wheeled to face her. He drew the revolver she had been unable to seize completely that had settled back into its holster. Extending it to arm's length, he centered the muzzle directly on her lovely face. "You've set me up good this time, haven't you? Giving away our location and leavin' me to make a run for it on a bum leg." The words came out between puffs of pain-quickened breathing. "Well, you've made sure it might be curtains for me, but by damn you're not gonna be alive to get any satisfaction from it!"

Pressed against the stone wall where she'd been slammed, Millie glared back at him, showing no fear.

Craddock stood there, his shoulders rising and falling with his rapid breathing. He continued to hold his arm extended. But slowly, his gun hand began to waver unsteadily, uncertainly. "Damn you!" His words came in a hoarse whisper, his teeth bared as if in disdain. "You're a witch, that's what you are. A witch who's had me under her spell from the first time I laid eyes on you. I never got the chance . . . and now I can't even —"

Abruptly, he lowered the gun and shoved it back into its holster. Then he made another awkward, jerky turn and moved toward the cave opening. A moment later, he'd pushed through and out . . . and was gone.

Millie stayed pressed against the wall, motionless. She kept her gaze locked on the vertical slit through which Craddock had disappeared. A belated tremor passed through her.

And then, from somewhere outside, she heard the sound of gunshots. Three in rapid succession, a slight pause, then two more.

And then silence.

CHAPTER 52

Millie emerged tentatively from the cave, blinking and squinting against the transition into sunlight. As her eyes adjusted, she was able to make out the forms of two men moving slowly toward her. Both were only a short distance away, coming at her from separate angles. Though she wasn't able to immediately make out the features of either one, she sensed no need for fear or a feeling of threat.

Raising one hand to shade her eyes and focusing on the taller of the two, Millie was able to recognize him as Luke Jensen. Her pulse quickened. He was the man she had at one time liked and romanticized over only to have him act so cold and say such dreadful things when he showed up to speak with Kelson.

She shifted her gaze to the other approaching figure. When she recognized him it seemed impossible to believe. Nevertheless, her feet were suddenly carrying her toward him. He also quickened his pace and they met in a mutual embrace.

"Russell! Oh, Russell," Millie said breathlessly. "I thought you were dead!"

"There was a time I believed I deserved to be, for my foolish behavior that placed you in the hands of that treacherous Craddock," Russell replied in an emotional rush, burying his face in her golden hair. "But I had to live. I had to, in order to make amends by helping get you back."

Millie tipped her head back and gazed up at him. "Oh, no. You had no reason to punish yourself with such thoughts. No one but Craddock was to blame for what happened!"

"Well, he ended up paying for it. He's dead. Him, Kelson, and the rest of the Legion of Fire," Luke said as he strode over to the pair.

Millie pressed more tightly into Russell's arms and turned her head to glare at Luke. "You! I'm surprised to find Russell and his selfless feelings mixed up with the likes of you."

"Millie!" Russell was quick to admonish. "If not for Mr. Jensen, it's almost certain none of us would have made it this far. And nobody's been more selfless when it came —"

"Hold on, kid. Don't sell yourself short," Luke interrupted. "Nobody pushed himself harder — not to mention the rest of us — than you. Plus, you saved my neck twice when I almost certainly would have been a goner."

Millie's eyes returned to Russell. "You, Russell?" she said, gazing up at him. Her gaze lingered for several beats and then she added, "Yes . . . Yes, I can see it. You've changed."

Luke could see a fierce blush flooding up the sides of Russell's neck, his ears turning beet red. Luke wanted to urge the bashful young pup to go ahead and kiss the girl, but of course that was up to Russell.

Before anything could happen, Millie swung her attention once more to Luke. "My father! What about him? You said —"

"Your father's not dead," Luke interrupted. "I deeply regret making that claim in front of you and for the rest of the way I acted that day. It was all meant to put Kelson off balance while your father and Russell were getting into position to deal with the men waiting in ambush."

"Your father is fine," Russell said reassuringly. "He's wounded, but not critically. He's back at the big cave with Miss Lucinda and the rest of the ladies. They're preparing to take him back to Arapaho Springs for medical attention, but I'm pretty certain they haven't had time to get headed out yet."

Luke nodded. "We can be back there to join them in no time."

"Oh God! That's wonderful news," Millie exclaimed. "After so much that seemed hopeless — *everything* is looking wonderful!"

Gazing down at her beaming, beautiful face so close to his, Russell murmured, "Yeah. Things do look pretty wonderful."

Luke smiled. He considered himself neither a romantic nor a fortune-teller, but it looked like his words to Russell earlier that morning might actually come true. Seemed there was a good chance of something deeper possibly blossoming between the young man and Millie. It was a thought that made Luke feel kind of glad.

Then the less sentimental, more practical side of him kicked in and he thought of something that made him feel even more glad.

Though he'd have to share them with Russell, the bounties on Craddock and all those Legion of Fire hombres meant his trip to Arapaho Springs was going to result in a mighty nice payday after all!

ABOUT THE AUTHORS

William W. Johnstone is the *USA Today* and *New York Times* bestselling author of over 300 books, including Preacher; The Last Mountain Man; Luke Jensen Bounty Hunter; Flintlock; Savage Texas; Matt Jensen, the Last Mountain Man; The Family Jensen; Sidewinders, and Shawn O'Brien Town Tamer. His thrillers include *Phoenix Rising, Home Invasion, The Blood of Patriots, The Bleeding Edge,* and *Suicide Mission.* Visit his website at www.williamjohnstone.net or by email at dogcia2006@aol.com.

Being the all-around assistant, typist, researcher, and fact checker to one of the most popular western authors of all time, **J. A. Johnstone** learned from the master, Uncle William W. Johnstone.

He began tutoring J.A. at an early age.

After-school hours were often spent retyping manuscripts or researching his massive American Western history library as well as the more modern wars and conflicts. J.A. worked hard — and learned.

"Every day with Bill was an adventure story in itself. Bill taught me all he could about the art of storytelling. *'Keep the historical facts accurate,'* he would say. *'Remember the readers, and as your grandfather once told me, I am telling you now: be the best J. A. Johnstone you can be.'* "

The employees of Thorndike Press hope you have enjoyed this Large Print book. All our Thorndike, Wheeler, and Kennebec Large Print titles are designed for easy reading, and all our books are made to last. Other Thorndike Press Large Print books are available at your library, through selected bookstores, or directly from us.

For information about titles, please call:

(800) 223-1244

or visit our website at:

gale.com/thorndike

To share your comments, please write:

Publisher
Thorndike Press
10 Water St., Suite 310
Waterville, ME 04901